THE BARCALOUNGER COWBOYS OF ST. COLUMCILLE'S

A WRITERS' GROUP ANTHOLOGY

This book is published by The Barcalounger
Cowboys' Press

Copyright © 2009 by Derrick Abromeit, Jason
Alberty, Nathan Frese, Jennifer Horn & Lisa
Roberts

www.barcaloungercowboys.com

ISBN 978-0-578-00332-0

Contents

Derrick Abromeit
2-27

Jason Alberty
28-78

Nathan Frese
80-144

Jennifer Horn
146-199

Lisa Roberts
200-246

Cover Art: Tara Marsh

The Barcalounger Cowboys
of St. Columcille's

For some people, writing is for the soul what pizza is for the tongue. And like a convocation of Cubs fans or classic car aficionados or — even — Magic the Gathering mavens, when the right mix of writers gets together, the whole becomes greater than the parts. As of September 2008, this Midwest writers' group has been rolling along, not always smoothly, for twelve years. When we started, we were all teachers...not so anymore. When we started, some of us were married and some of us were single; while that is still the same, it is now in a different combination (although, to clarify, we have not married each other). When we started, there was simply one child among us...now there are eight, perhaps nine or ten, if the rumors are right. And what do we write for? We write for ourselves, we write for each other, we write to receive the occasional rejection letter, we write to connect in the world. And we laugh...a lot. Following is the history of the Barcalounger Cowboys of St. Columcille's:

So, Jason and Jen met when Jason was student teaching where Jen was teaching, at Northwest Junior High. Jason and Nate met in the English Ed. program at Iowa. Derrick and Lisa and Jen met in the summer Iowa Writing Program. Nate and Tom met in the English department at West High.

In the summer of 1996, Jason and Jen said, Hey, we should start a writers' group, whatever that is. Jason said, I'll ask Nate. Jen said, I'll ask Derrick. Derrick said, Yes, and I'll ask Lisa. We would have to wait a long time before we would get to meet Tom, though.

So, in September 1996, Jason and Nate and Derrick and Lisa showed up at Jen's Iowa City apartment to begin what has become a fine tradition of meeting. And eating cheese and chocolate. And enjoying cold beverages. And laughing. And not disclaiming. And laughing. And sharing writing. And critiquing. And laughing.

Sometime in the first winter of the meeting and eating and drinking and laughing, etc., etc., Jen brought a story that featured mean boys from St. Columcille's school.

When the group met on Wednesday, March 12, 1997, Nate told a story, which somehow included a Barcalounger, about the perro that gives advice to Consuelo.

On Thursday, March 13, 1997, Derrick sent an e-mail that said, "I haven't laughed that hard in a long time. And the chocolate was better than sex."

In mid-May 1997, Jason instigated a naming project. Group names that were considered and rejected included:

Lonesome Flotsam
Express Yourself, Bob
Hump Day Madness
The St. Columcille Virgin Raiders
Bulbous Urge
*

Six-Inch Average
Holy Juxtaposition, Batman!

On May 21, 1997, a consensus was reached, and the group's name officially became the Barcalounger Cowboys of St. Columcille's.

Lisa tried out the name conversationally to make sure it worked: "No, I can't go bowling tonight. I have a meeting of the Barcalounger Cowboys of St. Columcille's." Jason and Nate thought that a good slogan would be "Write 'em, cowboy!" Nate brainstormed the idea for a convention booth giveaway of an official, logo-stamped rectal thermometer. Jen figured the giveaways/souvenirs could also be sold in the vending machines in the English-Philosophy Building on the UI campus. We were good to go.

Over the months that turned into years, Lisa brought personal essays punctuated with wry observations and well-timed, guffaw-inducing humor. Nate supplied the hipness factor and introduced Peter, the character you hate to love, into the shared history of the group. Derrick made us all think we might want to take up fishing after all and to cheer on Harold, hoping he'd make it to the end of the novel. Jason took us on emotional roller coaster rides via poetry, essays, one-acts, monologues, novels, ear-piercings, you name it. Jennifer mostly stuck to poetry, as it provides excellent camouflage.

Then, in the fall of 1997, Nate moved away. Not too far, though, so we thought we'd try to keep going with the occasional field trip to Nate's place in the Quad Cities and trying to lure him back to Iowa City with promises of, well, anything. But long-distance relationships are challenging. So there was a brief-ish and somewhat fuzzy period of Kat but no Nate, which also involved a collection of cat whiskers. It felt wrong.

Then, in the summer of 1999, Nate came back. And there was much rejoicing. Kat became a footnote. And it felt right again.

The Cowboys carried on basically happily, with only a minimal amount of sibling-like bickering that sort of peaked circa 2001. From Nate: "Maybe we need some kind of group magna carta or something." And from Jen: "I am not looking for anyone to sing the I'm Very Sorry Song or to make declarations of undying loyalty ... But I look at us as sort of like a band; we work best when everyone is there." From Jason: "Mommy, Daddy, please don't fight..." From Lisa: "You don't set aside time to write, Jason?? I am shocked! [Shocked and in good company]" And from Derrick: "I have 28 tennis meets in 59 days. / I have no balance. / I have little sympathy for whining. / I love the Cowboys. / I live and eat stress. / I try to write. ... Can't we all just get along?"

And we all just got along. Very happily. Till the summer of 2003, when Derrick up and left. For real and for good. To one of the rectangular states in the middle of the country. It was a big blow to the Cowboys. We had to sit and nurse our wounds a while. What were we going to do? How could we fill the gaping hole where Derrick used to sit? What kind of person could do this?

After a while, Nate made the call: I'll ask Tom, he said. And, lucky for the Cowboys, Tom had the intestinal fortitude to step into the clan and make the place his own; he said, Yes.

So, in early 2004, the Cowboys were back up to full strength and beginning to show a preference for being Loungers instead of Cowboys. And suddenly, with Tom rounding out the group, we had cultural commentary and political satire and a fictional satirical town to add to the mix, along with connections to a steady supply of political candidate bumper stickers. (You can also order T-shirts from his blog web page. Hurry — quantities are limited.)

And we continue meeting, and mostly not disclaiming. We're harder on each other than we used to be, and we can take it. We juggle more and whine less. And we show up at each other's important things. And whatever a writers' group is supposed to be, we wouldn't trade this one.

From the Archives:
E-mail Follow-Up to December 6, 2006, Meeting at Old Chicago

From: Jen
To: Jason, Nate, Tom, and Lisa
Date: December 7, 2006
Time: 8:50 A.M.
Subject: meeting minutes

It was good to see y'all.

Happy editing.

J

Reply From: Lisa
To: Jen, Jason, Nate, Tom
Date: December 7, 2006
Time: 10:06 A.M.
Subject: Re: meeting minutes

Revised minutes

1. Lisa arrives slightly before 8:00 and realizes she has no scraper in her car. She hopes for the snow to stop.

2. Jennifer arrives, stylish in her plaid coat.

3. Jason skids in, muscles still tense from slick driving experience.

4. Ty attempts to get drink orders as conversation begins.

5. Ty brings 4 waters. Loungers not ready with drink orders. Conversation continues, with an emphasis on beverages.

6. Bob replaces Ty. Great rejoicing in the booth. Orders are taken.

7. Drinks come, conversation continues.

8. Jason orders calzone, adds meat.

9. Food is served, drinks consumed, conversation continues.

10. Nate arrives with dark circles under eyes, semi-collapses into booth. Bob, so much better than Ty, takes order from Nate.

11. Conversation continues. Sprite arrives. Nate watches basketball game while conversing and uses the word "manservant." The word "manservant" is discussed.

12. The manuscript is brought out in all its glory. Jennifer lays down the law. "You have a month to edit your own fabulously well-written gems. Next month, we'll switch and have the intense pleasure of editing another person's work." (Quotation approximate.) After some discussion, this plan is agreed with and many hearty affirmations of its immediate implementation are heard.

13. Dates we don't want to meet in January are put forth. Jason will host. More information will be forthcoming.

14. Tom unexpectedly arrives. There is cheering.

15. We all leave.

DERRICK ABROMEIT

Derrick is a high school social studies teacher, and admitted history-geek. He lives in Lawrence, Kansas with his wife Deanna, the educated member of the family, two spirited children, Lily and Elliott, probably more intelligent than their parents, and the family dog, a black lab mix curiously named Scarlet Moonlight. Although Derrick occasionally thinks of himself as a writer, he most often imagines himself as a word-class fly fisherman.

A.M.

Warm under the covers in the fall crispness,
Snuggled in dark silence.

"Dad."

Lost, drifting toward the edge of clarity.
Instinct pulls. Get up, get up.

"Daaaaaaaaaaaaaad."

Eyes open to the blackness, hurrying ahead.
Then, pain. Bright and jolting.

"Daaaaaaaaaaaaaaaaaaaaaaaaad."

Partially open door impossible to see.
Like looking for the edge of a dime.

"Daaaaaaaddddyyyyyyyyyyyyyyyyyyyy."

Why was the fucking door open?
Is that blood on my forehead? Fuck.

"Daddy, Daddy, Daddyyyyyyyyyyyyyyyy."

Staggering, dizzy, holding one hand out.
It's okay, Sunshine.

"Can I sleep with you?"

Sure.

My Addiction

Every Halloween my addiction returns. This year was no exception. I found myself sneaking handfuls from the jar, hiding them in my jacket pockets and in my desk at work. I would take a quick drink of orange juice or root-beer to hide the smell. I couldn't stop. I have to come clean. I am an adult and I am a candy-corn-aholic. I know I shouldn't eat them before dinner, but I do. I know they don't make a very nutritional breakfast, but I just don't care. It's this phase I go through each year. When the leaves turn, I get the craving. I think I can stop with just that little bag of four corns that cheap adults give to trick-or-treaters. But I can't; I have to have candy corns by the pound. Not the ones with the dark brown section, those aren't the real thing. They must be white, yellow, and Orange, and there better be lots of them. Don't laugh, I have the canker sores on my tongue to prove it. I know, it sounds like some disturbing psychological affliction. I know what you're asking: is it triggered by some deep mental reaction to those little jack-o-lantern buckets that kids carry around to collect their spoils on All Hallows Eve? No, it's more simple than that, but it has been an obsession of mine since I was twelve.

When I was just a kid, my parents sent me to Camp Saint Malo in the mountains of Colorado, near Estes Park. It was a camp like any other I suppose. We swam and rode horses, we became archers and leather workers, and we even got to shoot real .22 caliber rifles. That was all fine, but the best part of camp were the Fridays when we got to go into Estes Park for the evening. Sure, they had gold mine tours, go-carts and a variety of different carnival games like skee-ball, but the best thing about it was this: you had your own money. It was actually money your parents left for you when they dropped you off the previous Sunday, but you had complete control of it on that Friday in Estes Park. It was a glorious adventure in freedom and the pursuit of anything you wanted.

It was that money that got me started down that steep and slippery slope to candy corn addiction. A friend from camp, who I'm sure, must have been the best friend I ever had at that time, and who I remember only the sketchiest details about now, decided that some of his money was going to the candy store. Since we both felt like we had far too much money to actually spend in one night, we were not shy on our orders to the small old woman behind the counter. My friend was drooling over, and never took his eyes off, the homemade fudge. He left carrying a very large bag. I, on the other hand, looked at every single type of candy in every single old fashioned jar on the shelves. There must have been hundreds of them. Of course I was twelve years old and in a frantic situation, so there may not have been quite that many, but I do remember smelling that candy in the warm store for a long time. Then, for a reason that eludes me to this day, I passed on all the exotic stuff and told the woman, "I would like some candy corn, please." She asked me how much and I said something clever like, "Oh, just one bag." She asked how much in pounds, and I said, with as much confidence as a twelve year old could muster about a topic he knew nothing about, "Three." I remember her staring at me, unmoving. Then she started filling the bag.

I changed my mind on the amount as she came to the top to the paper bag. I was reading the old fashioned scale as she went. "How about just two and a half pounds?" She stopped and checked the weight of the bag. I don't recall just how much it cost, but it didn't matter, money was nothing to me that night. My friend and I went to the go-carts and sat on the bleachers and started eating. Neither of us even considered sharing.

We spent the next several hours busily doing nothing, which seems to be the unique talent of twelve-year-olds, before finding the bus for the trip back to the camp. Just before it was time to leave, my friend and I ran back to the candy store. We were both feeling very sick, and we probably didn't really run, but it was important to have something for the bus ride back and for that night in the bunks. I didn't have enough money for another two and a half pounds, but I did manage to get almost another half a bag.

I figure by the time we fell asleep that night in our bunks, I had eaten close to three and a half pounds of candy corn, and I am proud to say I did not throw up. I don't think I could eat them for quite a while after that, but the next year at camp, I did the same thing.

I consider myself lucky that, unlike chocolate, candy corn really only comes out for Halloween now. It is not my constant source of temptation, but only teases me for a few weeks each fall. And this year I only ate one pound. That isn't much—I'm sure I could handle a few more, but I'm trying to cut back.

Changes

The kids in my class don't get it now. It just doesn't click. It was a fact of life a few years ago, and now none of my freshmen American history students grasp the concept. When I began the unit on the Cold War, I started by telling them that I was surprised, and also relieved, to be alive at the ripe old age of 43. They looked at me with a mixture of curiosity and skepticism. They know that I use gimmicks and stories to illustrate history, and they probably imagined that I was going to tell a story about an accident or a near-death experience. In a way they were right. At least I think they should have been.

It was just the way people thought when I was a kid. In junior high my group of friends, and I assume many other patriotic young Americans, never really believed that we would grow up and have families. It was like getting the newspaper off the porch every morning, or the mail carrier making the rounds, it was a certainty. We talked about it all the time. We asked ourselves why we should save our money and stay out of trouble if we weren't going to live long anyway. We were condemned; a death sentence with an execution date yet to be determined.

We were just kids, but we were forced to have adult thoughts. Along with discussions of the latest *Starsky and Hutch* episode, and the prospect of the Broncos beating the Raiders, we speculated on our future. Of course at that time our futures seemed as bleak as the Broncos'. Would we make it to 18? If we were still around then, we could drink beer. That was something to look forward to. What about that magical age of 21, was it within reach? We considered the rewards for reaching legal adulthood, like being able to gamble, and being able to vote. Not as gratifying as beer, but Las Vegas would be cool. As far as voting, it seemed like a waste of time. Our political destiny was predetermined. We were pawns. What if we made it to college graduation? Nobody gave that much of a chance. None of us really thought we would live another eight years.

By the time I related this to my American history class, the fourteen-year-olds were hooked. Finally the gimmick worked, and one of them asked the question I was waiting for. Why would you all die? It was the question that wasn't asked by kids when I was teaching this class in 1990. Somewhere between 1990 and today, the world had changed dramatically. The remarkable thing is that people didn't teach their kids that the fear is gone. I guess that's my job.

The answer to the question is probably obvious to everyone born before 1980 or so. We didn't believe the world would survive the nuclear war that was inevitable. The Soviets would start the war, the United States would respond, and then, before the firing was over, all life would end. It was not possible to win the war, and the only survivors, according to popular myth, would be cockroaches. It was a bleak prospect, but it was a part of life. Cockroach-like, we adapted.

The only unknown factor was time. When do the explosions begin? How long would we live after the attack started? How long would we live if we were unlucky enough to survive the attack? The most important question of all; how much warning would we have after the Soviets launched? This question was crucial, because every conversation included the "what would you do if you knew the world was ending?" question.

So, I asked my class the same question. What would you do if you were told that the world as you know it would end in 45 minutes? There was silence then, as kids contemplated not only the answer to that question, but also the strangeness and newness of the question itself.

My friends and I, in the middle of the heat of the Cold War, came up with the same type of answers. For us it was unanimous. We would find a beautiful girl and have wild sex. We were sure it would be great, although we could only imagine what wild sex really was, since none of us had actually had any. We also failed to consider that even after the wild junior high sex, we would still have about 40 minutes to kill before the big finale. The majority also concluded that if there were no girls available, because of circumstances beyond our control, then we would go into the mountains or to a park and just enjoy nature while it still existed. That was really just a fall back position, however, because we were all pretty confident that we could find some female when the time came. It was also agreed that living through the "Nuclear Winter" was not an option. None of us were going into a bomb shelter for the rest of our lives. We had seen *The Day After* on TV, and it scared the hell out of us. There was no way we wanted to be a part of that; death was definitely the better option. The conversations usually concluded with less weighty discussions and debates about the possible identity and qualities of the lucky girl.

Of course I didn't go into all this with the kids in my class. I just let their imaginations run for a few minutes before continuing with the lesson. I think it gave them something to think about for awhile. I'm pretty sure most of them came to the same conclusions as we did years before.

So today, with the threat of annihilation apparently over, I wonder what all the hype was about. Why am I still here? Why didn't the evil Soviets launch? What happened to the bad guys? I know they were bad, I saw *Rocky IV*. Rocky didn't really have a chance; Drago beat the crap out of him. Rocky was lucky he was a Hollywood hero. The Soviets had no hearts; they were machines. It was all inevitable.

The government did such an excellent job of preparing me for the end that I was, and am, a little shocked that no end came. We went from sending warheads to the Soviet Union to sending hogs to Russia. It's no wonder then that today's young people don't understand what impending doom is all about. The government has turned off the nuclear propaganda faucet. Books, television, movies, news-magazines, were regularly saturated with the "Evil Empire." Where has all the paranoia gone?

It is almost hard to believe then, that in the age of the New World Order, there is still enough news to fill the vacuum left by the falls of the Berlin Wall and Soviet Union. What is a government to do with an inactive propaganda machine now?

Saddam Hussein, come on down. Osama bin Laden, come on down. Kim Jung Il, come on down. You are the next contestants on the Threat is Ripe. Of course it really isn't the same. Even Bob Barker is retired.

Ron and God

On his way to the grocery store, Ron met God. He had gone out for eggs, milk, toilet paper and tarragon, all of which, he soon discovered, was unnecessary, due to his death.

The accident was still fresh in his mind, having only occurred moments before. He never would have believed that his Ford Explorer would have come out on the short end of the stick in a battle with a Dodge Neon, but it had. The Explorer had lost. He had lost.

Ron's first thoughts upon dying were not what he had expected, not what he had considered the previous 41 years. There was no bright light. His life did not flash before his eyes like a TV series reunion. There was no pain or any feeling of relief. Ron was dead, and he knew it, but that was about it.

He stood on the curb next to the crumpled pile of steaming navy-blue Explorer on his own feet, the same feet he had had his whole life, and looked inside at the empty driver seat where he was supposed to be sitting, but wasn't. That's when God first spoke to him, although he didn't realize it was God. Looking back on it, Ron was impressed with the speed with which God had come to him following his death. He also thought later that he was probably pretty special, getting a personal greeting from the Big Man, and not some angel.

"Hi Ron," God said.

Ron was caught by surprise. He assumed that none of the living would be able to see him, but here was another mystery. He had no idea who the stranger was. "Hi."

"Everything OK?"

Ron looked at the man closely, unsure weather he was kidding or not. "Well, I'm dead." He paused a moment and then continued, "I feel OK, but I'm dead. And, now that you ask, I'm not really OK about felling OK about being dead, I guess."

"That's perfectly understandable," said God.

"So, you're dead too I take it. Were you in the little white car?"

"Yes and no to both questions."

"What?" Confused, Ron asked, "Are you saying that you are both alive and dead and that you were in the white car and also not in the white car?"

"Yeah, that's pretty close. I think I have the best of both worlds."

"What worlds? What are you talking about? Are you dead or not?"

"Didn't we just cover that? Not. Are you?"

"Look, I think I'm dead, I just told you that I was dead, but I don't know how I know. I also think that you must be dead too, because you're here with me. If you are not dead, then why are you here?

"Its what I do."

"What is? What do you do?"

"I visit with the newly dead, answer questions, show them around. Sort of a tour guide for the place."

"This place is Iowa, and it doesn't need much in the way of tour guides. I know my way around well enough."

"OK."

Ron walked around to the other side of the accident and looked in the window of the small white car. There was a man with blood on his face, but he was still breathing. Turning back to his own vehicle he saw his new companion still standing on the curb where he had left him. The usual street sounds surrounded them. Ron could hear the hiss of steam and the distant sound of sirens, but when he asked a question of his companion, in a normal voice, the other sounds became background noise like the hum of lights or the gurgle of a fish tank. "What is your name, and where did you come from?"

"God. Here."

Ron laughed and looked at the man more closely. He was wearing faded denim jeans, a Green Peace T-shirt and a baseball cap. The cap was on backwards. "OK, God," said the skeptical and sarcastic Ron, "What team does the creator root for? Let's see the front of that hat."

"I usually root for the underdog. This is, of course, a Chicago Cubs cap," God said, taking it off and showing Ron.

A quick laugh escaped from Ron. "What about the Green Peace shirt? Are they the underdog too?"

"Yup."

There was a pause while Ron considered this. They guy seemed sincere. There didn't seem to be any sarcasm or malice in his voice. "This is very funny God, but not right now. I don't really understand what's happening to me here and you don't seem to be making things much better. In fact, you are making things more confusing."

"I know exactly how you feel," said God.

"What do you mean you know exactly how I feel? I'm the one who just died here." Ron was shouting over the accident, he could feel himself shouting, but the volume didn't seem to change. He walked back over to the curb, stepping on broken glass that didn't make a sound. Ron didn't notice.

He stood looking at the scene for some time without talking. The emergency crews began to arrive. One of the ambulance drivers looked in the Explorer's window, reached his hand in briefly, cringed and walked back to the Neon.

"What did he reach in for?"

"He was hoping you still had a pulse."

"I don't get your sense of humor. The car is empty, what was he really doing? Did I leave something in there?"

"Just your body." God took off his hat again and pushed his hair back behind his ears.

"Why won't you answer any of my questions?" Ron turned back to the scene. The paramedics were taping things to the person in the Neon, who was rapidly changing from a driver to a medical experiment. "OK, look, if you really are God, which I doubt, then you should be able to prove it."

"OK."

"Well?"

"Well what?"

"Well prove it already."

"What can I do to prove to you that I am God?"

"I don't know, you're God. Make something miraculous happen. Read my mind. Introduce me to Jesus. Anything. I just can't believe that God is in his mid 40s, and he definitely doesn't look like David Crosby."

"Hmm...David Crosby huh? Well, you never gave me much thought before. Are you saying I need a haircut, or that I should lose the mustache?"

Ron stared again at his companion. After a few moments he turned back to the accident and said, somewhat exasperated, "God looks like he is about 70, has a long beard and mustache. And he is BIG. He needs to be, because he's GOD!"

"You've always loved that movie. Frankly, that surprised me. Usually the only people that have that image of me are very religious people, or visitors to the Vatican." God nodded his head in a knowing way. "Of course it's one of my favorites too."

Ron was trying to hold himself together, which he thought was strange considering the circumstances. Together was starting to have an all-new meaning. This person was claiming to be God, which wasn't possible. But somehow he had guessed that the image he was thinking of as God was actually the face of God painted by Charlton Hesston on the ceiling of the Sistine Chapel in *The Agony and the Ecstasy*. How could this man have known that? It must be a common thing, picturing God as he is seen in the movies.

Ron turned to ask him how he had guessed when he was interrupted.

"George Burns, clearly the number one, especially in the United States."

"What?" Ron's mind was sifting through layers of logic, trying to find the answers. "What about George Burns? What does George Burns have to do with anything?"

"Because many more people think of me in that image than yours. I still get a few Charlton Hestons, mostly people in their eighties, but I don't believe I've had a David Crosby before today."

The semi-orderly chaos of the accident scene continued, more police, EMTs, a tow truck and a local television station van were crowding closer to where Ron and God stood. The living paid no attention to the dead, or apparently to God either. Life was going on for everyone, exactly as it was supposed to, everyone doing a job, everyone with a purpose. Ron's uneasiness was growing. He had the distinct feeling of intrusion. His mind was drifting in and around, back and forth.

"Oh, God? You mean the movie *Oh, God,* with George Burns and John Denver? Are you saying that people think God is really George Burns?"

"No, they just expect me to look like him."

"So," Ron said, "You're saying that you appear when people die and the way you look is the way they expect you to look? Is that about right?"

"Yes, precisely right," said God.

"Well, that explains it all then. You don't look at all like the God of Michelangelo. So you must not be who you say you are."

Before God could answer, a police officer walked toward them and swept some glass from around them. His broom made almost no sound. After he moved farther down the sidewalk, God said, "You are incorrect. You didn't really believe in me as the image from the movie. In fact you didn't really believe in me at all. At most, I was a passing thought, primarily guilt from your mother and grandmother. Once, however, when you were very young, I believe you will remember that a baby sitter said something to you. Think back."

"What do you mean I never believed in God? I have never said that." Ron felt a trap coming. He was being forced into a position, he was not in control.

"I know you never said it. Just think about the baby sitter. You were four. I think you were four. Well it doesn't matter, just think back to a baby sitter named Christy."

Ron was losing track of the conversation until the name Christy, and then the memory came back, as though it just happened. Christy was listening to music. Loud music.

"Isn't this far out Ronny?"

"What's far out Christy?"

"The music Ronny, the music. Crosby, Stills, Nash and Young. I just love Neil Young. And the harmony Ronny, I tell you, David Crosby is a god. This is the best band ever."

Ron was stunned by the memory. He could hear the music. He could feel the beat of the music pass through the orange shag carpet and into his bare feet. Tiny feet. He could see Christy. He could almost smell her perfume. He turned to God.

"How do you know that?"

"It's what I do."

Ron closed his eyes and lived the memory again and again. Each time the music was loud and his feet were tiny and Christy smelled like nice, like safe was supposed to smell.

"Can you do it again? Can you make me remember other cool stuff?" He felt like dancing and crying, but couldn't do either.

"I'm God. You're Ron. You make the memories. I just watch them sometimes when you think about me."

Ron closed his eyes again, just to check if the memory was still there. It was, and he opened his eyes. "So you're really God? You really do exist?"

"Yes. Yes."

"Wow. God." Ron shook his head, "Who would have imagined?"

"Actually, the vast majority imagine. And almost all of them more than you."

"Sorry."

"Why"

"Well," said Ron, "I'm sorry I didn't believe in you when I should have."

"That isn't necessary," said God. "I am seldom what people imagine. Although dolphins are surprisingly accurate."

"You mean to tell me that dolphins know more about God than people do?"

"No, but they guess better."

Ron stood, thinking, watching the front of the pile of steel that was his vehicle being lifted by the tow truck. "You know God, I'm still not completely convinced."

"You rarely are."

"This could be pretty cool. I mean if you really are God, I have some questions. I have a ton of questions."

"I had a feeling you might, that's why I came. I have just one for you first, then you can ask all the questions you like."

"You need to ask me a question?"

"Actually I have several, but I need to ask one first. Here it is: do you know that you are dead?"

"Of course I know I'm dead." He paused, "I'm not sure how I know, but I do."

"Thank you," said God. "Now you may ask your questions. We can stay here or we can go someplace else."

"I don't understand. Where would we go? Isn't this heaven?"

"Its Iowa." God looked around and added, "How about golf?"

"God golfs?"

"Of course, everybody golfs."

"Is it much of a challenge for you?"

"Yes. I'm fairly good. I'm pretty long off the tees, and I usually putt well."

Ron thought about golfing, swearing, wanting to break clubs, hitting balls into lakes. Would God shank his 3-iron too? What if a person won the match against God with a long birdie putt on the eighteenth? What does God say when he doesn't get out of the sand trap? "I think I would rather not play golf, if you don't mind. I don't have my clubs and I don't think my concentration is there today, having just died and all. Can we just sit down somewhere?"

"I understand. Yes."

The next instant they were sitting on a large rock overlooking a mountain valley, a small stream meandering through a carpet of pines far below.

"Oh my God," said Ron.

"Yours and everyone else's I'm afraid," God whispered.

Ron didn't hear the comment. He was dizzy with the height of the view and the suddenness of the transformation. The sun was bright, reflecting off the water in flashing pin-pricks. It all seemed familiar but not enough for him to place exactly. He guessed it was Colorado because he grew up there and hiked in similar spots, but it could have been anywhere in the West.

He could see the wind moving the leaves of scattered groves of Aspen trees, sweeping up the canyon and for the first time realized that he couldn't feel the breeze he was seeing. It was unfulfilling and disappointing.

"What questions would you like to ask?"

It took a few seconds for Ron to respond. He suddenly felt overwhelmed with everything. He took a deep breath and with a sigh asked, "How much time do you have?"

"That isn't really relevant anymore. So, take your time."

Ron turned away from the canyon and looked at God. "Was that a pun? Are you kidding around at a time like this?"

God smiled, looked out at the landscape and said nothing.

"First question. Did you make me die today?"

"No."

"Can you make me alive again?"

"I can't make you alive again, because you are dead. There is life, however, even in death. You will understand more later."

"Later? Will I be able to tell when later is?"

"Interesting perspective isn't it. Einstein thought so too."

Ron almost asked about the possibility of talking with Einstein, but instead tried to keep the questions going in some order that his mind had created. "Did you know I was going to die today?"

"No."

"Can you control anything that people do?"

God squinted at the sun and turned his cap around to shield his eyes. A look of resignation came to his face. "Of course not."

"What do you mean 'Of course not'? Why do you say it like that? You're God, no doubt a little different that most people think, but you are still God. You obviously have power."

"It's not what I do."

"So," Ron turned his back to the valley and looked up the mountain, "what's the story? Are you the benevolent or the vengeful God that I keep hearing about?

You sound like the isolationist God to me."

"You are sounding more like a dolphin every minute," said God with a smile.

Ron noticed for the first time that God's Green Peace T-shirt had a picture of dolphins on it. "So, if you are laissez faire God, how do you know when my time is up?"

"Time isn't as relevant as you, and Einstein and everybody else, make it out to be."

Confused, Ron said, "Are you an oracle? Did you used to live in Delphi? I'm not getting straight answers here."

"No, and I live always. You should ask straighter questions."

Ron looked back down the valley. He could just make out a bird soaring above a distant peak. Smaller and smaller it became as it rose on an invisible thermal. When he could no longer see it, he turned back to God.

"There must be people dieing all over the world, all the time. Don't you need to go and ask them if they know if they are dead?"

"Yes."

"Well, when? I mean we've been talking for awhile, and I'm sure somebody in Bangladesh or New Jersey or Patagonia just died, and you're still hanging out with me."

"I'll visit with them if they need it. Time is not a worry for me," said God.

"Okay. I think I understand. You answer questions like a lawyer, or a President." Ron was silent for a few more seconds, going over the questions and answers from their conversation. "Sorry about the President comment." He then asked what he considered a pretty good question. "What is your opinion of the bumper sticker I saw that said, 'God grant me wisdom and protect me from your followers'?"

"Dark comedy, but very clever. I wish I could. Isn't it obvious that I cannot?"

"That's what I always thought," Ron said, slapping the granite stone next to him.

"I know," said God. "I understand."

"You keep saying that. Do you really understand? Everything?"

"Yes to both questions," said God. "Your vulture is back." God pointed to a spot high in the sky to their right.

"Dark comedy?"

God smiled and said nothing.

"Okay, what about the other bumper sticker that says Born OK the First Time?"

"What are you asking?"

"Well I guess I'm asking if there is anything to this born again stuff."

"There is just as much to the born again movement as there is to the other religions of the world."

"So does that mean that they all get to heaven, no matter what religion they are?"

"Have you ever seen a dolphin in a mosque or a church?"

Ron shook his head, confused again. "Why do you keep bringing up dolphins? What do they have to do with Born Again Christians?"

"It is safe to say that they belong in the same category as Christians and your vulture."

"God, don't take this the wrong way, but sometimes you seem a little bitter. What do you have against Christians?"

"Have you seen the movie of the play *Inherit the Wind*?"

"Yes."

"People had the chance to make a break, but didn't. When Spencer Tracy picked up *The Bible* and *Origins of Species*, put them both together and carried them out of the courtroom, I knew an opportunity was lost.

"So is it mostly Christians that you are irritated with?"

"Have you been paying attention to the Middle East?"

"But you are God. Do something about it."

"It's not what I do."

"No offense, but you don't seem to do much"

"What would you have me do?"

Ron considered this. There were so many people suffering in the world. There was so much anger and unhappiness. And then there was the whole global warming problem. And over-population. And child abuse. And so much more. Surely something could be done.

"What about stopping wars? There seems to be a war going on all the time."

"I understand your frustration with each other, but it is much too complicated a world to make those kinds of decisions."

"But if you're God, and if you know as much as you lead on, then you should be able to figure it all out."

"Who should win these wars?"

Ron had to admit that could be a problem.

"Here's the thing that you and many others fail to grasp. You all have free will."

God stood up and walked to the edge of the rock, looking down at the descending mountain and the life beneath. He turned back to Ron. "You still do."

In an instant, they were no longer sitting in a mountain canyon, but in a quaint little coffee shop in Iowa City. Ron was sitting across from God at a small round table. There was a good crowd and he could hear the college student, working behind the counter, steaming milk. But he couldn't smell the flavors of the air.

"Nice choice," said God. "See?"

"I love this place. Or I used to love this place."

"Yes."

"Tell me about Jesus," said Ron.

"What exactly do you want to know?"

"Was he real? Did he really turn the water to wine and all that jazz?"

"He is a very peaceful person with a lot of ambition."

"But, was he right in everything that he preached? Should people still be quoting him?"

"He lived a short life that has been interpreted differently for centuries. Right and wrong doesn't really have anything to do with it any longer."

Ron thought God had a little tone of regret.

"But was he right or wrong? Was he the son of God? I mean, was he your son?"

"Right and wrong is really just a matter of perspective. He is my son in the same way that you are."

"And the dolphins."

"Correct."

They sat and watched the people in the coffee shop. They were all so alive. Ron didn't think they really appreciated it, and it was a little depressing. He couldn't have what they had, and they couldn't know just how valuable what they had was.

Ron thought about being in a different place, and then he was. He and God were sitting in overstuffed armchairs in a corner of a large bookstore.

"This is also nice," God said.

"I like places like this. I always feel strangely peaceful in bookstores."

"I know."

They were in the section of the bookstore devoted to history. "I think it's the ideas that are available to me. I always wanted to know everything in all the books. I felt a little guilty not reading, because I didn't want to waste time and miss out on some important information before I died." He paused for a moment and then added, "seems like I was wrong on that one."

"Time is more, and less, than most people can really grasp. And the desire to know everything is obvious."

They didn't talk. Both Ron and God sat in the well worn chairs and read the titles on the bookshelves that surrounded them.

Eventually, Ron broke the silence. "Is heaven the same for all?"

"It's a little like pizza. Everyone has access to the same ingredients, but every pizza comes out different."

"Sort of like the David Crosby thing."

"Yes."

"What about the non-believers? What's their fate?"

God tilted his head a little as he looked at Ron. "Like you?"

Ron hadn't thought about it like that. He had to admit to himself that he had, until very recently, been included in the non-believer category. "So this is my pizza?"

God just smiled.

"Do I get to hang out with other people? Can I visit my dead relatives? I would love to see my dad again. And Ben Franklin, and Erasmus."

"You can see them if you're available to them. Most are open to everyone, but some people don't have enough space."

"What do you mean? Why not? Haven't you told them what they are missing?"

"It's not what I do." Once again Ron thought God looked a little disappointed.

"Of course. I should have known."

After a moment Ron said, "In them, you mean. That's what you meant. They don't have enough space inside themselves?"

"Cleverly put."

Ron stood and touched the spine of a book on the shelf. It was a book on the Crusades. It felt ironic. "I think I'm nearly ready to begin. I think I'm going to have a long list of questions for a long list of people. And, perhaps dolphins."

"Yes," said God.

"I'll probably have more questions for you as well."

God smiled and adjusted his Cubs cap.

"How do I get started?"

And he was.

Superheroes, Knights and Pirates

I haven't actually seen the dragons. I'm sure they must be very large and treacherous. It's a wonder I can even get into some of the rooms in my house with all the slaying going on. The pirates too, I understand, are a tough bunch, although I think the British sailors are the evil ones. Then there are the Bad Guys. There are lots and lots of Bad Guys. In fact they show up more often at my house than the dragons. They never present much of a problem however, because I live with Superman. I know its Superman because he introduced himself to me and then jumped down from the fourth stair in our entryway.

I also live with Robin. Interestingly, I seldom see Batman. I'm not clear as to why Robin is more at home in my home that Batman, but that does seem to be the case. Occasionally Spiderman swings by, but I don't think he has what it takes to hang around our house on a permanent basis. One or two of the Power Ranges are ever coming and going. For some reason the Pink Power Ranger is at dinner far less than the Black Power Ranger, but sometimes they will all show up in the same evening. (We have established a rule requiring all dinner guests, including Power Rangers, Knights, and Pirates to remove their swords while eating. Unfortunately, it isn't always enforced.) My favorite superhero, at least my favorite local superhero was Metal Man. I had never heard of him, but he told me that he was really tough and strong, and nothing could break him. We talked about very high heat, but melting didn't really seem to worry him. His only real concern was rust.

I'm not sure when all this began, but my house has been, for quite some time, a hang-out for cowboys. Also, Buzz Lightyear sleeps in a bunk bed on the second floor of my house almost every night, in a Space Shuttle. Buzz is constantly talking to his wrist, or to some guy named Star Command.

The thing is, my family never knows who is going to join us at any given time of the day or night. The Superheroes, Knights, Pirates and others can be found with us at the library, grocery store or airport. Earlier this week, for instance, Superman was seen flying down the pedestrian mall, Robin was noticed outside the pool after swimming lessons and several witnesses saw a sword carrying Pirate riding a tricycle down Governor Street.

Of course I was, as most people would be I assume, concerned by these unusual events. However, one day at the Kirkwood School for Children I saw four Knights together in the same room. I decided then that it must be quite common. I left that afternoon holding the hand, and one of the swords of, a great, if somewhat short, Knight.

This morning, while making coffee in the kitchen, Spiderman informed me that he had lost his sword. I asked the obvious question. Does Spiderman need a sword? I was told that in fact I wasn't really talking to Spiderman, but to SpiderRobin, and SpiderRobin needed a sword. I told him that there were to my knowledge, four swords, two daggers and a light saber in the house some place, and that since he was the superhero, it was his job to find them. I felt pretty comfortable talking to SpiderRobin that way since he was unarmed.

On our way to the car to go to swimming lessons I asked SpiderRobin if he found his sword. The answer was, "Arrrr matey!" Of course I felt foolish having failed to notice that SpiderRobin had been replaced by a squinty-eyed Pirate instead. I told him I was glad he found what he needed, and to buckle his seatbelt.

I Am Spartacus
or
Derrick's Warped Sense of History

I have made a commitment on Halloween. Every Halloween for the rest of my life, or at least those that involve carving pumpkins, I will leave my pumpkins on the front step.

I showed parts of the movie *Spartacus* to my students this week. At one point Crassus, the Hollywood bad guy in a Roman toga, declares that all 6,000 surviving rebel slaves will be crucified unless he learns the identity of Spartacus. As the tension mounts, Spartacus stands to make his confession, but before he can say anything other slaves declare themselves to be Spartacus. "I'm Spartacus," rings out from hundreds. My students don't get it.

When I was a kid I went trick-or-treating with my friends just like almost every other kid in America. As I grew older, and stayed out later, I also became a bit of a hoodlum on a night that was made for them. My friends and I thought it great fun to grab pumpkins from porches and smash them in the street. If the curtains were open, or there was a dog inside, or there was some other additional element of risk, the caper would yield even more respect from the other smashers.

"Why don't they just tell them that one of the dead people from the battle is Spartacus?"

Good question. In fact it is the question.

The most legendary pumpkin caper took place in one of the last years I could reasonably pass for young enough to get away with trick-or-treating. One of my friends opened the front door, took a step or two inside, and took the pumpkin off the fireplace mantle. It makes me nervous remembering it.

In the end, Spartacus is hanging from the cross, watching his wife and his child escape to freedom. His sacrifice has helped only two people, at a cost of thousands of lives.

Some day I hope to watch, as some kid grabs a pumpkin from my porch and destroys my feeble Halloween art. I will know that I have done my part and those kids can carry on. I am Spartacus. A little.

The Long Walk Home

My daughter and I walked home from school today. It isn't often that I have that luxury. The afternoon is the crucial, and almost always hectic, errand running time of life. Before dinner, the groceries must be shopped, the library books must be returned, supplies from Menards are certainly needed, the post office closes early, and there is always something to pick up at Target. The lists perpetuate like bunnies. Work is done, time to go to work.

It is fair to say that my daughter has little appreciation for the important things in life. The fact that she is three years old gives her some leverage, but at some point she needs to see just how important it is to leave school without doddling so she can rush to stand in line at the motor vehicle department. Her misguided sense of values still insists that stopping to look at and then pick up worms is more important than getting to the repair shop to pick up the DVD player before they close. With enough modeling, I'm sure she will understand that going up and down on the teeter-totter is nice, but getting to JC Penny's to exchange the shirt that doesn't fit is a necessity.

But today she and I walked home from preschool. I remembered something today on our walk home. When I was a kid, I had to hold my dad's hand when we walked across the street. He always said, "Grab my hand, Bud." The only thing was, I didn't hold his whole hand, just his index finger. Today I found out how it felt to have a whole hand wrapped around just one index finger. My dad's was rough and strong, and if I held on tight, I could swing. I wondered if the feeling was the same for my daughter.

Today it took me 10 minutes to walk to the school to get her, and 45 minutes for the two of us to walk home. In between stops to look at flowers and bugs and dogs and trees and puddles and anything purple, and endless other unnoticeables, my daughter held my index finger. She walked along by herself if she had to scratch her head, the last remainders of her chicken pox, or to hold a cracker in each hand from her snack-to-go from the preschool, but mostly she just held my finger.

We stopped dozens of times, but only twice for significant periods. On the way home there are two mulberry trees. They are producing berries by the mouthful. Since she is too short to reach the branches and also because she was wearing a white shirt, I did all the picking. I held the little green stem and she ate the berry with out using her fingers at all. After we ate all the ripe berries we could find, as well as a few that could have used another day or two on the branch, we continued home.

By the time we got there, my fingers were purple. I was happy that I had shared the experience of eating mulberries with my daughter and had kept her clean at the same time. It seemed strange that I had no reason to rush home that was more important than that long slow walk. As it turns out, my daughter does seem to have a sense of the priorities. I sat on our porch swing and thought how nice it would be to be three years old again. The only negative side was that I wouldn't be able to reach the mulberries. I guess that's what dads are for.

I went in the house to find my daughter curled up on the blue chair with her Blanky, and I noticed that she didn't get away completely unstained after all, there was just the faintest purple stain on the palm of her hand.

Super Hero Sleepover

The Super Hero Sleepover was last night. Not everyone is aware that Super Heroes have sleepovers, but there are probably many things about Super Heroes that would surprise the average person, the first being that they hang out together. Last night, four of them gathered at the Red Power Ranger's house to watch videos of themselves, eat popcorn, go on a mole hunt, catch lightning bugs, and, most importantly, sleep in a tent in the back yard.

The modern Super Hero, contrary to myths developed over the years by people who don't know Super Heroes but merely conjure up stories about them, is really only five years old, is capable of shifting powers and the personas of many different Heroes and is most content when sword-fighting with other Super Heroes. Also, they have bossy big sisters, whom they generally listen to and occasionally attack without warning or malice.

Last night's gathering was unusual for the fact that Super Heroes rarely have the opportunity to have sleepovers. It was a special occasion, due mainly to the fact that the Red Ranger, from the *Mighty Morphin Power Rangers*, is relocating his main residence to Kansas in the near future. It was quite an event.

Most Rangers stay in their civilian clothes until danger stirs them to action, but not the Red Ranger. He was in his red suit with mask by 9:00 AM. The tent, having been borrowed from the family of a slightly older Indian War Chief and his older bossy sister, was in place by noon and the Red Ranger had sleeping bags, pillows (including his special night-time "Soft Pillow") and books in it soon after. While the other three Super Heroes were apparently spending their days fighting crime and not listening to their mothers at their own homes, the Red Ranger and his big sister spent the day reading books and playing in the tent. There is something extraordinary about a tent, even in the back yard.

After a hastily consumed dinner of Chinese take-out, in the midst of stacks of partially packed boxes and totes, the other three Super Heroes began to arrive with their mortal parents. The first to arrive was Spiderman. Although the youngest of the Super Heroes at four years of age, he more than makes up for his youth with size and enthusiasm. He is the strongest and most persistent; although when he walked in he was carrying his beloved stuffed animal "Toad," without whom he never slept. His parents and his older bossy sister, who rolled her eyes at the obvious lack of maturity of young Spidey, accompanied him. Spiderman's mother, lugging his backpack, reminded the Red Ranger's parents that as of that time, Spiderman had yet to make it through a complete sleepover and would more than likely choose to go home around 10:30 that night.

The next to arrive was Buzz Lightyear. Nearly as enthusiastic as Spiderman, Buzz tends to want, as is his nature in both film and life, to be in charge.

Unfortunately for them, the list of people that he commands also includes his parents, who were lugging his sleeping bag, backpack and baby blanket while he ignored them and immediately engaged in swordplay. Buzz, like all super-heroes, has a weakness. The lack of an older bossy sister, or any siblings at all, could certainly be considered his weakness, but Buzz was most concerned with the fact that he still wore a pull-up to bed at night. His parents related a special request that he be given some "private time" before retiring for the night so he could change into his pajamas alone.

The last of the Super Heroes to arrive was in disguise ... as a normal preschooler. The only hint at his true persona was his Wild Force Power Ranger T-shirt and his stack of Yu-Gi-Oh trading cards. The quietest of the four, he was at different times during the evening Batman, Blue Power Ranger and Superman. He carried his own sleeping bag, pillow and backpack, and in a clear attempt to display his independence, his mother carried his own single-hero pop-up tent. This Transformer Hero could be the twin of the Red Power Ranger and they are indeed best friends. Slightly nervous about the prospect of spending the entire night in a tent, the Transforming Hero got assurances from The Red Power Ranger that they would be sleeping together. The matter having been settled in a brief Hero-to-Hero heart-to-heart hushed conversation on the back porch, the party was complete and it was time for the four Super Heroes to do what they do best, wrestle and battle with swords and light-sabers.

The battles continued, on and off, in and out of the tent, over and around the swing set, in and out of the house for the better part of an hour. The rough-housing finally slowed somewhat when they settled in to watch videos of themselves in action on the small TV set up in the corner of the tent. They watched, and of course actively critiqued, three short movies, *Mighty Morphin Power Rangers: Goldar's Vice Versa*, *Batman and Mr. Freeze*, and *The Batman Superman Movie*. To replenish their ever-expanding energy needs, the four Super Heroes consumed two giant bowls of popcorn and a pitcher of lemonade.

Following the movies, and after yet another snack of graham crackers and pears, it was time for the mole hunt. The mole, a pesky dilemma for the Red Power Ranger for the past several weeks was, alas, safe for another night due largely to the fact that darkness had begun to fall and the bossy big sister and her friend (also spending the night) had decided that lightning bugs were easier prey and quickly transformed the hunt. What most people, who aren't necessarily associated with either Super Heroes or bossy big sisters, don't know is that to hunt lightening bugs, the most important skills are running and screaming at each other loud enough for every neighbor on the block to hear. This cacophony of shouting, flashlight-dancing spectacle lasted for more than an hour until, for their own well being, it was suggested by Red Power Ranger's parents that it was time for bed. The end result of the hunt was five captured lightening bugs, four living and one not.

Not surprisingly, Buzz was the first into his pajamas. He made a quick change in the bathroom before the other Super Heroes had even had a chance to get their backpacks from the tent. There was a clear look of relief on his face after his stealthy change. There was a brief moment of hesitation when young Spiderman at first showed no intention of getting ready for bed. He overcame his fear, at least for the moment, when the Red Ranger changed into his jammies. Spiderman reluctantly followed the Red Ranger's example and changed from his daytime-hero, Spiderman, into his nighttime hero Batman. Needless to say, with Super Heroes changing identities so often, it was difficult to keep track of them. The Transformer Hero transformed yet again into another Power Ranger shirt and a pair of shorts. Ready for bed, the four Heroes headed to the tent for stories.

Reading stories to four Super Heroes is an interesting experience. Aside from the fact that the reader needs to balance a flashlight on his chest and find a spot where everyone can see the pictures, it is almost impossible to find any story that all four have never heard. Also, being Super Heroes, they are very confident and very intelligent. So, to the story reader, this means a constant running dialogue with each other about the story, including additional facts about the book that the author failed to include, the subtleties of the relationships between characters and most irritating to each other, the ending of the stories. After 20 minutes reading the 27-page *The Underwater Alphabet Book* and discussing, in painful detail, the myths and truths about every creature from the Angelfish to the Xanthidae, (there was no Y or Z entry) it was time to move on to *Caps for Sale*. It was the only real trouble spot in the evening. After the peacefulness of the moment had been completely destroyed by the screaming attack of the flashlight wielding bossy big sister and friend, the other three Super Heroes got angry with Buzz Lightyear for constantly telling what was going to happen next in the story. Thankfully order was restored, and only the Red Ranger had heard the last story, *The Stray Dog*. It was a sweet story with a happy ending on two levels. One, the stray dog found a happy home, and two, both Buzz Lightyear and, most surprisingly, Spiderman (now Batman) were already asleep.

After a few minutes of quiet discussion of Yu-Gi-Oh cards, the Transformer Hero and the Red Power Ranger, on separate sleeping bags, but next to each other, fell asleep. The time was 10:45, and the Red Ranger's father, clearly not as comfortable as the powerful and exhausted Super Heroes, tried for some time to ignore the partying college kids in the next block before dropping off to sleep himself sometime close to 11:30. It was a peaceful sleep for all but the Red Ranger's father who swore to himself about positioning the tent in the least smooth and uneven part of the yard and swore at the college kids who revived the party at 2:30 after the bars closed.

It was a short interval of sleep again, because at 3:30 Spiderman (now Batman) woke up and with a look of terror on his face said he needed to go home. After a fruitless attempt to comfort him, and a quick call to his mom, the Red Power

Ranger's mom put him in the car and drove him home. The Red Power Ranger's father, after covering the lump-like sleeping Heroes with their sleeping bags, fell to unconsciousness again and managed to sleep until every bird in the neighborhood began to chirp mercilessly at 5:15. By 6:15, with the sun fully up, the Super Heroes were awake and ready for swordplay and pancakes, in that order.

By 10:00 the Red Power Ranger's mom had the three remaining Super Heroes in the car and they were returned to their parents. As for the parents of the Red Ranger, napping was definitely on the agenda for the day. Packing could wait.

JASON ALBERTY

The first thing I remember writing was a poem about the color green: "Green is the color of that new shampoo, Pert." God help me. I hope I've come further than that. I have a vague memory of a poem about a tornado that won some poetry contest for me in early elementary school. It seemed like a big to-do at the time. But my main to-do these days is working out what all this swirling life is about. I explore it with my wife and dogs, family and friends. I explore it through writing. I explore it through theatre. I explore it through the regular meetings with friends to discover each other's ever-deepening facets. And I explore it through helping students find some understanding in their own swirling and ever deepening self-concepts, their wonder at the flowering and confusing world that engulfs all of us.

The Kinder, Gentler Death
a monologue

Man sits on solitary chair, stage right, pinhole spot. Mottled blue and red swirling light on cyc. behind him which stretches along the back of the stage. The rest of the stage is in darkness.

The man is wearing a teddy bear costume with a red vest, buttons running down it. One of the buttons is noticeably loose. He is holding a clipboard with papers clipped to it.

He is bored, passing time, waiting, not happy to be there.

He sighs deeply, in the manner of exhibiting tested patience.

He notices the audience, acknowledges them with a quick raise and lowering of his head. Maybe he spouts a quick "hey."

He waits several beats. Exhibits some traits of impatience.

He looks again at the audience.

MAN: It's not easy, you know ... Death I mean. What? You think bing-bang and you're gone forever? Huh. Or better yet, you pretend that you're nice and you pretend that you have good thoughts about everybody, and, when you slip off into the great beyond, the white angels lift your soul to some cloud-carpeted suite where an old, bearded man says, "Enter, my child. Your soul shall rest in heaven."

Ha! There is no rest, my friend. We are in a constant state of movement—all based on our choices, of course. I mean, you die at the appointed time, I come down and pull you back up, you're debriefed, you fill out the next Pre-incarnation Application 1A42-17—you know, what dimension, life-station, the experience parameters you want—and then you wait your turn at the Department of Body Acquisition and Soul Placement ... (for decades) ... and they set you up ... theoretically. But they've been having some problems in Body Acquisition. There's no work ethic in that department. Every once in a while they'll slip a soul into the wrong body, you know. And then we've got to go in and fix it for them. You wouldn't believe the overtime we've been racking up. Not to mention the paperwork.

Oh, it's a bureaucracy, my friend, and Death is just one of the cogs in the greater wheel of this ether-filled, multi-dimensional universe. Sure, it looks easy: Death. You float, you know, kind of hover, not walk, but hover upright, slowly moving toward the lately departed, your black Armageddon robe billowing behind you in the otherwise still air. You stick out a bony finger, point it toward the newly deceased, beckon menacingly, then escort the bewildered dead to their next destination, whatever that may be. Right? Yeah, well, let me tell you 'bout that one, my friend: Jeptha of Sinon! No! Really, that was him: Jeptha of Sinon. That little idea got him moved up to Undersecretary of Receiving.

Well, it was timely, you know. I mean, hell, I wouldn't begrudge him the recognition, although I'd like to, the rat bastard. Okay, here it was: The Department of Inhabitant Management ordered up a new global restructuring program, complete with a new world-wide contagion, and yet, they forget to send a memo to Notification and Receiving? I mean, what the hell? That's the first place you send a memo. Come on, have you tried to handle a global catastrophe with an entire battalion of Death Notification trainees? Well, even a first year Notification Specialist can see "Cluster Fuck" written all over that plan. Jesus! I mean, you'd think they've learned that from the Extinction Meteor debacle. That was a nightmare!

On the other hand, we did have a decade notification for the Great Flood. Now, that was some good work there. People were on the ball with that one. None of this "Oh, by the way, tell your people we're wiping out humanity tomorrow." I mean, we had tactical and procedural manuals that thick. Training programs, exercises, live fire maneuvers. We were prepared for that one.

I don't know, I guess when you do something really well you sometimes get complacent.

Anyway, back to Jeptha—we were working the usual shifts, you know, I mean nothing spectacular. At that time I was working the Mediterranean. That was some nice work, there. Sun, ocean. Nothing too bad, you know. Some drownings, which are actually pretty easy. You know that whole back to the womb thing, breathing liquid. I mean they know they're dead (which helps us out in the long run). These souls who drown kind of go though this birthing reversal thing and it's like they're expecting you. Like they remember, you know? It's easy. It's when they don't expect you that things get rough.

Suddenly things start going haywire over in the Asian Sector. I mean, Jesus! The whole Department of Notification and Receiving was swamped, instantly understaffed, and they were pulling people from Africa and the

Near East. Well, they couldn't handle it. And, that was it. They actually went with a full multi-dimensional alert. They started pulling every Tom, Quag and Bedeeeeeeeeeetzwildtpk from the Ether to use them as Death Notification trainees.

But you see, the notification process ain't so easy. The procedure at that time was to just recombinate psychically to the new dead as a physicalized manifestation of a skeleton, and that was a pretty good clue for them that it was time to move on, you know.

Now a full body skeleton is pretty tough to put together psychically; there are a lot of parts you're trying to think together, you know? Well, we just didn't have time to train the new Notification Specialists thoroughly. Shit, we had boneless canaries, sentient clothing, and blue mists all over the fucking place. That meant thousands of unnotified walking dead.

Well, Jeptha had come up through Early Greece and Rome and was just released from a stint in Mongolia (I mean this guy had seen some shit come down). Well, he knew pretty well how to handle some major numbers of newly dead in a quick fashion with relatively fresh Notifiers. His idea was to simplify. Simplify everything.

Now a bony hand—not too hard to psychically recombinate, especially if you break it down into just five long, curved bones instead of trying to get all the carpal, metacarpal, phalange-pangy stuff, right? I mean, they see a floating set of hand bones coming toward 'em, they ain't gonna look hard enough to notice and say, "Hey! That floatin' hand bone ain't got no metacarpus!" Naw, they're gonna figure the jig is up. Clothing? Behind the blue mist, clothing is the easiest thing to recombinate psychically, and if it's a one-piecer, you can do it in your sleep. You see, the black Armageddon robe covers up the need to recombinate the rest of the skeleton; you just have the hand to deal with, you know. Pretty simple.

Now the scythe was another matter. You see, some newly dead did not take us seriously. And when we're dealing with the numbers of newly dead that the Black Plague was working up, they got to take us seriously... fast. Well, the scythe just added the punctuation mark to our get-up. Who ain't gonna listen to a freakin' Armageddon-robed, bone-handed guy with a big-assed scythe. My point exactly.

Yeah, those were the days.

But, you know the only constant is change. And, well, we had to change with the times.

Now we are working toward a "kinder, gentler" Department of Notification and Receiving. My ass. Apparently we were becoming a bit too disturbing while notifying our prospective newly deceased. Now the protocol is to notify the newly deceased psychically recombinated as A: a manifestation of some earthly departed loved one (you know, like in that scene from Ghost. Ah, that was a nice movie!), or B: as that which was ordained to bring about his or her Earthly demise (you know, if they're killed by a big city bus, we show up as a talking big city bus, kind of like a mass transit version of Herbie the Love Bug—kind of shake 'em into recognition), or C: as the newly deceased's most prized and loved possession (a hold-over from the 1980s. I can't tell you how many candy apple red Porsche 911s I've come back as), or D: any combination thereof (see, many times I am able to come back as their prized possession, which also was the thing that did in fact kill them—note the Porsche 911s).

Well, now you got to be creative. You got to do your homework, your background checking. You don't want to show up as a talking chicken bone to Melvin Blumberg when he has actually just had a myocardial infarction, you know what I mean? Oh, listen to this: we had this one kid, just got done with training, going out on his first solo notification, you know. Well, his newly deceased just died in Bangladesh of beriberi; you know, one of these nasty tropical wasting away kind of deaths. I kept telling the kid, the new notifier, "Do your research. You got to do your research." Well, this kid shows up as a talking bunch of big yellow berries off a Persian lilac. I mean, Jesus. Yeah, it is an Asian plant. Yeah, it is poisonous, but A: it's got nothing to do with how he died, and B: you never—never!—show up as anything remotely edible to a newly dead who has wasted away. Cause you know what? He's feeling a lot better, and he's fucking hungry. He had the kid half eaten before we knew what was going on! You only make that mistake once.

The positive is that it's brought out the challenge in the job again, you know. It weeded out the mediocre Notification Specialists and the other post-physical ne're-do-wells. So I guess it's a good thing. I mean, I can take pride in my job again, you know.

But I got to tell you, this over-time work is killing me. (*Looks at paper*) Case in point: my next notification, little four-year old Billy L. Wanamaker of Pawtucket. (*He fingers the unraveled button*) Look at this... another misbodied soul match. You know, you order one body incarnation and you're not expecting to be birthed into another. See, this guy ordered an hermaphroditic double-jointed Afro-Asian with enhanced physical acumen and ended up as a white Lutheran in suburban New Jersey. Well, it's not the worst misbodied soul match I've had to deal with.

Ding. Lights stop swirling.

Well, that's my cue.

He gets up, smoothes down his teddy bear suit and begins exiting into the darkness toward stage left. Stops, rips off the loose button, tosses it, catches it. Looks to audience.

See you 'round. [*Exits*]

Dance

The music fades away
to an airy wisp
and all that exists
are your eyes
your smile
and the joy behind them.

Even my seemingly
Atlasian concentration
—steptapsteptap
           rock—
melts into your
Athenian eyes,

so that,
swayed by the ocean-movements
of our dance,
only
we
exist.

Conversation I

Two men on a park bench.

PERSON 1: Do you, you know, make up rules for stuff?

PERSON 2: What do you mean?

PERSON 1: Well, you know, rules. Like you make up a game or something.

PERSON 2: Oh, yeah, yeah. Me and my friends, when we were younger, we'd like make up all these weird games, you know. Yeah, we had one, we had one, get this, we had one where we would all be on our skates and we'd have this tennis ball . . .

PERSON 1: No, man, no. Not like that. No, I mean, like now.

PERSON 2: What, right now?

PERSON 1: No, but like this year, you know. As your age is at this moment.

PERSON 2: I don't know what the . . .

PERSON 1: No, look . . . Eh, nah, you're just gonna haze me with it.

PERSON 2: No, man, I'll be cool.

PERSON 1: Shit.

PERSON 2: No, really, man. Let go with it. Go ahead. I'm cool.

PERSON 1: Yeah, all right. Okay, so like I'm getting up in the morning, you know, and, like, I go to the sink and I'm thinking, I'm thinking, "Okay, so if I turn on the hot water and it's like already warm then this is gonna be like an awesome day." Right?

PERSON 2: Uh . . . okay.

PERSON 1: Or, like I'm running down stairs and I think, I think, "So, okay . . .

if my right foot is like the first foot to hit the floor then so-and-so's gonna ask me out." Okay?

PERSON 2: Yeah.

PERSON 1: Okay, okay. Like the other day, I'm walking out of Tuff 'n' Eddie's, and—you know that thing they got in the parking lot?

PERSON 2: What?

PERSON 1: That thing, that thing, you know. In the middle of the damn lot: that, that, that grass thing.

PERSON 2: Oh yeah, that uh . . . that berm.

PERSON 1: "Berm"?

PERSON 2: Yeah, that grass berm.

PERSON 1: What the hell's a "berm"?

PERSON 2: It's that grass thing, that . . . uh, that humpy grass thing. You're talking about that thing with the tree, right? And that yellow curb?

PERSON 1: Yeah.

PERSON 2: Yeah, that's a . . . that's a berm.

PERSON 1: Yeah, okay, whatever.

PERSON 2: It is.

PERSON 1: Fine, yeah, fine. Anyways, I'm walking out of Tuff 'n' Eddie's, you know, and I decide I'm gonna cross that . . . thing. And I'm thinking, I'm thinking, "So, okay, I'm gonna cross this thing and if my right foot lands on the far-side crack between the grass and the curb I'm gonna get laid tonight."

PERSON 2: Really?

PERSON 1: Yeah.

PERSON 2: This is what you're thinking?

PERSON 1: Yeah.

PERSON 2: Does it work?

PERSON 1: What do you mean?

PERSON 2: Do you get laid?

PERSON 1: No. That's the problem; it never works.

PERSON 2: It never works?

PERSON 1: No, man. It's like never worked.

PERSON 2: So you're saying that your foot always goes onto the crack and you never get laid because of it, even though the rules say you will?

PERSON 1: Yeah.

PERSON 2: Well, then stop it.

PERSON 1: I can't, man. It's like an obsessive thing. It just pops into my head, and before I know it, the rules are laid out and everything is happening.

PERSON 2: It just pops out?

PERSON 1: Yeah.

PERSON 2: Well . . . .

PERSON 1: What?

PERSON 2: Well . . . if it never works just change the question.

PERSON 1: What do you mean?

PERSON 2: Well, you say . . . .

PERSON 1: No, no, you never say it out loud; you just think it.

PERSON 2: Okay . . . you just think, "Hey, I'm gonna walk across that berm there and if I put my foot on this here crack then I ain't getting laid." And cause it never works, if you put your foot on that there crack you're guaranteed to get laid cause it's directly goin' against your rule.

PERSON 1: What?

PERSON 2: It'll work cause it's directly goin' against your rule.

PERSON 1: You . . . you mean cheat?

PERSON 2: Nah, that ain't cheating, it's just reconstructuring the question.

PERSON 1: No, man, it's cheating.

PERSON 2: No, it ain't. It's a simple . . . uh, questionial reconstruction.

PERSON 1: Nah, look, it's no good. First, you're just plain cheating. Secondly . . . uh, secondly, you're being negative.

PERSON 2: How am I being negative when I'm guaranteeing you a guaranteed lay? That's about as positive as I can get.

PERSON 1: No, you've like changed around the question so it's asking it in a negative way . . . like, "If this happens, this won't happen." You can't do the "won't."

PERSON 2: Okay, then you say, "If I don't put my foot on this crack there then I will get laid."

PERSON 1: No, man. You're still doing it, you, you've just like changed it around.

PERSON 2: Look, man, I'm just trying to help you out. You lay this weird shit on me about making these randomal rule things. Then you, then you say they ain't working for you. I'm just trying to help you out.

PERSON 1: You know, man, I'm just making conversation here. I'm not asking you to help me.

PERSON 2: You seen a shrink about this?

PERSON 1: No, man! It ain't like that.

PERSON 2: You say it's all obsessible. I mean, that sounds like shrink shit to me.

PERSON 1: Why do I even talk to you?

PERSON 2: Look, you brought it up man. I'm just trying to help you hold your shit together.

PERSON 1: Hold my . . .? Jesus! I'm, I'm just gonna stop talking to you, man.

PERSON 2: I'm just trying to help you out with your affliction.

PERSON 1: Just shut up.

PERSON 2: Yeah, okay.
    [*Long Pause*] Hey, uh . . . did you want to hit the game?

PERSON 1: Yeah, cool, you ready?

PERSON 2: Yeah.

[*They both get up and walk away with purpose. Lights fade out.*]

Conversation II

A woman and a man on a dinner date. They sit across from each other at a small and intimate dining table.

HER: So, you discovered who you were at 26.

HIM: Now, that's not what I said.

HER: That is what you said.

HIM: I said, "At 26 I realized I didn't know who I was. I began to discover myself."

HER: Okay, so?

HIM: So what?

HER: So who are you? When did you "discover" who you were?

HIM: Well, discovery's a process. I mean, we're always changing. We have to rediscover ourselves with every change. As to who I am, explaining that's like trying to distill an essence. It's a complex thing, you know.

HER: Yeah, okay. Go on.

HIM: Well, how do I start? Who am I, the core of me? [*Long pause.*] Ocean.

HER: What?

HIM: Ocean.

HER: What the hell does that mean?

HIM: Well, how can we even begin to explain something like this, but with metaphor.

HER: Yeah, okay. Keep going.

HIM: Ocean. Depth with as yet hidden and unknown creatures, monstrous and beautiful, lithe and brittle. And I have to, with each newly discovered creature, catalog it and befriend it—even the hideous leviathans that scheme to overwhelm me and mold me to their darker purpose.

I'm millpond calm, glassy smooth, yet under, always, always, turbulence, undertows, and the giant squid, or that eternally infernal white whale, seemingly mythic, comes up for air and is seen, though I try to keep him down, unseen, in the dark.

Occasional tempest: love, yearning for love, to be loved, to love; righteous indignation, always for the "justice" of my beliefs, yet painfully close to my hypocrisy . . . painfully close—and yet (and this is something that prides me) I'm able to stare into the mirror of my own hypocrisy and recognize it, you know, be reviled and guilty of it, attempt to cleanse it from me; emotions, always run by emotions.

[*Long and thoughtful pause.*]

HER: You are so full of it.

HIM: Do you think so?

HER: No question. People don't talk like that. Did you memorize that?

HIM: Well, if that's what you think. I mean, it does me no good to argue with you about it. [*Pause*] You know, you have an odd and troubling gravity.

HER: What do you mean? I'm serious or . . . ?

HIM: No. You remember when we talked in the car that night . . . till three?

HER: Yeah.

HIM: You know I spilled my guts. I mean, I thoroughly embarrassed myself because I don't want to have to deal with the game any more. No more game. All out in the open.

HER: Okay. I remember.

HIM: I am pulled toward you. And I don't know whether it's chemical, desperation, interest, or what. But . . . . You know, Conrad wrote about Marlow looking at the Congo River like a bird looks at a snake, mesmerized by it, pulled into it, hypnotized. That's me.

HER: Okay, so who's the snake here?

HIM: That's not the point.

HER: No, really I'd like to know, and I think it's my right; am I supposed to be the snake in this little analogy of yours?

HIM: Look, okay, not the best analogy. There is no symbolism here, no Freud at work. It was just a simple and innocent analogy, okay?

HER: What kind of bird?

HIM: What?

HER: What kind of bird are you? If I'm, what, a garter snake, what kind of bird are you?

HIM: Okay, I'm going to go home.

HER: No. Don't.

HIM: Look, you're not taking me seriously. You . . .

HER: No. I'm sorry. You're just . . . you're just getting ready to go into a . . . thing . . . that I'm not sure I'm ready for.

HIM: Well, what do you want me to do about it?

HER: I don't know.

HIM: Look, I'm going to go. If this is making you uncomfortable you're obviously not ready for it, and I might as well . . .

HER: No. Stay. Go ahead. Go ahead. Please.

HIM: You know . . . whenever I see you, I leave more lonely than when I arrived. What the hell's with that? I mean, I'm starched, depressive, lonely. It's not a good feeling. It's not a good feeling. It's like seeing your mate with someone else; you know, that hungry empty, cold knot in your belly . . . that visceral loneliness. Except here there's no reason for it. I mean, you haven't committed to me, I haven't committed to you. Hell, I barely even know you.

I mean, I know you, but I don't really know you. But I want to. I want to discover who you are, unravel your mysteries so much . . .

[*With a slow, dreaded realization*] And as the words flow out, I can feel them pressing against you, pushing you away, or pushing at whatever is keeping you from it, whatever weight bears down on you. And that this confession, whatever the confession itself means, has already sentenced me.

HER: I'm reflective too, you know.

HIM: What?

HER: I'm a very touchy feely person: back slaps, hugs, arm rubs, closeness. But I feel that I can't with you.

HIM: Why?

HER: I don't know. I guess I don't want to lead you on or give you the wrong impression or something. I don't know.

HIM: Great.

HER: I see great potential in this relationship. Really. Whether it's really great friends or what.

HIM: Me too.

HER: I don't want to lose the possibility of a great friendship because we suddenly feel self-conscious around each other.

HIM: Don't we already feel self-conscious around each other? I mean, isn't that what this is all about? [*Long pause.*] Sorry.

HER: Now what?

HIM: What?

HER: Now what?

HIM: [*Pause*] Fate. I guess.

[*They sit back in their chairs and look at one another. Lights fade out.*]

Conversation III

Man or woman is sitting in a chair. Someone, unseen is in a hospital bed next to them. The speaker is holding the patient's hand in his or her lap, trying to warm the hand.

PERSON: The Bendricks stopped by the office today. They dropped off a casserole; you know that shepherd's pie of Erik's that you really liked. I guess . . . I guess they forgot I was allergic to carrots. Yeah, I thanked them, you know, told them how you were doing. All that. I thought you'd like that irony . . . the shepherd's pie.

Brad was going to take me to work today, so my car could have that alternator replaced, but Cameron ran away again last night. Brad and Sara are starting to get less freaked out when he does that. It still freaks me out. I mean I can't even imagine waking up and your kid being gone, you know. How can, how can that get to be normal? Anyway, they're spending today trying to find him with the police and whatever that . . . child services? I don't know, whatever that group's called. They were talking about getting him some therapist or something, and I guess that's what freaked him out.

You know, I get close to saying okay to the whole kid thing, so close. I'm like just on the verge of thinking I'm ready, thinking it would be cool, thinking we could do it, you know, and then Cam runs away, or the Washingtons' kid breaks his leg, or something like that and it puts me off again. But I'm getting closer, you know. I'll get there, probably sooner than later.

[*Long pause.*] You know, huh [*pensive and self-reflective*], you know what I thought of today? I couldn't believe it. You remember when we were at Disney World . . . what was it, Land or World, the one in Florida? Anyway, we were at Disney, at . . . Port R . . . Orleans, Port Orleans, right, and, I can't remember why we started it, but we were going back to the room and I said, huh, I said, "You know, if we've been robbed and the only things left are the toothbrushes, I'm throwin' those fuckers away!" And we could not stop laughing. And for the rest of the week, every day, you would somehow find new toothbrushes and hide them everywhere! I'd find one in a sock, or hidden in the toilet paper roll. Hell, you even hid one above the door jamb, "Just in case," you said. You wanted to be "totally prepared for any eventuality."

No, wait [*gearing up for the punch line*], then on the last day, when we were packing, I couldn't find a fucking one of them. You were driving me nuts. You smiling that shit grin of yours, laying back on the bed just watching me go crazy over a stupid-assed toothbrush. Then . . . I don't know why . . . I looked in the toilet, and you had taken my toothbrush and just caked the head of it with most atrocious brown shoe polish—Oh my God!—and you'd dropped it the toilet, and it was just sitting there. Thank God I was in the bathroom 'cause I nearly peed myself!

God, I loved you so much at that moment.

I never thanked you for . . . Well.

[*Long pause.*] Look at your hair. How can you do that? I mean, you don't do anything to it and it's still awesome. It's just . . .

[*Long pause.*] God, I miss you. I miss you so much. I have to . . . I have to believe you can hear me, cause if I—I mean, I mean I know you can hear me, I know you can hear me. I know it. Dr. Reese says you can. I mean, she would know, right? Why would she make that up if she didn't know? There's no reason, right? There's no reason to do that, is there? No, of course not.

Your new nurse is great. Well, it actually kind of freaked me out, you know. I mean he's a guy, a guy nurse. I, I don't know. Why is that so weird for me? I mean. What kind of equal rights advocate is like, "Yeah, female doctor good. Male nurse? What's up with that?" Oops, a little self-reflective kick in the ass, huh?

[*Long pause.*] Your hands are so cold; it always takes me forever to warm them up.

[*Long pause.*] Sometimes, I think . . . I think I feel you squeezing back. My God, my heart races . . . It's like when I was a kid and my parents were out; I'm in bed and hear a noise, you know. I'm all tensed and rigid, not breathing, all my concentration spiked toward my ears to hear if I really heard it, you know. All that same concentration piercing into my hand trying to keep it from moving, you know, but I can't. It's, it's shaking. And, and the more I try to stop it so I can feel if you really squeezed, the more it shakes. I, I want to, I want to feel the squeeze so badly, so badly, I can't stop the stupid shaking.

Jesus, when the police showed up, I thought I was going to die. They were good though, you know, Officer . . . I can't remember her name, she was good about everything. Shit, what a shitty job that would be, huh? It makes finance seem really, really good.

[*Long pause.*] I can't get over your hair.

Dr. Reese said the cuts on your face would only leave tiny scars. She said you were lucky you didn't lose your left eye. You know, your glasses were so smashed and the broken rims . . . well. We'll get you new ones when you wake up, okay? When you open up those big green eyes. You know they were the first thing I noticed . . . Well, you've probably heard that story, what, a hundred times now?

Oh . . . well, I guess they're kicking me out again. So I guess I'll see you tomorrow, okay.

I'll see you tomorrow.

[*The Visitor stands to go. Looks sadly at other person. Lights fade out.*]

Sonnet IV

I have felt you underneath me with a sigh,
when the spring of hope within me blooms
and sows the garden of my wandering mind
that fills with flowers all my wintry rooms.
I have felt you underneath me with a sigh,
when the summer brings its sultry rays
and shows the moon that cools the lovers' night
that calls them so to sleep away the days.
I have felt you underneath me with a sigh,
when autumn fills this world with colors gold
and casts long shadows in the fading light
that cools the world, once in the summer's hold.
       And yet my winter always rules, it seems,
       for all my thoughts of you are just my dreams.

Observations on a Captive Logophile

His eyes ooze over the words
like the smarm bubbling off
a gold-chained, polyester-encrusted, disco-pumping, wavy haired,
pencil-mustached, bushy-sideburned, I'm-a-Taurus-what-sign-are-you,
Don Juan on the make.

He slowly slips his quivering index finger
between the page and the
right-side bulk of
"The Ox"
as he calls it
(He might as well call it Pooky)
and slowly lifts its
diaphanous dried pulp
in orgasmic anticipation
even before he's done reading
the definition.

He pauses with concentrated joy,
looks hard at the type and says aloud,
softly,
"My-azzz-mah."
He licks his lips and reforms the new sound:
"Mee-azz-mah."

He smiles in satisfaction.
"Sweet. I'll have to make a note of that one."

And
I?

I must look away.

In Defense of Folding

I remember my father once said, "Son" (he used to call me son — now he just casually refers to me as "The Liberal") — "Son," he said, "real men wad."

I freely admit that, in the innocent, ne'er-do-well, wild days of my youth, I was a wadder. So much a wadder, in fact, that it precipitated a filial war of sorts with my brother who was not just a wadder, he was the veritable Nile god of our bathroom. He could make Noah shudder with a Post-Traumatic Stress episode just by walking into the room. We had Roto Rooter on the speed dial.

I'm not sure when I discovered the fine art of folding: the gentle three-turn wrap, *the retirer le main, the reunir les collines*, the agile quad-wipe[1]. It was, I must say, almost freeing. Some say that it is self-indulgent. Well, I have a friend who always uses Love's baby wipes — that is self-indulgent. I consider the folder refined. It is, in fact, a gentle art. Not like the almost bestial philosophy or *Toiletentechnik* of using the hard roll-pull and the *Arschputzstein* in the German style[2]. I am a wadder no more.

I think we can look at popular or important figures in our society to help us better understand the psychology of this choice. Franklin Delano Roosevelt was certainly a folder: those delicate hands. Stalin: wadder. Shakespeare was clearly a folder, as he has Lady Macbeth's gentlewoman say of her, "I have seen [Lady Macbeth] rise from her bed, throw her night-gown upon her, unlock her closet, take forth paper, [and] fold it. . ." (*Macbeth* 5.1) and has Helena say in *A Midsummer Night's Dream*, "Things base and vile, folding no quantity" (1.1), which clearly means that only the basest and vilest creatures fold nothing. On the positive wad side, Hemmingway was probably a wadder, when he wasn't using leaves.

I have wadder friends who are aghast at the folding style. "Don't you mess your hands. I mean, what if a finger slips?" Well, if a finger slips you should have someone else working for you. Sure, the wad has pure area coverage, and I agree to its nook-and-peak cleaning surface, but there is no control. No control. One wipe. That's it. Done. Go for the next hard roll-pull, or, for the more genteel wadder (if that's not an oxymoron), the finger-roll gather or, as Nietzsche put it in his seminal

---

1. *retirer le main*, the *reunir les collines*: " removal of the hand" and "creation of the hills" respectively. Robespierre in his *L'Esthétique d'Essuyer* uses the phrase "la main comme la roue d'eau" or "the hand as water wheel" as the inauguration of what he refers to as " le beau nettoyage": "the beautiful cleansing." However, I've found the roue d'eau to be a bit wasteful, and I have therefore opted to use Frederick W. Taylor's more efficient three-turn wrap (from Taylor's *Dual Use Pamphlet*, 1911). The quad-wipe is, as is well known, Stephen Hawking's addition to the craft.

2. *Toiletentechnik*: Now simply the German style. *Arschputzstein*: the act of balling the paper into a tight stone-like wad.

wadders' manifesto *Der Rohrenkrieg*, ***Klopapier Zusammenkrümmpeln mit den Fingern***[3].

I am a folder, and I am finally proud of it. There may be more of you than us. You may be stronger, bigger, louder, more forceful. But, aesthetically, wadding is just one step up the evolutionary chain from the famous Moroccan rock wipe.

3. ***Klopapier Zusammenkrümmpeln mit den Fingern***: loosely translated as "The marching fingers that crumple paper for the final onslaught."

My Father's Father

You were my distant Doric column
supporting my child sky
in made memories of family tales.

You were
my Forever Man:
scent of bacon,
sweat and cigarettes
and oil —
every day —
of oil you drew from the earth.

I saw, through eyes and thoughts of others,
you,
standing Hercules,
arms extended,
feat of strength
with my young parent lovers
swinging from your branches
as from an oak,
a fabled tree.

You were
my Forever Man:
vibrant, gruff
spirit of your Cherokee father,
earth and loam.

I loved to read
your bronzed warrior skin
laced with webs,
like Sanskrit
speak of wars and rivers,
soldier nightmares,
sun and things you never could reveal.

You were
my Forever Man:
story weaver,
hunter, fisher,
wolf in woodsman skin.

So much my Forever Man
I can-
not bear
to
see your weath-
ered face now
laced with
waste and sad-
ness, quiet
acquiesc-
ence,
breath-
ing from
the cart-
rolled cani-
ster,
waiting,
waiting
for the end.

You used to
wait for
no one.

Summer Song

Sometimes,
when the air is thick,
I like to say the name
Idi Amin Dada:
starting slowly
with its rising scenes
of sweat and heat,
oppressive weight of history,
glistening beads
on dark black skin:
repeat
repeat
tempo pushing faster,
simply to feel the clicking
undulating flicks of my tongue
in the beating cavity of my mouth
until the name is no more
than the sound of a train
clacking quickly on rickety tracks.

And as my quivering eyes
focus on the heat
rising from the melting street
I fight the force of a momentary need
for a public ululation.

Daydreaming

I slip the sea of sound,
cacophony of conversation
aimed into my ears
like sand into a sieve,
to expand a pinhole thought,
like the iris of a eye,
upon a fantasy
of you.

On Otto Dix's "Assault Troops under Gas"

Into my nightmares,
like politic worms at feast,
a certain convocation,
they slither
from trenches,
bathed in green and oily air
through him,
on paper,
to me;
the hapless
unprepared or slow
still writhing,
rolling eyes,
foaming mouths —
among the death —
lay the trenches.

The eyeless
demons,
grey-garbed,
black-souled,
white-faced,
impervious to pleading,
terrify my imagination
with what seems real
and whisper to my conscience,
"You can never truly know."

Nectarines

Passionate plums with a bad thyroid:
my nectarines,

my sign of summer
with its nectar
        (nectar-ines [youknow])
slipping down my chin
like a student escapee down a waterslide,

and my tongue hopping after it
                (the fugitive juice)
to bring it back to desirous buds
addicted from the very first
getting-your-boot-caught-in-the-mud-and-losing-it
suck-sounding bite
to the delicate last few
surgically
    precise
        nibbles
of the red-golden ambrosia
clinging fast to the pit.

My hazy sunset,
fuzzless,
tender,
sweet
and
sssssssexy
orb.

Pulp

i want these words to howl,
to leap from this white pulp
and spear into your eyes,
burst your iris with blinding light,
with searing pain,
to throw you back
into a blackness
so new it tears at joy,
it rips and claws at memories,
it hollows you
as i am newly cored
and flung upon the heap.

i wish to bellow,
"NO ONE KNOWS WHAT i KNOW!
NONE HAVE EVER
NOR EVER WILL
FEEL THE PAIN i FEEL!"

But that would be
just another lie.

For i know this pain,
this confusion,
this contemptuous,
fuming mix
is not mine
alone.

It has been suffered
by countless millions.
It will be suffered
by who knows more.
It was even suffered
at 8:03 and forty-seven seconds,
Central Standard Time,
in the evening
— exactly at that time —
by more than just me.

i know that hundreds,
even thousands,
all across this spinning world
had their defeat
at that same speck of time.

And because of that
i am lonelier
than this white page
can show.

Where's the Ram in my Rama Lama Ding Dong?

My girlfriend of the last few years and I have recently broken up. By "recently" I mean two months or so ago. But, like reverse dog years, it seems like yesterday. I am over the whole fiasco.

Fiasco may be a bit dramatic.

It was really more like the rotation of the Earth suddenly stopped, ripping my intestines from their cavity, depositing them somewhere in, I don't know, Madagascar. But I've come to the conclusion that this particular soul mate is not yet as ready as I to hook up in this life. So maybe next time around. At least that's what my spirit guide, Marcus, seems to be saying.

But I am over it...mostly. However — there is always an however, isn't there? — I have come to discover something, a sort of collateral damage, a personal civilian remains in this relationship bomb crater. While emotionally my stockpile of self-esteem is nearly replenished and my physical cache once again filled, to my great horror — horror, I say — I have realized that, upon her, I have blown the wad of all my good songs. This new understanding spun me into such a loathsome miasma of spirit and abyssmalia that the very fiber of my...well, it wasn't really that bad. But I am a bit dispirited.

Who now may wholly own my gift of The Hollies' "The Air that I Breathe" free and clear of emotional baggage? How may I hum the Coaster's "Smoke Gets in Your Eyes" sweetly into the fragrant and succulent ear of a new beloved without at least the faint vestiges of heart-shaped hot tub memories? How may I now illegally download, burn, and present a CD of Rex Smith's "You Take My Breath Away" without that ever present wisp of redolent banana pudding and mint chutney scented memories?

I have been struck song wadless!

But I have a plan. Necessity, as they say, is the bastard son of creative potential. I have created a new web site devoted totally to replenishing my song wad. Render unto the wad, say I! I have included a brief list of some 347 songs spent upon the aforementioned young woman that have now been rendered emotionally useless to me. Oh, perhaps I might use Kiss's "Beth" on an illicit one night of emotionless passion. But they are generally dead to me, in the sense of any real emotional future relationships. So please go to www.lovesuckscauseitbitmeinmyemotionala ss.org to peruse my song list. If you know of a useable song that is not on that list of Orphic flotsam, please click on the button entitled "Wad Redux" and add it to the new list. Your help in my musical rejuvenation is much appreciated.

Lieutenant Ruytenburgh's Glance

on Rembrandt's
The Shooting Company of Captain Frans Banning Cocq
and Lieutenant Ruytenburgh

You bombastic lout.

You ignorant peacock,
with your "Let me tell you this"
and "I think"s and "To the contrary"s.

You think you're beloved
as you pontificate,
leading the mob
along the Amstel
shooting.

But they are simply jackals
like your own dog hoping for the fox,
jumping at the scraps you drop.

They love you not.

You will say the wrong thing
                someday,
or give the wrong glance
or use the wrong whore,
and the next day
court will silence when you enter,
and you will finally know
what a little man you are.

I shall,
at your fall,
become the captain.

But I?
I
shall shoot
alone.

Reginald Dyhre

Reginald Dyhre was feeling. He was achingly conscious of his being, as if he were emerging from a thick pudding, only to float into darkness. He was floating. He thought he was.

He tried opening his eyes, only to create a minor flutter. It was no good. It only tired him.

Lying in the dark, he began to slowly realize several things. A constant and deep throbbing pain quietly made itself known. He discerned that there were several in different locations within his body, the most evident pain in his chest. It ran the width, from side to side. And it throbbed with every labored beat of his heart.

Then, like the slow flap of a condor's wings, a picture emerged in his mind's eye. As he remembered, the pain in his chest began to burn.

He had not seen the runaway team in time, of that he was certain. Reginald remembered the neighing and the shouts of horror coming from Foldad's Mercantile. He remembered turning to see the flared nostrils of Finn McHaughnahy's wagon team as they rode him down, trod upon him. Then his memory flagged, blanked out.

It must have been a wheel that got him. Now his chest burned with the very memory. And the smaller throbbing pains became more noticeable in his legs and stomach.

How long had he been unconscious? He once again tried to open his eyelids. A flutter and then... Were they open? He blinked. They were open. All was still darkness, darker than any night out at Rodney's farm when the moon had sneaked behind the thick clouds — darker even than his old bedroom in St. Louis.

Raising his hand to his head, he was shocked as it cracked on the rough wood ceiling. I must be in the hospital bunk, he thought. He felt the ceiling. It was rough unpainted wood. How shabby. Utterly pedestrian and, well, western.

He had come out here to help Rodney with the finances. This was not the city of St. Louis, and by no means the metropolis of his beloved Chicago. He remembered when Chicago was the West.

This hospital was cold, but strangely stuffy. It smelled like sleep and urine, decay, sweat. It was thoroughly unpleasant. But he was tired and in no position to do anything about it tonight. He would just rest this night and, with renewed strength, get up in the morning and see to his condition.

He realized suddenly that he was ravenously hungry, and with that recognition his stomach gurgled loudly and growled.

He brought his right hand up to his stomach to rub it soothingly as if to quiet a crying child. It was then an oddity clicked like the hammer of a gun within him. He felt his abdomen ... metal buttons. He felt higher and noticed the tell-tale apex of a vest at his mid-torso.

A slowly creeping, incomprehensible thought blinked momentarily from the shadows of his mind—a thought so horrid and oppressive that it made not one second attempt to be conceived. Reginald Dyhre was not a man who dwelled on, or even sallied with thoughts of the grotesque and morbid. No, his was a world of logical understanding, reasoned reality. Numbers were at the center of his world, numbers and funds, logical, clear, understandable beauty. The linear and crystal thought of numbers was his religion, one might say. Certainly his brother, Rodney, did.

When Rodney told Reginald of his plan to move westward and live with and off the land, Reginald responded with, "Brother, be serious. Are you willfully disregarding your financial responsibilities to you and your progeny for what is at best a pecuniary penumbra?"

Rodney replied, "Well you have certainly not lost your way with words, brother. But your spiritual path ... Well, your religion is no longer spiritual. It is purely financial. I only thank our Maker that you have not yet fallen in with the unethical of your religion. You still work for your client, I know that. But there are many who work solely for themselves. Please do not fall into the burning pit of their company."

That talk with Rodney had shaken him up, brought him back to the long and lifeless sermons of Father McPhar, the same, unchanging monotony of the Sunday Mass, the vinegary wine and stale brittle bread of the Eucharist that, for Reginald, was merely the pap of a dying religion, an antique of our older emotional selves.

He realized he was holding his breath. He slowly released it into the stale air. *Think*, he thought to himself. "Fine, now," he said to no one. I shall rest, he thought.

The feeling, for that is what the incomprehensible thought was becoming, swept throughout him again. It came like a scythe on an October morning, from his feet to his head; it coldly sliced him horizontally in two.

He cleared his throat nervously and moved his hand down the wool of his vest. He felt his hands shaking at the thought with which he had begun to battle. Slowly they moved down the buttons. That for which he was feeling and hoping against finding, made itself known below the third vest button. At first he felt the lapel come under his wrist. But it was the button — his suit-coat was buttoned, the black wool winter suit, the one he had brought to appease Rodney's Sunday church habit — that stripped his breath away and made sweat pour from his forehead. "My God," he whispered. He moved his right hand back to his side and, for the first time, noticed the wood upon which he lay. His palm was flat against the bottom, his fingers flexing shakily, feeling the rough wood grain below him.

He lay motionless, his throat parched, his mouth coated in a rank paste. He lay like a young boy in his bed at the still-dark morning when he wakes to a strange noise and feels the eyes of an imagined killer upon him — afraid to move to see the shadow only to find it is his coat upon the door, yet knowing he must move to end the play of terror within him, for good or bad.

Reginald's breathing was shallow and labored. His mind battled with itself, and the Titans of reason were finally succumbing to his Olympian dread. *No, no, no*, repeated over and over within his conscious; and yet he knew the conclusion before the climax was revealed. He now noticed the faint odor of the pine resin within the wood that surely surrounded him. It began to enclose his brain like an acrid fog. He shallowed his breathing even more, so as to keep the smell from him. He felt the pain in his chest most intensely, reacting to the fast and forceful beating of his heart. The pains in his legs and abdomen were now incessant pin pricks, fluttering like gnats. He wished to rub them, to squeeze the pain away, but he was too afraid to move, too afraid to confirm his most frightening hypothesis.

With resolve, he began slowly, ever so slowly, to move his hands shakily away from his body, hovering lightly above the wooden bottom. His hands touched the wooden sides of his coffin, and the vacuum of his fear sucked all the air from his lungs and they began to burn.

"My God," he whispered again.

"My God," he said louder.

Then, and with the sudden violence of an explosion, his hands burst upward against the roof of his coffin and began to pound and pound and pound. All the while he screamed, "No, no, I'm alive, alive! No, I'm alive!"

His feet kicked up and down and his body bucked inhumanely. He kept pounding with the hope against hope that he wasn't yet covered with the dirt he feared was above him. "No," he screamed, now with a high and painful pitch, a banshee wail of the wind. "I'm alive, alive!" His coffin was filled with the sounds of his screaming and the dull thud of his beating and kicking.

As the painful futility of his actions began to seep into his mind, he slowed his beating until he was spent, empty of energy. He lay quietly in the darkness of his coffin. The pain in his hands suddenly shot through his arms, making him flinch. He felt his right hand with his left and noticed the warm dampness and roughness of torn and bloody skin. He dropped them again at his sides.

No logic, no reason, nothing could aid him in this. His mind went momentarily blank.

He was going to die. He had never thought that before, even though it was the one surety, the one logical and reasonable truth for all humanity. It was the linear end to all living things. He had known that it was out there: Death. He had written his will before coming out to help Rodney. But that was only at the request of his attorney, due to the tidy sum he was beginning to accumulate. Never the less, he had not dwelled upon that certainty. Well, he was now going to have a lot of time to ponder his lack of existence. Too much time.

At this thought, he began to pound again at the roof. He pounded twice and ceased, mostly because of the futility, but also because of the intense pain in his hands. It overpowered the constant throbbing pain of his chest and the pin pricks of his other pains.

Time was now his enemy, he thought. Reginald had always believed he would die in bed, when he had considered death at all. He now knew he would never stand again. He would never see the sunrise over the river, smell the ink from his well or the starched collar of a fresh shirt. He would never eat again.

My God, he thought, *how long will this take!* He had read accounts in the newspaper of men being found nearly starved after a month in the western deserts. *A month*, he thought, *a month. That is totally unacceptable.* But what could he do?

Finally, he was overwhelmed by the utter sadistic futility of his end, like a blind worm buried in the mud. He began to cry, trying to hold everything inside him. For whom? He wept and screamed a pained and indescribable wail. Surely, if there had been a mourner at his grave, this scream she would have heard. He screamed one continuous lamentable wail. And he wept fully, with the abandon of a tired child, almost luxuriously. He had not wept like that for ages, possibly ever. Nor would he again, Reginald imagined.

He wept for the loss of his own life, for his many lost chances of love and affection. He wept for his regrets, for his failures. He wept even for his sins. *For my sins.* This thought slowed his weeping, until, finally, it stopped.

For my sins, he thought. When was the last time he had gone to confession? Ten, fifteen years? Certainly not since his apprenticeship, not since he converted to his religion of numbers and finance. Was this the retribution of some reviled Old Testament God? Was this his spiritual cleansing before the final personal Armageddon? Surely there was a reason, a reason beyond blind chance ... something beyond the self-determined rationalism of his former existence.

Reginald began to review his past. Who were the people he had slighted? Who were the poor he had ceased to help? What were his impieties and indiscretions and sins? He pined on his spiritual history. And yet nothing stood out as a grievous wrong against humanity or this God, this God he had been taught to fear and love.

Fear and love. They had never been able to meld within his ideology. He could not fear and love anyone at the same time. Either he feared and loathed or he loved and respected. And this God of his childhood he was taught to fear. Therefore this God ceased to exist within Reginald Dyhre's life.

Meaningless, he thought, *utterly meaningless.*

He no longer questioned his state. He had come to understand his situation. *It was*, he thought grimly, *a good idea about the will.*

This thought, the will, clicked in his mind. He searched for the recollection of it. He grabbed for his pocket-watch in his vest's right pocket. It was there, just like he had written. This discovery quickened his blood like a Christmas morning. *Is it there?* he asked himself. He licked his lips with hesitant expectation and slowly moved his left hand down to his side.

Yes, it was there, just like he had written on that god-awful paper back in St. Louis. "Well, you can't be too sure about what's a gonna happen out there, you know," MacKenzie, his attorney, had said. "You got to write down what you want done with your body. What kinds of keepsakes and memorabelios you want to take with you to the great beyond. It's all a lot of horse toddy, if you ask me. But it brings me some business."

He slid his hand into his left hip pocket, feeling the clammy cotton insides against his thigh. He felt the little derringer, cold and moist, and quickly grasped it, pressed firmly between his fingers and his palm, like some lost talisman.

"Thank God," he whimpered. *Thank God for that god-awful will*, he thought.

He pulled the gun from his trousers and moved it up to his chest. He rubbed the side with his right hand, lovingly, softly. It was his most outrageous, wild-haired purchase. The first thing, the only thing really, he had purchased with the spontaneity of a young boy's early summer skinny dip. He closed his eyes, now only from habit, to concentrate on its image: the silver, stubby barrel with the filigree of such intricacy it drew him in every time he looked at it; the mother of pearl inlay in the handle, its opalescence like milk on a mirror. It loaded like a shotgun, but it was a gentleman's gun, a sophisticated gun. He had never even fired it. Indeed he had slipped it into his pocket so often along with his coppers and nickels, handkerchiefs, and pocket-watch and all the other trinkets he adorned himself with mindlessly in the morning, that he had forgotten it was a prized and cherished possession.

And now he knew what he would do. Was this the way he was going to leave? Was this what his mother meant all those years ago? "God has a plan, Reginald. You just remember that." The imagined sound of his mother's voice no longer carried a mother's love. Now it was the sound of his end, the sound of mocking. Was this God's plan? Reginald was angered now at this thought. Even though this God was no longer in his heart, this God still dug into his brain.

"What the hell did you want from me?" he screamed. "What did I do? To whom? To what? What?" He began to cry in a sudden burst and writhed within the coffin like a larval moth.

"What?" he screamed again.

"What?" he wept.

"What?" quietly, the torrent over.

Resolve, he thought to himself. It was, of course, against the law of God. But God had left him now. He could not imagine anyone more alone in the world.

He wiped his nose with the back of his hand.

Christ was said to be alone on the cross. But he had Mary and his mother and his kingdom. He wasn't alone. *I am alone*, he thought, and stifled a cry.

The sooner you do this the better. Come, now, resolve. His fingers could not grip the gun. His hands, shaking, could not do the work now. He violently slammed his hands against the sides of the coffin. "Work, damn you!" he yelled. "It's all I ask."

He shook them out and grasped the gun with his right hand and weakly pulled back on the hammer, hearing and feeling the light click he loved so much when cleaning the gun.

"Now," he said through clenched teeth.

He brought the gun barrel up under his chin and pressed it into the softness of his skin.

He rested the top of the barrel on his Adam's apple, and it wavered there.

"Now," he said again, a little more determinedly.

He swallowed hard and the thought of a blessing, a prayer, something just in case, went through his mind.

His eyes began to water profusely and the tears ran like rain down a window into his ears and along the bottom of his neck at the hairline.

"Now," he said again, in a squeak, nearly inaudible.

He pulled on the trigger as Samson at the columns. He pulled and pulled, so slowly, pulling ever so slowly.

"Now, damn it."

He felt the trigger snap back.

Click.

A sudden rush of fear swept through him. He pulled the trigger again.

Click

Again.

Click.

It was a sound more painful to him than the pain of the whole universe. It was a feeling more empty than death. He grabbed the barrel with his left hand and cracked the gun at the middle, and without a beat, stuck his right forefinger into the butt-end of the empty barrel. His lungs exploded outward with his held breath. "No," he breathed.

His elbows dropped to the hard wooden bottom of his coffin, his hands sliding down his chest, his belly, to fall at his sides. His prized and worthless derringer thudded on the wood beside his thigh.

He stared silently into the darkness.

Life Lesson at Sixteen

Only one of three alive
in stillness lay
broken,
burnt,
ripped from the short ride home
on her crisp orange autumn day
at the corner
where my high school stands,
and the powder green pines grow—
at the corner
where the flag whips the air
from the platinum pole,
bright contrasts to pools of red
and metal wrung like wet rags
against the asphalt gray
they were.

All blood and blond,
their beauty stripped
by a quick-ran red,
an auto-ram impacted sides
with screams and squeals
and sweet-burnt rubber
and shimmering glass like
a giant's shaken salt
on the gray road-plate—
their flesh offered
raw
for his consuming.

Monet Morning

The flowered earth
in singular beauty
lays open to my
soul,

and the sun
slits my eyes,
creates the shimmer
in the speckled hill
of cornflower,
faded lemon,
pale lime,
in languid
slanting lines
soft as the brush.

She turns to see me,
and all she needs is a white parasol
illuminated by the sun
to silvery sheen
as she stands atop the hill
in her flowing
white translucent dress,
repeating flowers so small,
so bright,
with sun behind
revealing her lines,
soft and feminine.

She shapely smoothes a strand of hair
away from her cheek
and smiles her face,
closing my adoring throat to speech.

Nocturnal Omissions

Felt your hand last night,
fingers soft as air.
We held hands as we walked along the beach.
You and me,
happy and free,
as we walked along the beach.

Touched your face last night,
Moonlight in your hair.
The warm wind blew as we danced by the sea.
You and me,
happy and free,
as we danced down by the sea.

> You and me on that long deserted beach,
> holding hands in the night,
> listening to the waves rolling in and rolling out,
> falling in love under the moonlight.

Kissed your lips last night,
senses rolling 'round.
Looked deep in your eyes and you kissed me again.
You and me,
happy and free,
as we made love in the sand.

> You and me on that long deserted beach,
> holding hands in the night,
> listening to the waves rolling in and rolling out,
> falling in love under the moonlight.

Woke up in my room,
my dog right by my side.
He looked at me with his sad, sleepy glare.
Him and me,
alone as we could be.
Baby, you weren't anywhere.

Dreamt of you last night.
Shook to clear my head.
I took your picture from inside my pillowcase.
You and me,
never to be.
I sat there staring at your face.

       I cut your picture from a *Cosmo* that I bought:
       A low-cut neckline, velvet, red.
       You don't even know that I just might exist,
       So I put you back and went to bed.

Felt your hand last night,
fingers soft as air . . . .

Sonnet IX

The heavy, liquid sweet of blood Merlot
seduces with your all consuming kiss
and steeps in the scents of nonresistance,
heightens senses sleeping from before.
Vanillin neck, rose fragrance tender ear,
strawberry hair, bouquet all, piercing point
that stings into my sense and so anoints
my reason with your warm beguiling air.
All musk and ginger earth alluring me
into your arms of cinnamon and shell
that wrap me in your loam, that I may be
bewitched with your perfume so easily.
Released of all resistance to your spell
I slip into your safe and warming sea.

Christmas in the Fall

Our neighbor's Christmas lights
flash slowly out of place
on our Halloween street:
flashing blues and greens and reds
amid our lighted orange gourds,
gray straw-stuffed ghouls,
and the fake spider's webs
that soften the fingers of our barren trees.

Last month she found
that cancer had come
and would take her by
Thanksgiving.

The Spoken Dream

When prose sings, the earth will die. The revolution is just a part of the chaotic circus that turns the world on its dime and slings us into Einstein's theory, for all is relativity, and nothing hinges upon the fall of a sparrow. The readiness will hinder you. A flight of sparrows is simply another of nature's mathematical formulae.

Nothing more.

Beauty? What is it when the piper chooses to dance by the infernal fire of universal solitude instead of, like the skipping kern and gallowglass he is, picking up his pipes and playing with grace? Amazing?

No.

Is that all there is?

Should we not now wash our hands clean of the filth that covers us? Yes, and let us turn the multitudinous seas incarnadine.

But the bright sea of singleness of mind will move us through the No of all things. We will dry our wetted eyes when our feet move through the clean, fresh and long grass of the newly open fields through which we can now play.

That is all there is.

Yes.

An amazing grace of song that rises on the wind, that amplifies within the waves as we, the dancer, jump and spin in the sky's white clouds. Beautiful.

Nothing less.

The formula for our dance is imbedded within us, and, like the sparrows of spring, it will always return to us, if we are ready to accept it. For all is relative when pleasure is the prize, not dime nor dollar, but the simple sparrow can sing out our euphonic joy that is the festival of all that revolves around us. For we can live, when poetry speaks.

Christmas Memories

I remember
my family Christmas traditions:

My parents' bubbling laughs,
the bells jingling on their
multicolored night-caps,
as I giddily lay down
in the cinnamon scented
teak-wood box,
and them
gaily pouring the traditional
cardboard box
of living large-eared
and wondrously furry
angora rabbits
on my trembling,
glee-bursting body.

And the rabbits,
forty or fifty,
would romp
over my wriggling form
to the faint strains
of "The Marseilles"
playing on the living room
stereo.

Ah ... Christmas!

Amphetamine

I'm tired to my bones.
Sleep comes to me,
dressed in flowing crème and satin,
and begs me to take her
to my cheek, kissing my eyelids closed
and breathing onto my mouth.
She embraces me and coaxes me
and folds me into her warm, soft
body, tempting me to succumb
to her desires.

But at the sight of you
she slinks away
into the forgotten shadows.
Your touch is my amphetamine,
a sun that rises
though my bedroom blinds
and slants into my drowsy eyes,
rousing me for your desires.

Sleep must stay
curled in the dusk
and wait.

Sweet Heart

Her self-esteem
hangs above the dining table
like a plump piñata
waiting
eyes down
for his indifference to come
crashing into her belly,
to rip her open
and let her
red heart
candy
spill upon the floor.

A Poem for Beth on Her 54th Birthday

Verdant truth,
a green like no other
in the ferns of her misty hills,
the dark fairy forest,
hairy moss floors,
eyes in pine knobs,
enchanting me,
entrancing me;
deeper into her
I'll always dream:
my mistress,
my Caledonia.

Spheres

How do I take back the moon?
How do I recapture Orion,
seduce the seven sisters to return
to their indifferent, memory-less
pinpricks?

If I were medieval man
I would shatter the glass spheres
where they reside,
shatter the firmament with
my wail,
a profound pitch,
bouncing off the rock and water,
slashing to the sky,
beating against the spheres
that once held promise—
that once held communion—
like a crystal bell,
tolling
tolling
tolling,
vibrating the stars and moon
and you from the glass spheres
that cage me in this universe.

But I am a man of now.
Still the sisters remind me
of what was,
Orion hunts me with memory.
And the moon?
The moon, like the whole
of the night sky,
still has a face.

Graduated
Elegy to Dylan

I've seen death,
but never so young—
never so wasted,
waxy and gray
and fake.

Twenty years old.

Was he bored
or just trapped
in his own experiment?

He tried to mainline life —
instead of living it —
right into the caving vein
of his left arm.

But the needle was a scythe
and he was the golden grain,
golden,
the color of his hair,

with the sad, gray clouds of Autumn
reflected in his skin.

NATHAN FRESE

"How would you describe him?"

"I don't know," is the perplexed reply. Palms open to the sky, voice slightly pitched, "Jack of all trades, master of none?"

"Jack of all tirades? Does he have a temper or something?" Clearly something has been misinterpreted here.

"No, 'trades.' I guess he's passable at a lot of different things: he teaches high school English (his favorite course being AP English), coaches high school basketball, writes (infrequently), runs a couple of summer sports camps, plays the drums in a pretty mean cover band, does impressions, loves the cinema, has done artwork for several t-shirts, goes to concerts whenever he can, plays euchre, enjoys a pint now and then, throws a mean Halloween party, travels and really seems to fit in with just about everyone he meets (as long as they don't mind a little double entendre in their conversation)."

"Really? He looks like some kind of arrogant, preppy wannabe," is the astounded reply.

"I guess you could say that. His parents raised him right, though. He can thank them for his wit and intelligence, them and maybe cable television." A shrug is added at the end. "He went to the University of Iowa to be a doctor, but wound up as a teacher instead. He decided to teach high school, got married to an incredibly tolerant woman named Nikki, and set up shop in Iowa City. Then he got his Master's from Graceland University. He says he likes words and messing with them, just as he likes people and, well, I suppose he likes to mess with them a little, too. Above all else, though, and I think this is a more recent development, he loves his daughter Ava Marie. She offers him no end of enjoyment."

"Well, I guess you never really know someone until you get to know someone, I mean, really."

"That's profound." Sarcastically.

Never Land
(a novel fragment)

The urgency moved him to that frantic state, again. His complexion, once tinged with the glow that intoxication brings, began to pale. The color left his cheeks and nose. His eyes seemed to clear at once. "Fuck," he muttered. The figure now panned the room and its every detail. His focus was still a little hazy, but his intent was real enough. He turned and looked over the shelves above his desk—old baseball photos, trophies (some of them his brother's), a few knick-knacks which held minimal sentimental value, but nothing would serve his purpose.

"Shit." His pulse quickened with each breath, adrenaline gushing throughout his body. His hands began to shake. His eyes widened as he lunged at his bed, opening the drawers in the headboard, rifling through them like a common burglar.

The fear, which had been ringing in his ears now, re-established itself: the footsteps overhead moved with purpose. These harbingers of doom echoed through his adolescent ears—booming, ominous, deadly. He knew he had precious little time to find the antidote for his wrongs, the mask to hide his telltale visage. Ten seconds, maybe fifteen—no more than that would he have. "Shit." The word escaped in a high-pitched half-whisper. His head jerked about, begging to catch a glimpse of some kind of savior. He knew that hiding under the covers wouldn't work this time. He had been too clumsy, too noisy this time. Knocking over the small table, which held the TV remote, had been his first mistake, bounding to his room and slamming the door in a moment of fractured "logic" had been his second. If he made a third, it would be fatal. He mustn't get caught. One of his parents, most likely his father, had heard the clatter.

In the vernacular of the time, "he was screwed."

Peter's life flashed before his eyes, well, some of it did. There was the memory of traveling to Canada with his family, of "midget" football, of being locked in the living room closet while his brother had sex with the babysitter, of being hung upside down by his shoelaces by his brother's friends, of letting his friends cut his hair any way they wanted at a slumber party. There was the memory of tonight, of the party, of the pretty high school girls, of the alcohol. Damn, if only he hadn't made so much noise. He wiped his forehead anxiously.

"Peter?" bellowed his father.

Peter didn't answer. His eye had stopped on a sliver of hope: IcyHot. The red lid from Peter's IcyHot ointment peeked out of his gym bag. It was the only product in his room capable of being consumed, and it certainly had a smell strong enough to cover beer and Mad Dog. It was edible, even if the container's warning opposed that notion.

The father's footsteps loomed louder as he descended the stairs. Peter grabbed the small container; he spun the lid off and plunged his fingers into the analgesic cream. Thank God his muscles had been sore after practice. His hand quivered. He paused and thought about the consequence of putting this cream (meant for exterior use only) into his mouth. He had to cover up the stench of alcohol on his breath, though. All four fingers of his left hand cupped slightly in the wet goo, taking out almost a full handful. He deposited this jiggling white gelatin into his dry, waiting mouth. His upper lip curled. His eyes teared. He winced as he swallowed it whole, struggling to keep the mentholated mass in his stomach. He spun the lid back on and dropped the IcyHot as his father opened the door.

"Peter?"

Peter turned. His lips trembled slightly. "Yeah."

"What the hell're you doing?"

"Nothin'."

"Doesn't sound like nothing." His father's voice snapped at him like an old Smith Corona.

Peter held his father's gaze for three blinks then sat down on his bed. He began taking off his shoes, hoping his father would shut off the light and leave him alone. This would not be the scenario, however.

"Where have you been?" asked the father, his hands in the pockets of his flannel robe. He stepped closer to his son. He eyed his second son knowingly, he had experienced all of this before.

"Out," replied Peter. With that utterance there billowed forth a bouquet of mediciny, training-room odor, not like any other.

"You smell like an ashtray at a brewery," noted his father. This had been only half-observation. He assumed, by the look in his son's eyes, that he had been drinking. He noticed a slight mediciny odor in the room.

Peter continued to remove his weathered tennis shoes, thinking the IcyHot would still conceal his breath, even if his clothes reeked. "Some people were smoking where I was at," he mustered.

"And you with them, I suppose. You're goddamn half-loaded," accused his father, glaring at the top of his son's blond head.

Peter quickly looked up. "No I'm not," he blurted defensively.

"The hell you're not. Your eyes look like they've been dilated and glazed, and you're knocking all the furniture over. Coming in at one a.m., tell me you're not drunk, hmph." He turned to walk out. Peter figured he was getting off easy. Maybe a lecture in the morning, the silent treatment for a little while, nothing major would come of this. The IcyHot had worked.

"You're grounded for two weeks. We'll talk in the morning." He closed the door before his son could respond. He walked briskly back up the stairs, shaking his head in bafflement. The grandfather clock ticked monotonously on the top floor of the suburban split-level home. He paused at the piano in the front room, gazing thoughtfully at the 8 x 10 of Peter from third grade.

Peter pulled his shirt off over his head brusquely. The sound of stitch ripping penetrated the quiet air. His teeth clenched. His ears burned with rage. The awful taste lingered in his mouth. He stripped off his pants and looked at the bright red numbers of his radio-alarm clock. "Fuckin' bullshit," he muttered. He walked over and turned off the light, hitting his knee on the edge of his desk on the way back. He took a deep breath and exhaled heavily through his nose. The throbbing in his head began to match the throbbing in his knee. He crawled into bed. As he lay on his side he could see the half-empty container of IcyHot in the glare from the clock radio. His rage subsided and he dozed off a while later.

The next morning found Peter rising slowly, half out of a minor hangover, half out of dread for the coming tirade by his parents. His stomach had a pain in it, one he would rather forget. He pulled on some cutoff baseball pants and his favorite purple t-shirt. He put his glasses back on. He could hear the television going upstairs. The noise from the T.V. was the only sound in the house. His parents weren't talking—he wondered if that meant they were mad, or if they were just acting normal.

Mr. and Mrs. Darling sat in the kitchen drinking coffee and reading the paper. They seldom spoke to each other, and when they did it was to discuss their three children or bills, or any upcoming dates on their social calendar. They had been married for almost twenty-five years and had mulled over virtually every minute detail of life that they could glean from their existence. Now they had settled into the basic tenets with which all humans must contend—eating, sleeping, working, etc. These were added to the task of raising their youngest child, Peter—a sometimes daunting endeavor. But they had raised one daughter and one son who were already functioning members of society, so they figured number three wouldn't present them with any major obstacles they hadn't seen before.

Peter brushed his teeth in the downstairs bathroom, washed his face and neck and slapped on some deodorant. He hoped that he didn't smell too bad, but the shower was upstairs so he would have to see his parents before he could cleanse himself of last night's decadence. This meant any disguising of his aroma short of eating IcyHot would be beneficial. He made his way out of the bathroom, past the fireplace and snooker-pool table, took a deep breath and headed upstairs to meet his doom.

Peter entered the kitchen and went to the refrigerator. His father didn't look up from the paper. Peter said good morning to neither of them. His mother set her paper down, sipped her coffee and looked at the black and white television on the table.

"How did you sleep, Dear?" she inquired in her unique voice. It could coo with the best pediatric nurses, or it could pierce with the precision of a hypodermic needle. Peter had become immune to any change in intonation and, therefore, always answered in one of two ways: bored and monotone, or irritated and confrontational.

"Fine." He opted for monotone. There was hardly enough juice left for half a glass. He poured it into a tumbler and put the pitcher back into the refrigerator.

"Did you have a good time last night?" she asked. Her eyes watched the weather report on one of the local stations.

Peter shrugged his response and began drinking his orange juice. He watched the unmoving newspaper floating in front of his father's face. He knit his eyebrows in worry. The pain in his stomach grew sharper for an instant. He waited for the eventual double-headed blowup by his parents. He waited the entire glass of orange juice then set the green plastic glass in the sink.

He looked at the eggs in the frying pan on the stove. His stomach kicked from the inside, crushing the impulse of hunger.

"Where did you go?" asked his mother, now looking at her son. She removed her glasses and put them in her robe pocket.

"Out," was the surly reply.

"Where?" She stood up to grab a plate for Peter's eggs from the cupboard. Peter moved in unison with her so she wouldn't come too close and smell his foul odor.

Mrs. Darling did not notice her son's shuffling and began scooping some eggs onto Peter's plate with her favorite spatula, the one with the burn divot in the middle of the plastic handle.

Peter walked out of the kitchen and turned on the stairs going down. Only his head was visible, looking as if it was sitting on the top step. This was the bizarre view through the kitchen doorway.

"We're leavin' at 9:30?" Peter asked the man behind the ink curtain of newspaper.

"Mmm, hmm," emerged from over the top of the periodical, deliberate and accusingly.

Peter waited for more, but nothing was said.

When Mr. Darling and his son got in the car Peter became afraid, not so much of the potential of his father having a stroke from yelling so hard, but of the odd manner in which his parents acted this morning. Normally there would have been yelling and a re-statement of the punishment. Neither occurred and this frightened young Peter.

Mr. Darling had been coaching baseball since his eldest son, Shawn, had played little league. Now Mr. Darling was Peter's Colt League coach. Some players whose fathers were coaches participated in every game and played whatever position they wanted. Mr. Darling removed himself from the mere notion of nepotism by going to the other extreme—he rarely played Peter at all in the games. This frustrated Peter, but he enjoyed hanging out with his teammates and had taken on the designation of team jokester.

The two Darling men sat in the car. Mr. Darling started it up with a quick jerk, revved the engine twice and pulled out of the driveway. Peter stared at the dashboard.

"Your mother thinks I grounded you because you were so late last night, that's why she didn't say anything. I told her your watch had stopped." Mr. Darling turned the huge Oldsmobile onto Washington Street.

Peter looked at the polyester carpet on the passenger side door. He was thankful for his father's decision to withhold information from his mother. He felt a little guilty for his earlier thoughts of ill will toward the old man. He looked at his wrist then, puzzled, and blinked rapidly. "I don't have a watch," he said.

"I know," said Mr. Darling. His expression never changed. They sat in silence the rest of the trip to the local park where the West Side Colt League diamonds were. As they got out of the car, Mr. Darling reminded his son that he was still grounded for two weeks, then turned and smiled to himself.

The game moved along as most of them did. Peter sat on the bench and chewed sunflower seeds. His team won the game and Peter thought he might get in, but his father had considered it too late to insert a substitute. Peter figured out what was going on in the social circles for the Saturday evening. He didn't tell anyone he was grounded yet.

As Mr. Darling and Peter turned off of Washington Street and headed home they noticed three of Peter's friends hanging around in front of Peter's neighbor's house. This neighbor had been friends with Peter due to their close proximity in living arrangements. The other two boys had known Peter since he was five, having both been in his kindergarten class. It looked as if Max, the most athletic of the bunch, was shooting baskets while David and Nick sat on the front step and watched. They all three waved at the passing car, recognizing Peter and Mr. Darling.

Peter liked all three of these boys, although he considered David and Nick to be "dorks." They had always been nice to him and Peter felt superior to them when they played basketball or touch football in the street. He could beat them at something, so he didn't mind hanging out with them. Max was in the same social circle as Peter and was more his equal, athletically, although neither were superstars. Max was almost as hot-tempered as Peter and the two of them got along fairly well. They often discussed girls—something Peter never did with Nick and David. Nick and David had never had girlfriends.

After Peter changed out of his baseball uniform, he walked the five houses' distance in the direction of the big field behind the junior high. You could see the boys' school from Nick's front lawn.

"What's up, fellas?" asked Peter, stopping to stand under the basketball hoop erected by Nick's father. Nick's older sister had gotten more use from it than the doughy Nick ever would. Nick hated playing sports and only did so at the behest of two of his closest friends—Max and Peter.

"Nothin'," replied Max. He rattled one off the rim that Peter rebounded and bounced back to him.

"What's up, Peter?" asked David.

"Hey," mumbled Nick, who almost always avoided eye contact. His introverted nature had sometimes been a source of frustration for Max and Peter and other times they took advantage of that insecurity.

"Where were you at?" asked Max, spotting up for another jump shot. This one went in.

Peter pulled the ball out of the hoop. "I had a baseball game." He snapped the worn "indoor/outdoor" ball back to Max.

"Cool. Did ya win?" Max asked in mid-shot, this caroming off the backboard with a thud but finding the bottom of the net. Nick and David seemed interested, but they really were just bystanders.

"Yeah, but I didn't play," said Peter, his voice encased in nonchalance.

"You guys wanna play?" asked Max, turning to Nick and David. It was apparent they had already played something, as both boys had mild sweat rings at the necks and underarms of their t-shirts. Max had some color in his face but little else.

The two boys looked at each other and winced. They had fallen prey to Max and Peter's games of two-on-two football before, which they loathed, but they had never tried basketball. They each shrugged. David sighed heavily. "All right," he finally said, realizing that they would probably be brow-beaten into submission if they said no.

"I'll take Jansen," said Max, circumventing the problem of choosing the lesser of two evils. He knew Peter wouldn't really care. He might even think that having David was an advantage due to his being slightly taller than Nick Jansen.

"Okay. Come on, Dave." Peter motioned to David. David loped to the driveway. His shoulders were slightly rounded and he had little self-confidence. He didn't really like Max or Peter, he was better friends with Nick. He had grown tired of the condescending tone Max and Peter took when he was around.

Nick did not exude any aura of supreme assurance either. His toes pointed outward as he made the short journey from the front step to the uneven pavement in his driveway. He had dark skin, like both of his parents, but that was about where the heritage ended. He never embraced his Latino roots, a point which never seemed to bother anyone, expect maybe Max, who was also Latino.

"Your ball first. Play to eleven by ones. That crack is the take-back line." Max pointed to the small crevice made by the shifting pavement in the driveway. He flipped the ball to Peter and moved into his defensive position, the one Coach Baldwin had showed him. Nick and David stood next to each other, not moving.

"Come on! Move!" yelled Peter.

David bounced up and down but didn't really go anywhere. Nick mirrored him. Peter was irritated after only a few short seconds. He had little patience, especially when it came to competition. He did not want to get beat by Nick and Max.

The game progressed slowly. It was more of a one-on-one game with the extra men as either rebounders or passers. Neither Nick nor David shot the ball more than twice in the game. It wasn't really fair. Max was slightly quicker than all of them and had a better shot. He ended the game mercifully with a lay-up. The final score was 11-6. Despite their inactivity, both Nick and David were winded. They sat down to rest.

"I'm thirsty," wheezed Nick.

"Me, too," said David. He pulled on the front of his shirt, letting the air billow throughout. His dark, thick hair made his head hot on this early June afternoon.

"Why don't you get us something to drink?" offered Peter. He was still a little irritated about the game. He was shooting no-look lay-ups while Max, who had worked up a sweat scoring all eleven points for his team, sat on the Chemlawn-treated grass in the front of the house.

"We don't have anything," mumbled Nick, looking around. He wiped the sweat from his brow with his gray shirtsleeve.

Max darted a look at Nick. "Whatever, dude. You've always got Kool-Aid or pop or somethin' in there." This was true. Nick's mother always purchased more than enough sugar-laden goodies. Nick, a selfish person at heart, was rarely willing to share. This led to the aggressive nature of Max and Peter. They basically just took what they wanted to eat and drink whenever it was just the guys.

"No shit, Jansen. Go get some pops for us," ordered Peter, still intent on his no-look shots.

Nick, realizing he had lost, tried his next defense—laziness. "I ain't goin' to get you no pop," replied Nick, with slight assurance. "Get it yourself." He felt the prospect of work may turn the boys off to the desire to quench their thirsts.

"Awright," was the unisoned, immediate response from Peter and Max. They darted through the open garage door to the kitchen doorway. The door was locked.

"It's locked, Fat Ass!" yelled Peter.

"Oh no, I don't have a key," said Nick, with mild surprise. He shot a knowing look to David, who smiled meekly and looked at the two boys at the door.

"Bull shit. Give me the key," barked Peter. He was still upset about the 11-6 loss. He felt he was owed this soda as compensation for playing basketball with such inferiors.

"I don't have it," muttered Nick. He looked away, grinning a little. This playful cat and mousing was a way of getting back at the two more popular young men. It seemed that he actually had some control if he withheld something they desired.

"You want me to come over there and beat it out of you?" Peter clenched his fists. His brow furrowed.

Nick began to chuckle his nervous chuckle. His shoulders shook but the sound was suppressed to a barely audible, broken sound from deep in his throat. It remained oddly high-pitched however. Nick frequently laughed like this around Peter and Max. He knew that Peter could never, or would never, "beat it out of him." Nick was too much bigger and their parents had been friends for too long. This didn't seem to stop Peter from hurling threats, however. Nick finally shrugged.

Peter began walking out of the garage, toward Nick. He gritted his teeth, mumbling angry words under his breath.

Nick stood still and reached into his pocket. "Oh, Jesus, you are a spaz. Here." He handed the house key to Peter.

"I knew you had it, Jack Off." Peter relaxed a little once he felt the metal hit his palm. He turned without a thanks and headed back inside the garage and to Max.

Max watched this brief scene play out. He usually felt sorry for Nick, but never said a word. He thought Peter was always too gruff and insulting with not only Nick, but with other people outside their clique. Max' face looked innocent, expressionless as Peter came closer.

"I knew he had a key, fuckin' Jack Off." He let himself into his friend's home and was followed by Max. They headed right for the fridge and grabbed two Mountain Dews. Max stopped at the cupboard where he knew the licorice was. He took out the tubular Tupperware container and grabbed three red licorice strips. Peter scanned the fridge for anything else to consume. He walked past Max to head back outside with his soda.

"Hey, aren't you going to grab one for those guys?" asked Max. This seemed like a natural gesture, after all, Nick was letting them into his house to drink his soda.

Peter stopped and looked, dumbfounded, at Max, as if this never occurred to him. "No," he said, as if he had been accused of something.

Max rolled his eyes as Peter turned to go outside. He went back to the refrigerator and grabbed two more Mountain Dews and went outside.

Peter flipped the key to Nick. He did not say thank you for the beverage.

"Here," said Max, handing a cold Mountain Dew to Nick and then David.

"Thanks," muttered David.

The boys sat on the front step drinking their sodas and making small talk. They discussed classes in common, teachers who handed out "worthless" assignments, and the mentally disabled. This last topic was a source of humor for the boys, Nick especially. After about fifteen minutes of this light banter, Nick had to use the restroom.

"I'll be right back."

"Where're you goin'?" asked Peter from his spot on sidewalk.

Nick didn't answer as he moved past him, digging in his pocket for the house key. David stared at the wooded area across the street from the house. The fireplace wood was neatly stacked and covered with a tarp, no doubt the work of Nick's father. David smiled to himself at the thought of Nick even trying to chop firewood.

Max could see Nick from his spot on the driveway pavement. The chubby boy ambled through the car-less garage and began to unlock the door. He glanced out at Max as he pushed the button to close the automatic garage door. He looked frightened. Max sprang to his feet.

"What are you doing?" asked Max as he hurried toward the closing garage door. He could hear Nick's distinct chuckle from inside. Max ducked and squirted under the door. It shut with a thud. Both boys could hear the muffled profanity of Peter from the other side of the door. Then the banging. They both stood there.

"Open the door, fag!" bellowed Peter. For some reason he was uneasy being left out in the sun with David. He pounded on the door.

Nick moved inside, through the kitchen and to the front door. His house was quiet, except for the cool hum of the vents kicking out conditioned air. He opened the front door, knowing that the screen door was locked. For some reason he felt like playing that cat and mouse game with Peter again. He yelled through the door, "Don't pound on that!"

Peter stamped toward the front door. David, positioned directly in front of it, moved. Had he not he might have been trampled. "Open the door!" urged Peter as he jostled the handle of the screen door.

"Quit pounding on it," said Nick, in mock seriousness.

"Open the door, Jansen," said Peter. His irritation was growing. He liked and disliked Nick. He resented him for getting everything he asked for, but he knew that he could easily bully him into giving up some of his spoils from time to time.

"Settle down, Peter," admonished Nick. He liked to pretend he was Peter's father sometimes, just to piss Peter off.

Peter punched the screen and the metal behind it.

Nick was slightly unsettled by this as he looked at the genuine rage in Peter's eyes. He regained his childish grasp of what he was doing. "Don't hit my door," he cooed as he shook his head.

Peter pounded on door.

Meanwhile, Max had tired of listening to the muffled voices and waiting for Nick to come back to the garage. He entered the kitchen and could see Nick at the end of the front hall, talking to Peter. "What's going on?" he shouted.

Peter answered first, "Nick's being a retard!" He punched the screen more gently this time. His knuckles still hurt from the first show of aggression.

Nick slowly turned. "He won't quit pounding on the door," he sniffed.

"I'm gonna pound you, fat ass, if you don't open the fucking door!" Peter's eyes were sharp. His brow was furrowed and his face was turning red.

David laughed out loud.

Peter, feeling that he had an audience with David, grew more steadfast in his conviction. He knew he was right to insult Nick. He knew he needed to get inside. He knew that any means necessary was appropriate.

"Just let him in," said Max, as he walked toward the door.

"I'm not letting him in till he stops pounding on the door," said Nick, crossing his arms. The grandfather clock chimed loudly.

Peter pounded on the frame of the screen door many times in succession, yelling, "I'm not going to stop, fat ass, until you let me in!" He repeated this two times, then turned it into a song, with his pounding as the beat. "I'm not going to stop, no, I'm not going to stop, until you let me in, faaaat, aaaass!"

This was mildly amusing to both Nick and Max for the first three times, then it became annoying, then unsettling. Nick looked worriedly at Max. Max shook his head and looked at Peter, who didn't seem to be looking at anything.

"Quit pounding on the fucking door!" screamed Nick. He had reached his breaking point. He ran his hand through his greasy black hair. His eyes were wide.

Peter enjoyed this. He stopped and smiled and moved away from the door. "Are you going to let me in?"

There was no reply.

"Fine." Peter moved to the garage door. David watched him with intrigue.

Neither Nick nor Max could see Peter once he disappeared to their left. Seconds later they heard Peter. A loud bang echoed through the garage and carried its piercing message into the kitchen and then the hallway. The air was silent for two seconds. Then an identical sound filled their ears. The sound was quite menacing, and sounded damaging—like someone dropping a tool box full of tools.

"What is he doing?" Nick asked David through the screen. A car rolled by and the noise stopped for a moment. It started back up with a jolt. Max moved to the garage.

David, the only one who could see Peter, had an odd look on his face, perplexed, confounded. One of the corners of his mouth slowly raised into a half-smile. He couldn't believe what he was seeing.

"He's throwing the basketball against the garage door. Now he's doing it again. Again. Again. That's the sound you're hearing," David delivered in his monotone. He couldn't take his eyes off of the spectacle of Peter.

"Motherfucker," muttered Nick, but he did not move. He craned his neck to see the culprit. He could catch a glimpse of him only when Peter would gather in the ball from the recoil of hitting the big brown garage door.

Max was wondering when Peter would stop. After about the thirtieth bang, he thought about the dent Peter might be creating. He knew (they all did) that Peter wouldn't care about damaging his neighbor's property, let alone his friend's.

"Knock it off, Peter!" warned Nick. His friend paid no heed. "Oh, real cool, my dad will love the new hole in the garage!" yelled Nick, sarcastically. This had no effect. "That's enough, asshole!" screamed Nick. He never moved, though.

David's face softened to an almost dull serenity. He just stared at the now-sweating Peter. He was in awe of this young man's determination. He thought of the saying he had seen somewhere: a fanatic is someone who redoubles his effort when he has forgotten his aim. He wasn't sure why he knew that quote.

"Leave my fucking door alone, Peter!" screamed Nick. He was beginning to sweat and worry and wish his father would come home.

Max couldn't stand it anymore. The steady pattern of the basketball slamming into the garage door was interrupted by the chug and churn of the automatic garage door opener. Max readied himself, expecting one last basketball to come flying in at him once the door was raised.

Peter stood holding the ball under one arm. He wiped his brow with the back of his hand. He entered the garage, expressionless and passed Max.

Nick, upon hearing the garage door open, had let himself out the front door, not wanting to face Peter inside. He figured David offered some modicum of safety.

Peter moved calmly to the front door and locked the screen door, in clear sight of Nick. Then he ran back to Max and touched the button to close the garage door. As Nick tried to enter, Peter whipped the basketball at him, hitting him in the legs. Peter laughed like a hyena at the sight of Nick falling down. He didn't realize Nick had done this on purpose.

Nick rolled under the door just as it shut behind him. He sprang up, singing the Indiana Jones movies' theme song. Remarkably, he was smiling. He was impressed with his accomplishment and that seemed to overtake the fear he had experienced on the heels of Peter's recent actions. Both Max and Peter stared intensely at Nick, then a smile began to creep across first Max' face, then Peter's.

"You are a freak," said Peter. His anger began to subside as quickly as it had begun. He smiled at the playfulness of Nick, not realizing the courage the portly young man used in confronting Peter in a closed garage.

Nick stood up, proud of himself for making his two guests laugh.

"You been practicing that one, Jansen?" asked Max.

"Naw, just something I picked up from the movies," came the nonchalant reply of Nick. He looked somewhat nervously between the two young men. The aroma of motor oil arose from the stained carpet squares laid down by Nick's father. The acoustics of the garage were vastly different from the warm summer afternoon outdoors.

"Bet you couldn't do it again," challenged Peter. The words seemed boxed and fuller in the shadowy garage.

Nick shrugged and looked at the flat tire on his ten speed, leaning against the garage wall. The challenge hung in the air, waiting for a reply.

"I'll give you a dollar if you do it again," said Peter loudly.

Nick smiled halfheartedly, knowing the kind of odds Peter gave—if Peter knew he could win, he'd bet. If he couldn't win, he'd figure out a way to cheat out a victory. Nick was reluctant, then. But he couldn't see the harm in this bet. He knew he could roll under the closing garage door with ease. There was no way Peter could manipulate the conditions.

"So?" Peter was smiling. His eyes were wide behind his glasses with the prospect of winning a game of chance. He enjoyed winning and felt "by any means necessary" was just as appropriate in gambling as in anything else.

Just then a gentle knock came on the garage door. Peter pushed the button to open the heavy brown door. It creaked with the ten years of age it had acquired. David stood there, the same dull look on his face, waiting, as the two-car garage door slowly revealed his slumping frame. He scratched the thigh of his cut off camouflage shorts.

"Did you see my Indiana Jones roll?" Nick turned and asked David.

"Is that what that was?"

"I bet Fat Ass a dollar he couldn't do it again," interrupted Peter. He tapped nervously on the workbench located right below the garage door opener. He stared intensely at Nick. He did not have a dollar on his person.

Nick chuckled slightly and rolled his eyes. "Tsk, I don't wanna take your money that easily, oh, wait a minute, yes I do." He looked at David for approval of this humor.

"Then do it, Jansen," chided Max. He was actually impressed by Nick's quickness. He knew Nick could be agile—he was the only one of his friends able to put both legs behind his head and walk around on his hands—but Nick's weight gave the impression of an oaf. Max secretly wanted Nick to win the dollar he knew Peter didn't have.

"All right," said Nick. With that he strolled past David. He decided that some flare was needed for this undertaking. He walked all the way to the end of the driveway, squinting in the hot sun, to the smoothly curved edge of the street-curb. He pretended to stretch his hamstrings and bounced several times up and down on his toes. He removed his glasses and wiped his forehead, replacing the smudged spectacles on his perspiring nose.

"What a fuckin' dork," Peter said meanly to Max, quiet enough so that not even David, who had moved just inside the garage, could hear.

Max ignored the remark and smiled knowingly at Nick. He was enjoying the theatrics and could easily appreciate them. David echoed that sentiment.

"Whenever you're ready!" shouted Nick as he pointed at Peter and went into a shoddy looking sprinter's crouch.

"You better have my dollar!" yelled Peter as he emphatically pushed the narrow, chalky rectangle which served as the garage door's catalyst to open.

Nick approached with his unique jog, toes pointed outward, arms close in, head bobbing. He crouched as the garage door made it halfway down. He began to hum the Indiana Jones' theme song as he went into his roll. He moved from crouched to prone in an almost frightening amount of quickness, but his audience could tell he was careful not to soil or rip his shorts or the gray Iowa t-shirt he wore.

The three boys on the inside watched as Nick rolled just under the garage door and wound up on his side as the door closed behind him, a mere two inches from his backside. Peter frowned slightly. Max laughed out loud. David shook his head and admired.

Nick jumped up and into a ready-for-action position. He was still humming the music. The garage door made its final two clicks as the extra links in the chain were pulled taut.

"That wasn't like the last one," said Peter as he shook his head. He had no intention of losing a dollar, let alone his dignity, to this loser. "You got in way under the door, it wasn't even that dangerous." Peter crossed his arms.

Nick rolled his eyes as he stood up straight. He knew there was no real danger in his derring-do. The garage door was touch-sensitive. If it met any resistance on the way down, it would automatically recoil to the open position. He was rather disappointed in Peter's reaction, however. Hadn't his flamboyant approach had at least earned him minimal kudos? He honestly did not expect the dollar wagered, just a little credit where credit was due.

Peter was incredulous. "Do it again," he barked.

"He just fuckin' did it, Pete," huffed Max. "Give him the dollar."

"I'll give him the dollar when he does it exactly like the last time," explained Peter slowly. He furrowed his brow and looked at Max as if he had been accused of some heinous crime.

Max sighed and looked at Nick, as if to apologize for his friend. He wondered why Nick had even agreed to the bet in the first place. All of them knew that Peter would make Nick perform the stunt over and over again until he won the dollar. He would make up excuses or claim "do-over" for as long as it took to prove himself right. Only he would be satisfied. Only he would think himself the winner.

Nick looked for a moment at Peter's skinny legs, then shrugged. "All right," he muttered.

"Thought so," said Peter triumphantly as he pushed the button.

Nick turned to walk out and caught David's eye. He smiled a little and then looked at the elephant-gray pavement of the garage. The brown door clicked on its chain rhythmically as Nick ducked under and stopped in the middle of the driveway. He turned to face his task again and took a deep breath.

Max looked at the intent Peter, who's hand was poised over the glow-in-the-dark button mechanism screwed to the wall. He was not surprised at Peter's immaturity, but it still disappointed him. The air had been let out of the whole affair.

David watched the door rise and kept his gaze fixed there, waiting for something unexpected to happen.

"Go ahead," said Nick, as if a bully had offered to punch him in the face if he wanted to use the drinking fountain.

Peter obliged and smiled wickedly. He knew he could keep this up; it was only a matter of time before he had Jansen's money.

Nick began to sing the requisite theme song as he crouched, more prematurely this time. He rolled under the door, in no real danger, to the inside of the garage, then back to the outside and then back to the inside, as if he were rolling about to put out a fire. All of this in about two seconds—before the door closed completely.

This freestyling artistry in the realm of garage door opening had yet to be seen by the innocent eyes of young men like David, Max, and Peter. The feat would have been quite entertaining and skillful had it come off without a hitch. But sometimes hitches appear when they shouldn't. Sometimes things don't go as planned. Such was this third effort by Nick Jansen to impress Peter Darling.

As Nick executed his third roll under the impending weight of the metal garage door which loomed like a huge portcullis, he had miscalculated. This being the first time he had attempted the triple-Indy roll, he wasn't exactly sure how it would play out. But he did know that if any part of him was touched by the descending door, it would automatically go up and Nick would escape without harm. This caveat of information was assumed by all, which, in turn, led to the surprise when the door did not automatically rise up. Instead it kept pushing downward, with Herculean might, on the now split-lengthwise body of Nick Jansen. He had attempted this dangerous move figuring that if he failed Peter might give him another chance, and if he succeeded Peter might relent a little and drop the bet.

Of course, he had not figured on the weight of the door pressing down across his left collarbone, slightly angling across his sternum, running parallel with his genitalia and pinning his right ankle to the cement of the driveway, on which side his head lay. The garage door pushed heavily on the flabby body, somehow not obeying its usual course of action and then stopped its clicking and humming. Nick had also stopped his version of the Indiana Jones theme song. He was most definitely in shock when the door's weight pressed against his body.

Peter laughed hysterically, like a hyena. He pointed at the left leg, flank, and arm of Nick as it flailed about. He could hear Nick's shouts to open the door. This was music to his ears.

Neither Max nor David could restrain an initial laugh, the kind which escapes when witnessing someone fall on the ice or trip on stairs, the guilty kind which is as much out of nerves as of pleasure. They both knew they should help Nick, but they had been ridiculed by him before and thought a few seconds of enjoying this would be nice. They both wondered why it couldn't have been Peter under the door.

Peter laughed like a cartoon, hooting and howling. He held his stomach as he pointed at the awkward sight of a headless half of Nick. He looked at Max and David and noticed that they weren't laughing nearly as hard. It did not bother him and he kept on. After about ten seconds he wiped his eyes.

"How's it going, Indy?" he bellowed, followed by another laugh.

"Open the door, Peter!" came the distant response from Nick. He sounded calmer than any one of them expected.

"Look's like you owe me a dollar, Dr. Jones," came the short-breathed reply, followed by more laughter.

Max and David were now smiling, watching the moving arm and leg. It was odd to see Nick's body without the head, still moving. Like some freshly decapitated animal. It was slightly unsettling.

"Open the door!"

Peter laughed again at the spectacle. "Look at that retard." He invited his companions to join him in his mirth.

David was now watching the limbs with great intrigue. Max spoke up. "Push the button."

"My ass. I'm gonna enjoy this for awhile," Peter stared at Nick. His eyes were like a small child's at a fireworks display.

"Open the fucking door!" screamed Nick from the other side of reality.

"Hmmm, where have I heard that before?" asked Peter sarcastically.

David moved past the two boys at the door to the kitchen and into the house. He said not a word and looked only ahead of him.

Peter watched him coolly, expecting him to try and press the button. He lunged to cup the piece of plastic with both hands, protecting it from any evildoers.

"Where're you going?" asked Max.

A few seconds later, Peter and Max heard the front screen bang shut and the barely audible voices of Nick and David. Max went over to Nick. He bent down on all fours and spoke through the six inch gap between the floor and door near Nick's left shoulder. "You okay?"

Apparently Nick could not turn his head to answer, or would not, because he still sounded far away, even at this range. "I'm fine, but I don't like being stuck here."

"You look kinda funny," said Max, hoping to add some levity, however lame.

"I feel funny," replied Nick.

"What the hell were you trying to do?" asked Max.

"Win a dollar," replied Nick matter-of-factly.

Max looked over his shoulder at Peter, who was still giggling to himself. He got up from the hard floor and moved toward Peter. "We should let him out," he said.

"Oh, come on, we'll just have some fun for a little bit," said Peter mischievously. He tried to wink at Max, but both eyes opened and shut. Peter had never been able to wink.

Max looked at the blond-haired boy standing opposite him. He knew there was no point in arguing with Peter. The door could only be opened when Peter was ready or through some physical altercation, and Max despised fighting. He walked past Peter into the kitchen and out the front door.

The sun shone brightly off of Nick's glasses. David stood with his arms crossed and looked at the head, right arm, and bent right leg (down to the ankle) of his friend.

"Will you tell that dickhead to open the goddamn door?" Nick asked Max as soon as the more athletic boy came into view.

"Open the door, Pete!" yelled Max. There was no reply.

The image of the fat Latino boy, pinned under the painted-brown metal of his own garage door struck Max as comic and tragic. Nick had tried so hard to impress, to carve out his piece of individuality that this gross failure would likely do considerable damage. Instead of having someone to blame, however, Nick was entirely at fault for the screw-up—he shouldn't have tried to do more than he was capable.

"Dude, you do look kind of funny," offered Max, stifling a laugh. David laughed out loud.

"You do look weird, man, like modern art," chuckled David.

"Well fuck you, Picasso, and get Peter to open this door!" Nick yelled the last three words so Peter would surely hear them. Again, silence.

"What the hell were you trying to do anyway?" asked Max, giggling.

Nick looked at him over the top of his spectacles and gestured with his free arm. "I was trying to get asshole to drop this stupid game and give me the dollar... this fuckin' hurts y'know."

"It doesn't look like it hurts," said David, smiling wryly. He pushed inward on the garage door and shook his head. The sun was beginning to go down and he was cooling off.

"Well it does, David, it does!" shrieked the prone boy.

"Where's your other foot?" asked Max leaning down to inspect the trapped appendage that was Nick's right leg. He hadn't seen it on the other side.

"It's under the door and probably broken by now!" came the panicked response.

This sent David into hysterical laughter. He had been trying to hold it in for too long and this last remark proved the final straw. He exploded at the notion of a boy having his bones crushed, or even fractured by an automatic garage door. He had never fancied himself a tough guy, but this was ridiculous.

"You pussy," said Max mildly.

"It fucking hurts!" screamed Nick. His face showed no real pain, just an intensity to be removed from that difficult predicament.

"Well, you shouldn't have been jacking around underneath it, dip shit." Max shook his head and poked Nick's flabby calf, pressed against the brownish, paved driveway like a beached whale.

"Hey!" shouted Nick.

Just then Peter came out the front door. David and Max looked at him, awkwardly. The moment hung in silence—curious, unsure, scared about where it would go. Neither of the boys knew Peter's state of mind, but they figured he'd be up for maintaining Nick's captured situation as long as possible. They were right.

"Is he still there?" asked Peter, knowing the answer. He had a look of sheer pleasure on his face. "I could hear him whining about something from in there, but I thought I'd come out and see for sure." He knelt down near Nick's head, far enough away from Nick's flailing grasp. He poked Nick. "What are you whining about, Indy?" he sneered.

"Go open the goddamn door," ordered Nick. He tried desperately to reach Peter. If he was going to be down, his assailant was going to be down with him. His hand swatted helplessly at the summer air.

David chuckled again at the sight of Nick's lack of mobility. Max poked the flesh again and jumped back.

"Knock it off!" Nick's order pierced the air.

"Ooooh, somebody's a little sore," taunted Peter. He joined Max near Nick's leg and began prodding vigorously and then jumping back. Each time Nick admonished him to quit, and each time Peter cackled like a mad scientist. After about ten minutes of various taunting and torture, David, Max, and Peter began to grow bored. The late afternoon was making its daily sojourn into the cicada symphony of dusk. Nick's parents would be home soon.

After a while Nick had accepted that he would be tormented by these boys. This did not mean that he liked it, however. He cursed them at each new transgression, especially Peter, as the pain grew in his ankle—minor though it was.

"You can let me out, assholes," suggested Nick. The boys had made several trips from inside the garage to the outside. They found it easier to poke and prod from the inside but more fun to receive the verbal lashings of their quarry face to face. The cat and mouse game had returned, with a twisted vengeance.

"How the hell did you get stuck under a fucking garage door?" Peter finally asked, shaking his head. He was only growing tired of the hijinks because it was nearing evening—the time when he would go out with his friends and party.

This last pastime seemed to take precedence over all others, especially in the summer.

"No shit, Jansen," added Max. "Aren't these supposed to go up automatically?"

Nick did not answer. He had laid his head back and was staring at the sky, waiting for one of his parents to return home and rescue him from these evil boys.

"How's the foot?" asked David.

"Fucking hurts," muttered Nick in a monotone.

"You fucking pussy. Are you still whining about your fat foot?" asked Peter. His pitch shifted from normal to angry in just under one second.

"You'd be whining too if you had a fucking garage door on top of it!" Nick's voice crescendoed.

"We figured you were just being a pussy," said David, with genuine sincerity.

"Yeah, we figured your belly had taken most of the pressure off everything else." Peter laughed heartily at this jab. The other two boys smiled briefly but felt the joke too lame to dignify.

"Well, it really hurts, I'll probably have to go to the hospital," claimed Nick.

"The hospital! The hospital? Are you a moron?" asked Peter. He resented Nick for being spoiled. Ever since they had been small Nick had always been pampered. At the earliest hint of pain Nick would go running to his mother or father and they would cater to his needs. Meanwhile, Peter was expected to follow in the footsteps of the invincible thoroughbred that was his brother. He was not to cry or complain or make a scene. He was to endure injury and become stronger. These were the rules in his home which later became the rules in his mind. Nick stood for weakness in Peter's mind, and it ate him up when his friend exemplified it.

"If you go to the hospital I'll kick your ass," said Peter, as if it was a tempting offer.

Nick looked up and realized that Peter might have meant it. He looked down his body and sighed. Just then he heard another car turning the corner onto his street. He wondered what the travelers would think when they saw this odd scene. Then he wished it was one of his parents. His wish came true.

David, Max, and Peter watched the maroon Honda turn the corner and saw the female driver's jaw drop as she gazed upon her son trapped under the garage door and three of his closest friends standing idly by. They couldn't see her eyes behind the huge tinted disks that were her sunglasses. The amber-colored frames and dark brown lenses couldn't hide the shock, though. She pulled slowly into the driveway, unsure of what might happen and reached cautiously for the opener clipped to the visor above her. The three boys stood motionless.

Peter had never been wronged by Mrs. Jansen. In fact, she had been a friend of Mrs. Darling's and often tried to treat Peter as one of her own. This thought flashed briefly through the young man's mind. Then he remembered that she was not his mother and could therefore not punish him. He relaxed slightly and thanked God it was not Mr. Jansen.

"Thank God," whispered Nick. The weight of the door began to lift as a huge "ka-chug" sound signaled the opening of the huge brown door.

The boys moved slowly out of the way of the car and over to the sidewalk in front of the house. Nick rose slowly and limped near them. Mrs. Jansen had the window rolled down.

"Nick, what are you doing?" she asked, as if he had held the boys under the door all that time.

Nick looked at the three boys standing next to him. Each face was expressionless. Nick looked back at his mother. "Nothin'," he said. "I was just messin' around." He leaned down and rubbed his ankle.

"Tsk, you're gonna get hurt," scolded Mrs. Jansen as she pulled the car in.

Peter smiled and looked at Nick and the others.

It had been several weeks since the garage door incident. Peter had served his detention time for coming home drunk and was excited to hit the scene again. Although he was not allowed out at night, he had been permitted to leave during the day. He frequently went over to Kim's house. Kim was the girlfriend of one of Peter's best friends. Peter would hang out and watch T.V. before and after baseball. He might go to the pool with Kim, Tom (her boyfriend), and a varied assortment of their peers, depending on the day. He enjoyed this, because he still felt like a part of the crowd, even if he wasn't allowed to party with them at night. Peter always wanted to be part of the crowd and never wanted to miss out on anything. In his mind, missing a party was like another fall of Rome.

So Peter got his social fix during the days. Sometimes he'd have a friend steal some alcohol from the local convenient store and he'd get drunk with Kim and the girls. Sometimes he'd sneak a bottle from his parents' liquor cabinet and he and a couple of buddies would have a few tugs while Mr. and Mrs. Darling were at work. Most times he just enjoyed the company, though. Over these several weeks he had enjoyed the company of one friend in particular—Julie. Julie was tall and thin and had blond hair. She had soft skin the color of lifeguard-tan. Her blue eyes were close set and her smile was quick. She was one of Kim's closest friends and was generally around when Peter was. They started to see each other toward the end of the summer.

Peter had never been especially suave with the ladies. He had a winning smile and generally befriended them before expressing any amorous intentions. Of course, most of the girls he knew would then claim that he was "too good of a friend" to date. This frustrated Peter, but he liked the female companionship, on whatever level, so he endured. He had had several girlfriends in his fifteen year lifespan, but now he was entering high school. This step meant he had to take the hand holding and heavy petting to another level. He had to prove himself a man the only way all of his friends claimed was possible—he had to have sex with someone. This new endeavor seemed the mature thing to do, and Peter assumed he would eventually find a willing enough mate. Julie offered the opportunity to test this new goal.

Peter and Julie had made out a couple of times after his baseball games, but nothing serious. He was beginning to grow quite fond of her and thought about her more often than not. He was still awkward around her, however. He remained quiet and shy as a boyfriend, unsure of what he should say, not knowing what words might ruin his chances. Conversation was started and led by the soft-spoken Julie on almost every occasion. Peter thought that she didn't mind—maybe she liked the quiet type.

One thing loomed on the horizon as the close of summer approached—Julie's birthday. She was young for her grade and would turn fifteen in August. Peter, almost a full year older, winced at the thought of having to buy her a gift. He hated buying gifts for people. Finding the right gift was frustrating and not very self-satisfying. The holiday season was an absolutely gut-wrenching experience the older Peter was. He had been expected to take more responsibility in choosing and paying for his gifts to other people, a duty formerly reserved for Mrs. Darling.

Julie had decided to have a birthday party at her house on the fifteenth anniversary of her birth. This happened to fall upon a Friday. Peter, the boyfriend of three weeks, grew exceedingly nervous as the day approached. He had no idea what to buy her. Candles, beer mugs, and McDonald's gift certificates (last year's Christmas gifts to his family) would not suffice. The acid in Peter's stomach increased and irritated the yet-to-be discovered hole created by the IcyHot.

After two weeks of assuring Julie that he would be there, Friday arrived. The sun rose and beat down upon the tiny section of the planet holding Peter's hometown. He rose from a particularly restless night with $7 to his name and no gift for Julie. Peter's day passed quickly with a fruitless trip to the mall with Tom and several phone conversations with various friends covering the matter of what to buy Julie for her birthday. The afternoon rolled around and Peter was tired of thinking. He needed a diversion—one that would help him come up with an idea.

"Hey, what's up?" Peter asked lazily into the receiver.

"Nothin', just watchin' the Scrubs," replied Max.

"Who's over there?" asked Peter, fearing he was missing out on something else. Tom's mother had dropped him off after the mall excursion and Peter had been home for at least twenty minutes—a maddening amount of time.

"Just Felder," said Max. "Oh shit, and another one bites the dust," shouted Max, holding the phone away from his mouth.

"What?"

"Nothin', another Scrub just struck out, Felder's starting to whine about the size of the strike zone, too."

"Oh," was the short reply from Peter. He wanted to do something, but watching baseball was not what he had in mind. He needed to burn off some nervous energy. He looked at the clock on the stove. Its ancient second hand clicked and shivered, clicked and shivered. Each second drew him closer to Julie's party. It was only 3:30, though. The party didn't start until 7 p.m. He had plenty of time.

"You doing anything tonight?" asked Max.

"Yeah, it's Julie's birthday party. Aren't you going?" Peter figured for sure Max would be going.

There was a pause. "No, I wasn't invited. Guess you have to have a girlfriend or somethin'," came the dejected reply.

"Wha...oh, yeah. Naw, I'll bet Julie just forgot." Peter was quickly learning the proper rhetoric in covering up mistakes. He was surprised momentarily by Max' lack of an invitation, but then it seemed to make sense. Max and Julie had dated in seventh grade and had not broken up on the best of terms.

"Right," said Max, cynically. "Uh oh, nothing and one on the big hitter!" barked Max, again holding the phone away from his mouth. "Swing and a miss!"

"Who's up?" asked Peter, remembering that if he had to follow a team, it might as well have been the Cubs.

"Who cares? They suck."

"Yeah, what are they 15 games back?" asked Peter, trying to avoid thinking about Julie's gift.

"Something like that...here's the pitch...oh you're fucking kidding me! That was a strike!"

Felder said something in the background but Peter couldn't hear it.

"What'd he say?" asked Peter.

"He said 'watch out, now'," answered Max, re-iterating one of Felder's favorite phrases.

"So what are you guys doing now?" questioned Peter. He leaned against the wall in his basement and absentmindedly shot the weathered orange sphere into the Nerf hoop. It back-rimmed and came back to him. Peter caught it and whipped it at the plastic hoop in one motion, the frustration rising to a boil and cooling with equal quickness.

"We're watching the Cubs," said Max, slightly irritated. "What time's the party?"

"Seven." Just then a plan occurred to Peter. "You guys wanna play football?" he asked anxiously.

"Strike three!" Max said to Felder and Peter. "Sit down, loser!" He launched a taunting laugh into the August afternoon. "What did you say?" he asked Peter.

"Why don't you guys come over and play football? That game's probably over anyway, knowing the Cubs."

Max mulled the offer over for a minute and figured that he might as well do something. Felder wasn't going to Julie's either and was spending the night. They could work up an appetite before they came back and ordered pizza.

"Feld-man, you wanna go over to Pete's and play some football?" The reply sounded muffled to Peter, but lengthy.

"What'd he say?" asked Peter, twisting the phone cord with one finger.

"He said 'doesn't Darling realize that the boys of summer are in full swing and to shake down the thunder prematurely would do a disservice to this great game and make a mockery of the other?'" relayed Max.

"What? Tell him to quit being a pussy and come over. I'll call Danny and you call Nick and David. See you in a little while." Peter stayed on the line.

Max covered up the phone and only the stifled sound reverberations, traveling through Max' hand, could be heard. He uncovered the phone. "Alright," he sighed. "We'll be over."

"Don't forget to call Nick and David," Peter reminded.

"You call'em, you're the one who wants to play. See ya," said Max, hanging up before Peter had a chance to argue.

Peter tried to protest into the phone, but no one was there. He would call Danny, but he knew Nick and David would only come if Max asked them. If they weren't there, that was okay. They weren't part of the plan anyway. Peter had not thought to ask Max, Felder, or Danny about Julie's gift. These were three of the smartest people he knew but he had somehow overlooked their usefulness in this matter. He called Danny, who assured Peter that he would be riding his bike over. His plan was not much of one, it was more like gathering together the resources and hoping they turned into something tangible.

As the nautical clock over the basement fireplace ticked on, Peter formulated an idea and a backup idea. Danny, Felder and Max would come up with something just right for the occasion—they were smart. If Max and company could not come up with a suitable gift idea (one that cost under $7) he would have no choice but to forgo the party. He knew this would be a major transgression, but he also knew that going to the party without a birthday present for his girlfriend might prove equally dismal. He opted the way he always did, to deal with the fallout and hope for the best. This was "Plan B" of course. He had faith that the boys could come up with a romantic yet frugal gift in the time between they arrived at his house and the start of the party. Peter looked at the clock and waited.

The boys arrived at Peter's and began a game of two-on-two touch football in the street. It wasn't the Super Bowl, but the boys were having fun. Danny and Peter were on one team. The four boys knew that this was only fair, although they never voiced it. Danny was the fastest and quickest of the four, Peter the slowest and least athletic. For this reason, Danny and Peter knew they had to be on the same team. They played by ones to seven. It was 4 to 3, Felder and Max, when

Peter asked the triad for any suggestions on what to get Julie for her birthday. The boys were taking a break, sitting on the curb.

"Isn't her birthday party tonight?" asked Danny.

"Yeah, it's at seven," replied Peter as nonchalantly as possible.

"You still haven't got her a present, dude?" asked Danny. He was leaning on a mailbox but stood at attention with surprise.

"No," said Peter, sheepishly.

"What the fuck are you waiting for? The present fairy?" Danny began to laugh, not so much at what he said, but more at Peter's ineptitude. He generally viewed Peter as inferior, but still a good friend. He didn't agree with the Darling boy's tendency to make poor decisions and then try to fix them after the fact. This seemed very illogical to him.

"I dunno," said Peter, slightly embarrassed now. He felt like he was always having to meet Danny's standards. When he didn't it irritated and frustrated him.

"How much money do you have?" asked Felder, spinning the ball on the pavement.

"Seven dollars," replied Peter hesitantly. He knew the reaction to come, and he was not disappointed.

"What?" blurted Danny. He began laughing and pointing at Peter, whose face turned red.

"Seven dollars, dude?" asked Max. "You can't even buy her beer mugs for that." Max remembered last year's Christmas shopping.

"I know," was the sharp comeback. "That's why I asked you guys."

Felder let the ball spin to a halt. He was deep in thought, pondering the possibilities of gifts under seven dollars. "You could get her a tape," he offered. Felder was bright and sincere and wanted to help Peter.

"Tsk, what tape costs seven dollars?" snapped Peter. He scrunched up his nose at the idea, appalled by its suggestion.

Felder looked sideways at Peter then quietly said, "You're right, man. What the hell was I thinking." He returned to spinning the football and thinking about the upcoming school year.

"Don't you have any old tapes you could give her?" asked Danny sarcastically.

Peter perked up at this idea and actually gave it a little thought.

"You're not actually considering that?" asked Max. He rolled his eyes when Peter looked at him.

"Well I fuckin' gotta do somethin'," yelled Peter.

"Hey, don't get mad at us! You're the dipshit who had the past month to buy her something," said Danny. His voice was scolding, intense. His eyes dared Peter to up the ante.

Peter looked at the ground. "There's got to be something for seven dollars. If you guys can't think of anything then I don't think I'm going."

"Whuuut?" asked Danny. "Are you nuts? How are you going to explain that one to her?"

"I dunno," mumbled Peter. "I can't go to the party empty-handed, though."

"Tell her you had a nervous breakdown trying to think of something to buy her and you'll be staying at the hospital overnight for observation," offered Max. He chuckled, as did Danny. Felder was concentrating on the spinning football.

Peter forced a laugh, out of courtesy, and nodded. He knew Max was only kidding. There was something that intrigued him about the suggestion, however. His mind began to whir.

"Yeah, tell her you couldn't come to the party on doctor's orders. He didn't think the stress of fifteen year old girls' tits and tight asses would be good on you." Danny laughed at his armchair diagnosis. Max also laughed.

"Und you vill see zat too much of zee pussy could rrruin zee treement," blustered Max in a thick accent. He walked around gesturing into the air, as if he was giving a lecture. He went on and on about female genitalia and having one's tongue sucked and how stressful it was, considering the pain this young boy was in. Danny kept laughing. Felder finally joined in.

Peter chuckled slightly but felt that this was somehow at his expense. He listened to Max for a minute or so and then said, "You know that might work." The boys stopped and looked at Peter.

"You're joking, right?" asked Max.

"No, I could tell her that I'm not feeling well and really need to stay home."

"Oh. Right. Lie to her. That is actually the perfect way to keep a relationship going strong." Felder's facetious comment was veiled in a calming, mellow voice. He pursed his lips and nodded.

Peter glared at him, trying to figure out if he was serious or not.

"Oh definitely," added Danny. He shook his head and laughed. "How are you going to get sick in August?" he asked.

Peter thought for a minute. "Heat stroke!" he said triumphantly.

"Yeah, right!" said Max. "It's like 75 degrees out here. She'll never believe that."

Peter thought again. "Allergies," he said as he slapped the top of the mailbox on which he was leaning.

"What are you allergic to?" asked Danny.

"Pollination or something," replied Peter, waving his hand, his voice trailing off.

Felder laughed to himself. He looked knowingly at Max. "Oh yeah, I heard pollination was really bad this year. She'll go for that," he said and winked at Peter.

Max and Danny covered their mouths while they chuckled. Peter tried to figure out the reason for their sudden laughing. He looked at all three of them in turn.

"Yeah, you don't want to mess with pollination," nodded Danny. "You might get some flower pregnant or something." All three boys privy to the faux pas cracked up.

"What's so fucking funny?" Peter was irritated at not knowing what was so funny.

"It's pollen," said Felder. "Pollination is when bees help flowers reproduce."

"Wha—screw it. Dumb idea," barked Peter, anxious to stop the boys chortling.

The four of them sat in silence and pondered in and out on Peter's dilemma. Sometimes their thoughts would wander away from the quest for the seven dollar gift. Max thought back to when he dated Julie and how sweet that first kiss had been. Felder wondered what kind of boyfriend doesn't buy his girlfriend a gift on her birthday. Danny thought about which guys would be there and if any of them could sneak alcohol in past Julie's parents. Peter's mind tried to focus on a solution but it would sprint towards that ever-present safety blanket—anger. He would dwell on frustration and anger and impatience whenever a task with no ready solution presented itself. These consumed his brain like a dense fog. He couldn't see clearly under these circumstances. He would have to find a solution, but none jumped into his head. This only angered him more. His frustration increased exponentially.

"Fuck it," Peter finally said.

"What?" asked Danny. "Did you think of something?"

Evening was upon them. The working fathers were beginning to return home to their suburban split-level homes. The mothers had started preparing their roasts and meatloafs and fried pork chops. The afternoon talk shows were ending and the opening music to the news filled the small, black and white televisions in neatly decorated kitchens everywhere. Small dogs named Fluffy were raising their heads at the sound of cars pulling into garages. High school kids talked on the phone in low voices, figuring out where the parties were. Boys mutated from the sports-driven competitors to the sex-driven predators. Girls stood at their open closets, hands on hips, weight on one leg, wondering when they could go shopping for "new school clothes." All was right with the world. Except that Peter still had no gift.

Peter shook his head. "I think we may have to try the breakdown idea. It's all that's left," he said half-heartedly. He looked at his three friends and sighed.

Danny and Max began to smile but stopped once they realized Peter was serious. "What? That was a joke," said Max.

"I know, but I think we could make it so ridiculous that she might think it was funny," explained Peter. This began to sound reasonable to him.

"And?" asked Danny. The boys moved out of the way of the mini-van approaching from the far end of the street.

"And if she thinks it's funny she'll forgive me." Peter shrugged, as if this was the only logical way to go about this. He was becoming more and more convinced that this idea might work. "Yeah, this could work."

"Yeah, in Bizarro world," said Max. Felder chuckled.

"No shit," added Danny. "This ain't Neverland, moron."

Peter bristled but kept his cool. "I think it will work. The only thing is that I need you guys to help."

"Hi, Retardo, this is a stupid idea."

"Well it won't be so stupid if we do it right!" yelled Peter.

Felder looked at Peter in amazement. He wondered why he got so angry so quickly.

"Chill out," warned Danny.

Peter complied and took a deep breath. He knew better than to fly off the handle at Danny. He actually feared a physical confrontation with him.

"What's this idea, anyway?" asked Max. He looked at Peter sideways, ready to not go along with him.

"All right, let's see," began Peter nervously. He then began unraveling his plan to convey to Julie the sudden tragedy of his nervous breakdown. He explained how the guys would each play a role and how they would do all of the talking. There were two phones in the basement so two people could listen at once. They were to play the roles of concerned friends who had been with Peter the whole day, trying to ease his scattered sense of self. Peter was in no condition to speak, so his obligation to the project was nothing. He explained that if it didn't work Julie would probably be more upset with Max and Danny (the nominees for the task) than with him. Max was a little uneasy at this killing-the-messenger ideal. Danny didn't care and his attitude eventually convinced Max. Peter's excitement and nervousness grew as he wove the plan from mid-air, on the spot, over the next five minutes.

"What time is it?" asked Max.

"Probably about five," said Felder. He had decided not to partake in this charade and wanted to watch Sportscenter instead, hoping that the Cubs had come back and won.

"Well, what do you guys think?" asked Peter. "Should we try it out?" His eyes were alive and dancing. The corners of his mouth tugged upward, feeling around for the beginnings of a grin. Peter stood up and began walking toward the house. Max and Danny shook their heads, knowing that the outcome was going to be disastrous, but aware that they weren't the real culprits. Felder meandered behind them, spreading his hands over the laces of the football, thinking about gunning touchdown passes to one of his beloved Steelers.

"Hi boys," came the cheery greeting from Mrs. Darling as the foursome entered the home. She came out of the kitchen to the top step of the landing and stopped. "How are we doing?" she asked, as if speaking to one of her elementary students. The monotone response was that the boys were fine.

"Danny, how's your mother?" she asked.

"Good," said Danny.

"And yours, Max?"

"Just great," answered Max, staring down at the cream tiling on the landing. Peter was already downstairs.

"Your mom okay?" she asked Felder, out of courtesy. She had never met his mother.

Felder smiled broadly, knowing that Mrs. Darling was just being polite. He nodded. "Her job working third shift at the quarry is keeping her real happy, Mrs. Darling."

"C'mon, Mom, we got stuff to do!" yelled Peter from downstairs.

"I'm just saying hello, Brat," she replied with a slightly piercing voice. She rolled her eyes and looked one last time at the three boys on the landing and returned to the waiting cutting board.

Danny, Max, and Felder tramped downstairs to Peter's room. As Peter dialed the number Felder went out to the rec room and turned on the television. Max was to talk first and set up the whole thing. Danny would be on the phone in the rec room and would affirm his friend's story, then he would tell his version. Surely Julie could appreciate a story corroborated by two of her peers. Peter hoped.

"Hello?" It was Julie. Her slightly nasal voice sounded tinnier through the phone.

"Uh, hi, Julie?" Max had remembered that voice from seventh grade when they dated. He had enjoyed talking to her for hours about nothing of any consequence. He momentarily forgot what his mission was.

"Yes."

"Uh, I'm calling to give you some bad news," said Max shakily. Peter looked at him hopefully. He stood right in front of Peter, leaning slightly forward, as if he wanted to hear Julie for himself.

"Who is this?" asked Julie, bewildered. "Is this Pete?" She thought she was on to something.

"No, but, but, uh..." Max panicked. He didn't want to give his name and then dump this whole bullshit story onto the girl upon which he still had a crush. He didn't want to be the messenger who was killed. He tried to think of an alternative. His mind raced. He was certain that she would hate him if he told her it was him.

"Pete?" Julie asked again, more unsure than the last time.

"Well, not exactly, this is...this is..." Peter looked at Max with concern. He thought his friend would blow the whole scheme to pieces before it even got off the ground. He had wanted Max and Danny because they would remain the most composed under pressure, in case Julie became hostile. This wavering from Max was a surprise. Then it happened. Max clicked.

"This is Peter's doctor," said Max, slightly deepening his voice and trying to sound official. "Yes, this is Doctor," Max glanced around the room quickly for a false name, "Intendo from the psych. ward at Mercy Hospital."

Peter was utterly perplexed. He knit his brow and his lower lip jutted forward. His eyelids fluttered in awe. "What?" he mouthed to his accomplice.

"Yes, I'm one of the doctors in charge of Peter's case," affirmed Max into the phone.

There was a pause and Max feared she would hang up. "What did you say your name was?" asked Julie.

"Dr. Intendo," blustered Max. Peter's face showed disbelief.

"Like 'Nintendo'?" asked Julie, chuckling slightly.

"Nintendo? What the deuce are you talking about?" asked Max, full on into his new persona.

"Okay. Who is this really?" asked Julie. She was curious and knew it must be somebody from school messing with her.

"I'm Peter's doctor," answered Max, with indignation.

"Peter's doctor?" asked Julie. "You're Peter's doctor?"

"Yes, quite right."

"At the psych. ward, did you say?" Julie's voice peaked at the end of her statement.

"Mmhm. We have Peter under observation. He's had a mental breakdown," offered Max very matter-of-factly.

"What?" asked Julie shortly.

"He's had a mental breakdown."

"I'll say," muttered Julie.

"It's nothing to be terribly concerned about; he'll be right as rain in a couple of days. The only reason we contacted you was because he kept repeating your name, claiming that he couldn't stay for treatment. Kept mumbling about some damnable party for your birthday or somesuch." Max drew upon his deepest yearnings to be in the performing arts.

After staring blankly at Max, Peter gave a thumbs-up signal when he heard the bit about repeating Julie's name. He felt this would ingratiate him to his somewhat jilted lover.

"Uh...what is going on?" chuckled Julie in a bewildered tone. "This is very weird."

Max was only a little nervous. His plan was to keep yammering on about Peter and then have Julie agree to it and hang up, or, at the very least, Danny would intervene and relieve Max' obligation. He gave no real thought to Danny's reaction to this new direction for the production. Peter was now urging Max to continue.

"So you see, Julie, it would be extremely dangerous and downright suicidal if Peter were to venture off to some social affair at a time like this. You understand, don't you? It is in the interest of the patient which I give my advice." Max waited.

Julie laughed heartily. She apparently wasn't buying any of the story.

Max was momentarily stunned. He looked at Peter and shook his head, a worried look on his face.

Peter wanted to know what was happening. He asked the question of his good friend Max with a desperate expression. Peter did not want to have to get on the phone and talk to Julie. He would do that tomorrow. Right now he wanted the problem to just go away. He had found someone else to deal with his shortcomings and that was how he preferred it.

"How dare, uh, that you laugh in the face of medicine. I'll not listen to anymore of this contemptible rubbish. Laughing at me...sheer rubbish." Max was holding out hope on keeping up the ruse, though he knew it was a sinking ship. Then Danny spoke up.

"Jes, hello, is dees Yulie?"

The laughing died down. There was a pause as Julie attempted to figure out why Max had changed his accent. Max tried to figure out why Danny was speaking in a Latino dialect—a muddled one at that.

"Yulie? Can jou hear me? Jou should not be hlaughing to Senor Doctor Eentendo. He is bery knowing of de patient Peter Darling."

A brief silence was pierced by tear-inducing female laughter. It sounded almost as if Julie was in pain. Her laughing was intense, uncontrollable.

Peter could hear what Danny had said in the other room. He went to see what the hell was going on. Danny wasn't smiling. His accent was intended to be serious. He shrugged at Peter and mouthed the words "what the fuck did you want me to do?" at him. Peter glanced at Felder sitting on the floor. The docile young man seemed to be paying no attention to the unraveling of Peter's love life.

"My dear, you should control yourself, lest we have to admit you into the psych. ward as well," offered Max. "I should say that wouldn't be a bloody bad idea on the whole anyways," he muttered.

"Jou are right, Senor Eentendo. Dees girls es loco. Sometimes I yam having trouble understanding why my client is needing to date them."

Peter furrowed his brow. He didn't understand what Danny meant by the word "client." He was incredibly anxious to see how this would turn out.

"Quite right, old chap. I daresay all women should stay away from young Master Peter until he is fully recovered. But I do know how charmed he is with this hysterical creature on the other end of the phone and I wouldn't feel right depriving him of the company of such an obviously easily entertained companion."

Julie's laughing died down a little. She had now ascertained that there were two different people talking to her and was curious as to the new performer's name and relationship to her boyfriend.

"Whu, whu..." she tried to start a question, but her laughing stifled it. "What... is...your...name?" she finally managed through her chortles and guffaws.

"Are jou speaking to me?" asked Danny.

"Jes, I mean, yes," said Julie.

"I yam Pancho Cisco, Peter's...manayjer and ayjent," Danny announced. He wasn't watching Peter's reaction, though it would have been entertaining to say the least.

Peter's jaw dropped. He was more astounded than he had been when Max had announced he was a doctor in his stuffy pseudo-British accent. Now Danny had disclosed that he was a fifteen-year old's agent in a horrible Latino accent. This was becoming a disaster, but one off which Peter could not take his eyes. He was spellbound by his friends' refusal to give up the charade and Julie's apparent willingness to listen to it. He knew the original idea was blown to pieces. Perhaps Julie might find the humor in it, however, and forgive him for not coming to the party. He sat down and stared at Danny with baited breath.

Max was giggling in the other room, his hand over the receiver. He had not expected this surprise from his comrade and found the accent increasingly more ridiculous with each word uttered by Danny. He hoped he could keep it together long enough to disguise his voice and leave the conversation unscathed.

"His what?" asked Julie.

"Hees ayjent," Danny proudly announced. "Jou know, I handle hees bookings and calander and other tings of dat nature, jes?"

"His bookings? All right, what the hell is going on?" Julie's tone was moving away from entertained and toward annoyed.

"Jou have quite a mature tongue for such an elegant lady. But Peter has warned me not to be surprised by jour eentense passion for eberyting jou do. I soospect de language ees no different, si?"

There was no immediate response. Peter's face showed his perplexed thoughts. Felder was still oblivious. The Cubs had lost, but one of their outfielders had been badly injured and Felder was eager to find out how long he would be on the disabled list.

"Tell me who this is," demanded Julie.

Max heard the slight irritation in her voice and quelled his giggling. Danny's expression never changed. He was serious and all-business. He wasn't going to give up that easily.

"I told jou, I yam Pancho Cisco, Peter's..." but Julie cut him off.

"Bullshit. You're one of his buddies."

"But of course I yam his boody. He's a nice fellow, thees Peter."

"Seriously, you can stop with the accent. And that goes for you too Dr. Sega or whatever your name was."

Max recovered. "How rude," he blustered. "I've never been so bloody insulted..."

"Enough!" said Julie in a harsh tone. "It was funny at first, but don't run it into the ground."

Neither of the players knew how to react. They knew they had two options: hang up (in which case Julie would surely call Peter, forcing him to come clean) or stop the horrible ruse and hope their humorous attempt would allow Julie to forgive Peter's "illness" and subsequent absence at her party. Both alternatives had several shortcomings, but what could they do?

"Sorry, just having a little fun," said Max, in his normal voice. He was genuinely sorry for duping her. He didn't really like deceiving people.

"Yeah, you know, just messin' around," added Danny. His mind was racing on about how to extract Peter from this predicament.

Peter sat nervously on the hassock in front of Danny. He was frightened and a little upset, but he knew he did not want to handle the situation himself. Danny and Max had agreed to the original task, therefore it was their responsibility to keep Peter from getting into trouble. That was how he saw it, anyway. Peter had rarely had to handle his own dilemmas. Someone invariably came to his rescue, or he coerced a friend or family member into handling it for him. Peter saw nothing wrong in this shirking of responsibility. He felt he was clever.

"I thought that was you, Max. When you started in with the accent I knew it was you. Who else is there? Hello?"

"It's Danny." His eyes focused on Peter.

"Hey Danny. That was a pretty mean Mexican impression there," complimented Julie. She was beginning to lighten up to her usual self—a pleasant, budding, teenage girl with her feet firmly on the ground.

"Well, we just thought we'd put you in a good mood, you know, for your party," said Danny.

Julie paused. She couldn't tell if this comment was a little backhanded, knowing that she had neglected to invite either Danny or Max to her party. "Oh, yeah, it's no big deal, though, just a few people," Julie sputtered quickly.

Danny sensed this uneasiness. "Really? Who's going to be there?" asked Danny. His voice was pleasant, nonchalant. Max was probably more curious about the guest list than Danny.

"Oh, just a few people." Julie did not want to have to invite Danny or Max. She liked them, but felt that they might feel out of place. They were both single and none of the girls invited to the party were interested in them at the time.

"Who?" Danny persisted.

"Well, uh, Tom and his girlfriend, and Mitch and his girlfriend, you know, Tara. Of course, my little honey Peter will be there." Julie tried to make the party sound as if it was couples-oriented.

"Yeah, about 'your little honey', that's why Max and I called," Danny began.

"Yeah, we did actually have something to tell you about Peter," added Max.

"I suppose he's now a brain donor or something. Spare me the phony accents," guessed Julie.

"No, he is a little under the weather, though," claimed Danny. He was making this up as he went along. He was hoping Julie would accept this news and hang up.

Peter's eyes widened as he heard Danny's words. He knew that the success of this little endeavor now depended on Julie's reaction to Danny's latest statement.

"Really?" asked Julie.

"Yeah, he wanted us to call because he couldn't bear to hear the sadness in your voice when he told you. He's really not feeling well, though." Max thought this might actually work. They hadn't thought of playing up the sincerity angle of things. This could make Peter look like a thoughtful, kind-hearted, naïve boyfriend—if she believed it.

"Peter said that?"

"Yeah, you know he really is a nice guy," said Max.

"Yeah, he's funny and cool," affirmed Danny.

Peter clasped his hands in mock prayer. He couldn't tell how the conversation was going, but he figured a little help from above couldn't hurt. He closed his eyes and turned his face upward toward the paneled ceiling of his basement.

"Peter! Come take out the trash!" yelled Mrs. Darling from the kitchen.

Peter's eyes shot open and looked at Danny. Felder looked over his shoulder at his startled friend. Max had barely heard Peter's mother and did not realize what was going on. Peter had hoped, though, that the boys could finish the conversation without letting Julie know that they were indeed at his home. She might want to talk to him if she knew.

"Shit," Peter whispered.

"Was that Peter's mom?" Julie asked Danny.

Danny wasn't sure how he should handle this one. He had no idea how to explain away Mrs. Darling to Julie. He took a deep breath.

"Who?" asked Max. "Peter's mom? Is she over at your place?"

"Wha...no. She's not here. It sounded like she's there...at Peter's," said Julie.

"At Peter's?" asked Max. "We're not..."

"At Peter's for just any reason, we're here looking after him. He's very fragile right now and needs lots of support," Danny finished.

"Fragile? If he's there then why didn't he just call me?"

"He's bedridden," Max blurted.

"Peter! Get up here and take out the trash. And put the lawnmower away, too," came Mrs. Darling's voice from the top of the stairs.

"He's bedridden but his mother wants him to do chores? Right," said Julie incredulously.

"She's very demanding," said Danny. He looked at Peter and shrugged. This ship was spinning out of control.

Peter tore himself away from the drama and tramped upstairs. Everyone could hear the door slam as he angrily took out the garbage and noisily put the lawnmower into the garage.

"How that boy survives I'll never know," added Danny. "So, anyway, Peter is going to be doing his best to get better."

Julie did not readily reply. She was trying to figure out what was going on. "Peter's not coming to the party, then?" she asked pensively.

"I'm afraid not," said Max solemnly. "His health won't allow it."

"Yeah, right. I want to talk to him."

"I don't think that's a good idea," said Danny. He watched Peter come back downstairs.

"Well, I don't give a rat's ass what you think," said Julie sweetly. "Put him on the phone."

"You don't want to put him through the misery of hearing your little heart break, do you?" asked Max.

Peter sat down. Danny put his hand over the phone and whispered to him, "She wants to talk to you." At this, Felder turned around to watch the performance. Peter shook his head vehemently. He felt no obligation to talk to his girlfriend about why he wouldn't be at her party.

"This is your show, you do the talking," he whispered to Danny.

Danny glared at Peter and breathed deeply through his nose. Peter went to see how Max was faring.

"Now really, you should wait until he's better. The sadness in your voice might upset him."

Julie sighed. "Max, knock it off and just put him on the phone."

"I can't. He's asleep," stuttered Max.

"He can't be asleep, he just took out the garbage. Peter, are you listening?"

"He's not listening, it's just me and Danny. Peter's lying down now. The extra labor has depleted his already weakened energy reserves. He needs rest. And he's very sorry."

"I'm sure he's sorry. In fact, I know he's sorry, he's sad and sorry. Put him on the phone!" yelled Julie.

Max paused and looked at Peter. He held the phone out to him. Peter looked at it as if it were a deformed appendage. He shook his head disgustedly as he shoved the phone back at Max.

"I can't," said Max softly into the receiver.

"Why? This is so stupid. Just let me talk to him."

"I'm sorry..."

"What is wrong? I mean, why won't he talk to me? What did I do?" Julie began to sound frightened.

Max did not like to see Julie agonize. He especially did not like the thought of her agonizing over another guy. She didn't seem too broken up by the end of their seventh grade romance, so why should she worry so much about Peter's inability to perform boyfriend duties?

"What was that? Peter, is that you? What's going on?" asked Julie frantically.

Danny had hung up the phone. He came into the room where Max and Peter were, Felder followed.

"That was Danny hanging up the phone," said Max.

"Oh. Please let me talk to Peter," she begged Max.

"He really is not well. You can call him tomorrow, though," said Max somberly.

"What did I do? Why are you...is he doing this?" Julie was dumbfounded and obviously distraught.

Max wanted to tell her, but Peter's presence halted that notion. "He just needs to get better," he finally said.

Peter began to smile as he looked at Max' weary face. He felt a sense of relief that his good friend was shouldering the guilt and remorse of this heinous affair. Peter didn't see the need to feel bad if it could be avoided. Max was such a good friend for bearing the burden, too. He shouldn't forget how nice it was to have friends like Max around. He glanced at Danny and Felder and gave the thumbs up.

"I know it's hard to understand, but he just needs to gather himself," Max continued.

"But this is so sudden, so weird."

"I'm sorry. I don't like being the bearer of bad news."

Peter was grinning widely now and went over to his two friends who were standing in his bedroom doorway. "This worked out perfectly," he whispered triumphantly.

Neither Danny nor Felder smiled as they looked at Peter in disbelief. They both turned around and went back into the other room to watch television.

"You mean you don't like being an asshole," corrected Julie. This stunned Max.

"What?"

"An asshole, 'cuz that's what you and Danny and that piece of shit Peter are—assholes. Thanks a lot for ruining my party!" Julie slammed down the phone.

Max shook his head and looked down at his wrinkled gray shorts. He contemplated what had just transpired then hung up the phone.

"She okay?" asked Peter in a giddy tone.

"She says you're an asshole," said Max slowly. "She said we're all assholes for ruining her party."

"Was she crying?" asked Peter. It was as if he was asking his parents what his surprise birthday present was. He was mildly curious, but the joy in his voice was unmistakable.

Max looked up. "No, she wasn't crying."

"Awesome. Is she going to call me tomorrow?"

Max stared for a long time at Peter, his mouth open in wonder. "What do you think?" he finally managed to ask.

Peter shrugged. "We'll see, huh, man?" He cheerily left the room and joined Danny and Felder in the rec. room. When Max finally joined them Peter was ruminating on how he couldn't wait for the upcoming school year. This would be their sophomore year and there would be students from three junior highs pouring into one big high school.

"It's gonna be fuckin' awesome!" said Peter excitedly.

CHAPTER 2

Peter watched the ancient metal hand wind its way around the graying-white face of the industrial wall clock in seventh period. He was desperately awaiting the final click of the "big hand" to the 6. That meant 2:30--the end of the long hot day and the beginning of another Friday night. These were cherished times, especially now that Peter had entered high school. He played football and still had practice and a game, but they were merely speed-bumps in his ultimate weekend quest— drinking and partying. This had become even more of a ritual now that he had found a whole new pool of sociable teenagers with which to relate. Before he had only his junior high comrades, but now three junior highs had been combined into the school with the second largest enrollment in the state. It was mildly diverse, yet homogenized and safe. A young man like Peter could experience many new and exciting relationships, if he wanted, or he could maintain his current course. The choice was his.

Peter was not only excited to get out of school, but he was excited to partake in his new privilege—driving. Young Peter Darling had just taken his sixteenth spin around the sun and was ready to hit the pavement for a little while before he had to be back in the lockerroom. His parents had sprung for summer driver's ed. classes so that their son could take the old family car to the brink of destruction, chauffering his peers around. They had allowed him to use the car as long as he didn't damage it and kept it clean. He was to also keep it full of gas (from the money which they supplied), but this was quickly the exception and not the rule. He found that gas money spent just as easily on alcohol as on petroleum. This, added to his allowance/lunch money, made for a nice little "paycheck" each week. He could then pay the exorbitant amounts for beer and Mad Dog that the older guys with fake IDs charged for purchasing the contraband. Driving had opened up a whole new avenue of potential responsibility...which Peter shirked at every turn.

As the instructor droned on incessantly about the descriptive paragraph and the importance of being succinct, Peter only heard the clock ticking. He had drowned out his teacher's even-toned delivery and was certainly in no mood to hear about a thesis. His books had been closed for the last five minutes (every period ended five minutes before the bell rang) and his concentration centered on trying to move the clock faster by some sort of Uri Geller-ian mind trick. It wasn't working.

"...and, of course, Mr. Darling will be able to relay all of this pertinent information on Monday next, when a quiz is apparently in order." This subtle hint from the teacher was lost on the young man.

"That's right," said Mr. Lindsey, "due to Mr. Darling's lack of attentiveness, we'll be having a 100-point quiz over the importance of sensory details."

Still no reaction from Peter.

"Mr. Darling. Mr. Darling!" The teacher knocked on his desk.

Peter finally broke his attention away from the clock and looked unknowingly at his English instructor. "What?" He looked around at his classmates, all of whom were staring at him.

"You'll be ready for the quiz, then?" asked Mr. Lindsey.

"Quiz, what quiz?" asked Peter.

Just then the bell rang. "Never mind," said the teacher, rolling his eyes at Peter's ignorance. "No quiz. Go home."

Peter had not heard the last two words as he bolted out the door. He nodded casually at one or two of his fellow football players in the hallway on the way to his locker. He had to meet Weiland and Donny in the commons area. They were going to head to the local convenience store and load up on sugar and soda before their game. As Peter hurriedly went through his books he decided upon which classes had homework which absolutely had to be done by Monday and which ones afforded the option of lying to the teacher or doing it Monday morning before first period. He left all of his books in his locker. He glanced up at the clock in the hallway, oblivious to the maddening throng of people bustling through the hallway, banging lockers and shouting out plans for the evening. Peter felt the urgency to be in the commons before Weiland and Donny.

As Peter raced around the corner, a mere three minutes after leaving 7th period, he was struck with the one fear which most new high school students face during the school day—the appearance of "mother" outside of her natural element. Peter had never felt comfortable when his mother attempted to converse with his friends or even ask about them. It was his opinion that his mother knew nothing about him, despite her living in the same house and her raising him over the past sixteen years. Under this delusion, Peter believed that his mother would never have occasion to come to his school, especially unannounced. Mrs. Darling had somehow broken a rule known only to Peter and every other adolescent boy but somehow never made obvious to her: Moms don't come to school to see their sons.

Mrs. Darling stood smiling at the passersby. She nodded sweetly, intermittently. She said "hello dear" to the ones whom she recognized from

Little League or whose parents she had in quilt-making class. She stood near the benches and seemed to be waiting for Peter, knowing that he would be in the commons area. She waved as she saw Peter come around the corner of the main office. The secretaries watched from behind huge panes of glass, one of them pointing and smiling. She had seen Peter's expression change abruptly from anticipation to shock.

Peter slowed his pace and shifted his duffel bag from one shoulder to the next. He reluctantly approached his mother, trying to think of the most expedient way to get her out of there before anyone saw him with her. His mind was racing, but rage kept creeping in at the edges. It overran the few remaining outposts of calm, rational thought which held on. He counted the thirty, egg-shell white floor tiles that separated him and his maternal influence, his head down. By the time he got to her he had succumbed to anger and frustration. His jaw clenched and his brow furrowed. He breathed heavily through his nose. Now the object of his glare was not privy to her son's state of mind.

"What are you doing here?" Peter whispered harshly. His gaze shot quickly around the commons, looking for any upperclassmen. Two blond senior girls in short-skirts pointed over their pink binders at Peter and his mother. They giggled to themselves.

Accustomed to such a warm welcome, Mrs. Darling only grinned and tilted her head slightly. "Well, you're father dropped me off," she cooed.

"What?" Peter acted as if he were speaking to a secret agent.

"You're father dropped me off."

"Mom!" Peter uttered harshly through his gritted teeth. He looked around again and noticed Donny and Weiland approaching. He took a deep breath as he finally caught his mother's gaze. "What do you want?" he asked deliberately.

"Well, you're father dropped me off..."

"You said that already, get to the point!" Peter interrupted. His voice raised.

Mrs. Darling shot a finger in Peter's face. "Don't take that tone with me, young man!" she admonished. Several students standing nearby whirled to watch the drama and several heads swiveled as they heard the raised, middle-aged voice. Peter wished he did not have his football jersey on. Now everyone who went to the sophomore game would know it was him that got bawled out by his mother.

"Well, what do you want?" asked Peter, calmer this time. He saw Donny nudge Weiland as they walked closer. Both of them began to laugh.

"I need the car."

"What? Why?" asked the surprised and irritated Peter.

"I have some errands to run and your father is going out of town. You have a game anyway, don't you?" Mrs. Darling did not seem to be fazed by the growing number of people in the commons area. It was as if she was having a conversation with her son in her own living-room.

Peter had no idea what to say. His mother had infiltrated his domain and was now threatening to take away his one means of freedom. "You can't," he blurted.

This surprised Mrs. Darling. She started and gave Peter a puzzled look.

"I can, Mister, and I will. Give me the keys." She stuck out an open-palmed hand.

"But I was supposed to go to the store with Donny and Weiland before the game."

"Why?"

"We need to get some energy for the game." Peter's tone was short and irritable. He did not want to have this conversation, he did not want to talk to his mother, and he did not want to relinquish the keys to the car. In the back of his mind, he knew she would eventually win, and although handing her the keys might have hastied her exit Peter chose to quibble. "Why can't you just wait here while I go to QuickStop?" he asked.

"The QuickStop across the street?" asked Mrs. Darling. Donny and Weiland were now behind her.

"No, the one on the east side," was the sarcastic reply.

Mrs. Darling sighed, tired of the boy's attitude. Peter sighed right back, tired of dealing with his mother. "Hello Mrs. Darling," said Donny and Weiland in unison. They each shot a sly grin at Peter.

"Ohhh, hello boys! How are you?" This boisterous greeting heaped more attention upon the quartet. Many of the varsity football players had filtered into the area, as well as some of the sophomores. Some looked over and could relate, others laughed, still others couldn't care less.

"You both look well," continued Mrs. Darling.

"Mom," whined Peter.

"Well, I'll just take you boys over to QuickStop right now then. Give me the keys," she demanded.

Peter, who had been dangling the key ring from one finger, slapped them into his mother's waiting hand. It was more forceful than he had intended, but he almost hoped it had hurt. At least that way his mom would understand his displeasure.

She led the way through the hallway, the three boys lagging behind. Donny and Weiland didn't mind how they arrived at QuickStop. They liked to watch Peter squirm, though. Peter was fuming and trying like mad to avoid his mother's repeated attempts to talk to him. It seemed to him that her inquiries about homework, his lunch, and the décor of the trophy showcase were inane and only meant to enrage him further. Mrs. Darling tramped ahead, though.

As each set of eyes noticed the smallish, white-haired lady and the three, jersey-clad boys behind her they drew their own conjectures. Peter knew he'd have to explain to each and every person whom he saw at the party that night who the old lady was and why he was walking with her. To those who knew that Mrs.

Darling was his mother he would have to tell them how she had come to school and utterly embarrassed him and how stupid she was. He shook his head and pouted, mumbling under his breath as the foursome exited the huge side doors of Kallow High School and squinted into the sun.

The next few months moved along quickly. Peter dreaded school with each minute, but he began to develop into one of the more popular sophomores. He had made friends with most of the juniors and seniors through his constant attendance at parties and other gatherings. Peter always seemed to know what was going on and where. He began to relish this limelight. People were always calling him or stopping him in the hallways on Fridays to see what was happening. Usually he would withhold information, depending upon the person. If they were one of the cool people like Weiland or Donny or Tom he would gladly give up the night's itinerary. He looked up to these young men—and why not? They were handsome, athletic, humorous. They were what Peter wanted to be. The beautiful people in high school seem non-plussed by their celebrity. To them it is a way of life, nothing more nor less. To people like Peter, who was actually very well-entrenched in this circle, this fame was the mountaintop in high school. This popularity was assuredly the road to out, the cure for what ails, the path to paradise. But if someone not on Peter's list of idols inquired about a party or social occasion Peter might direct the query to another student, or give him vague information, or flat out lie completely about his knowledge on the matter. Peter was becoming quite a spin doctor in his young age.

Peter enjoyed Kallow High School. The basketball team was mildly successful. Peter had tried out but eventually decided against staying with the team as the 19th man. This gave him more time to party before games anyway. Although most of his close friends played basketball or wrestled in the winter, Peter was not bored. He developed new relationships and re-visited old ones. Kallow High had 1600 students enrolled in the three grades it serviced. Want of human contact was a non-issue if someone was willing enough. Peter was willing. He went to the basketball games on Friday nights with a different group of people each time, it seemed. His sophomore classmates would finish their game then join him in the stands for the varsity game. Peter's buzz had not started to wear off by this time, so he was usually quite entertaining. Somehow the school officials did not notice the intoxicated minors at basketball games unless they threw up on the concession stand or started a fight in the bathroom with one of the opposing team's fans. From the varsity game, people would head off to various parts and resume the party. This was pretty much how winter evenings passed on Friday and some Saturday nights. Peter loved it.

As the year wore on, Peter garnered the attention of teachers as somewhat of a class clown and of fellow students as the same. He had avoided any traffic violations and so his parents trusted him with the car each weekend. He had

argued for a 12:30 a.m. curfew and usually stretched that to 12:45 with an
elaborate excuse to placate his parents. On other nights he would spend the night
at one of his friends' houses. He tried to find the friend whose parents had the
most liberal curfew.

On one cool March evening Peter found himself behind the wheel of his
mother's huge, gray Oldsmobile. He had been drinking for several hours and
knew that he was a better driver, more relaxed, with a few drinks in him, so he had
offered his friends a ride home. As a ritual, most of the "cool" students of Kallow
High stopped at the major fast food restaurant on their side of town (open 24
hours) Some students did this because they were hungry; some students stopped
to meet their peers; some wanted to fight; some were dropped off and looking
for a ride home. In any case, the place was busy from 11 p.m. to 2 a.m. with high
school students in a constant ebb and flow. Peter and his friends decided to stop
at this establishment for food and to see if any girls were there. The last part of
this expedition was illogical, as the sophomore boys were rarely able to carry out
any plans once they found members of the opposite sex. They hadn't earned
late enough curfews or the guts to stay out until they wanted and deal with their
parents in the morning. The girls were the same, as far as that goes.

"I wonder who's with Sara and Michelle," wondered Marty. He was trying
to peek around Mitch, who was on his lap. Despite the Oldsmobile's size, seven
sophomore boys did not fit comfortably in it.

"Why?" asked Danny.

Marty paused. "I dunno."

"Is that Tony?" asked Mitch. Tony was one year ahead of them in school. He
came from a notoriously tough family. He was no exception. Peter had known
him since Pony League baseball and felt that he was on good enough terms with
Tony to call him a friend.

"Where?" asked Peter. As he turned to look he jerked the wheel, as if it were
attached to his craning neck. The car swerved momentarily but sharply.

"What the fuck?" asked Weiland.

"Hello, Drunk," said Tom. "Nice to meet you, I'm Sober and am usually a
better driver than you." Tom was not sober, but his sarcastic tongue was as quick
as any other time.

Peter laughed nervously and peered into his rearview mirror to check for any
cars he might have thrown off. He also looked for any police. Apparently the one
uniformed officer inside the restaurant had not seen Peter's move.

"Park the car, dumb-ass," said Donny. He was seated behind Peter and, being
large, couldn't wait to get out.

"What do think I'm doing, fuck-wad?" retorted Peter

Donny punched the back of Peter's headrest, causing the driver's head to
snap forward. A momentary sense of rage welled up, but Peter knew better than
to have words with Donny. He swung the car into a spot. All seven boys piled out.

They waved to a few people they knew hanging around their cars. They stopped to talk with a few of them and gradually made their way to the entrance.

"I gotta piss," said Mitch.

The rest of the boys ambled inside and grabbed a booth. There were no waitresses, but the boys would get their food eventually. They would take turns heading up to the counter to order. The smell of alcohol on them might overpower the on-duty policeman if they ordered en masse. Staggering their trips to the counter alleviated this problem. Peter had come up with this pearl of wisdom.

"There's Tara and Julie," said Danny. Peter turned to look at the two girls. They were splitting some fries. They waved and smiled. Peter nodded awkwardly and gave a quick half-wave. He still felt odd around Julie. She had obviously moved on and seemed to forget about Peter. She had a serious boyfriend.

"Damn Julie's hot," remarked Marty.

"No shit," said Weiland. "Didn't you date her, Pete?"

Danny and Donny got up from the outside of the booth and went to the counter to order. The line was only five people deep and only half the booths were full. The fluorescent lighting gave the dining area the feel of an operating room. The gray and maroon color scheme was plain and simple. There were a few fries and ketchup packets strewn about the floor, several empty hamburger wrappers and cups of ice on some of the tables. The low hum of conversation drowned out the Muzak from overhead.

"Yeah, I did," said Peter. His buzz was wearing off slightly. He hadn't had a beer in over thirty minutes. His eyes were still squinty. His nose still tingled.

"What happened with that?" asked Weiland. He grabbed the salt shaker and began pouring it on the table. A tiny hill began to form. He watched the salt, as did Peter. "Well? What happened?" repeated Weiland.

"She said I was too immature," said Peter, as if it didn't bother him.

"Too mature?" asked Marty. "You? That's a fuckin' laugh."

"No, dickhead, immature, IMMATURE," Peter enunciated loudly. His intoxication enhancing his quick temper.

"She just looked over here," muttered Weiland. "Must have got her attention, stud."

"Goddammit, Marty, see what you made me do," scolded Peter. He couldn't see Julie, as she was several booths behind him. This didn't stop Peter from doling out punishment to Marty for what he felt was a wrong. He reached under the table and clamped onto his thigh, just above the knee. He then squeezed the muscle. Marty looked at him, as if he couldn't feel anything. Then he jumped.

"Ow, fag!" he yelled and turned and punched Peter in the arm.

Peter cackled and tried it again. Marty moved his leg out of the way and raised his fist. Peter quit reaching for the leg and cowered. He slid over and off the seat of the booth onto the floor. Weiland laughed out loud.

"She just looked again," Weiland muttered.

Peter sat on the floor and glared at Marty, who was also laughing. He leapt to his feet with as much grace as he could muster and stood over his friend who couldn't stop laughing. Julie and Tara were laughing as well.

The small hill of salt in front of Weiland had become a decent size. Peter reached for it and wiped it into Marty's lap in one motion. Marty was too slow to move out of the way, but he stopped laughing. Almost as abruptly as his laughing stopped, Peter's began.

"Real funny, asshole," said Marty as he pushed the salt out of his lap onto the floor under the table. Weiland reached for the pepper shaker and immediately began work on another hill.

"That'll teach ya," admonished Peter as he smirked and tried to look cool. He was checking the corner of his eye to see if Julie was watching.

"Teach me what," asked Marty, "that you're a dumbfuck?"

"Your mom's a what?" asked Peter.

Marty stared at him in stone silence. An unnerving stare, Marty had perfected this look after years of watching his father, a reputable hard-ass. There was no way of telling what schemes and horrible fates were conjured behind the dull blue eyes aimed in the receiver's direction. It was best to look away. The uncertainty of what Marty was capable of was even scarier than anything he had actually done.

Peter held Marty's gaze for about two seconds, bit his lip nervously and then sat back down. He could feel the stare as he sat down. Peter wanted to end things. He liked Marty, but his obsession with all things bizarre had worried him slightly. This was one battle he might do better to let end quietly.

Danny and Donny returned with their food on a tray. Before they could even sit down Peter was reaching for one of Donny's fries. In his low voice, Donny calmly said, "Touch it and die."

"Oh, Don, come on," pleaded Peter. He had run out of money and was no stranger to mooching off his friends. He didn't grab a fry, but kept his hand hovering over the pile as Donny put his tray down and pushed his way onto the bench.

"Take a fry and we're going to have words," Donny said calmly. Danny giggled slightly as he sat across from them.

Just then Tom and Mitch appeared. They sat at the booth behind the others, seeing no room. Tom reached from behind the boys and grabbed a handful of fries from Donny's tray. Donny didn't seem to care.

"Hey, what the...aren't you going to have words with him now?" asked Peter. He had since removed his hands from over the fries, but was ready to pounce at a moment's notice.

"No," was the simple response.

"Why not?" Peter raised his voice and knit his brow. He was genuinely irritated. The police officer at the counter, having finished his conversation with the manager of the restaurant, looked over in the direction of the boys.

"Pipe down," said Mitch slowly, as if he were a ventriloquist.

Peter whipped his head around to glare at Mitch. "What?" he snapped. "I don't think I was talking to you."

"Shut the fuck up," said Mitch, holding his hand over his mouth as if he had to cough.

"Fuck you!" said Peter, loud enough for the policeman to take a step in their direction. "I'm trying to get some fries over here and unless you plan on helping you can take 'pipe down' and shove it up your ass!" Peter was angry now. The alcohol did this to him sometimes. He was never sure why.

The police officer, whose son had gone to Kallow High School and had graduated the year before Peter and his friends graced its halls, sauntered over to the booth. He was casual, knowing what boys do on weekend nights. He was more interested in keeping the peace, rather than making a bunch of arrests.

Peter noticed the figure in blue making his way toward him and huffed. His pulse began to quicken. He knew he didn't need to draw attention to himself in this condition.

"Evening, how we doing tonight, fellas?" asked Officer Fletcher. He looked at each boy in turn.

"Fine," they all muttered, keeping their heads buried in their chests, as if they'd been sent to the corner for pulling some girl's pigtails.

Officer Fletcher nodded. "Good." He stayed standing over the table. "How's your brother doing, Darling?"

Peter was startled to have been addressed and didn't respond immediately. He could pretend not to hear him, that sometimes worked with his mother, but he knew Fletcher was too close. He kept his head down, but his eyes darted everywhere around the tabletop looking for some answer to present itself. He had almost forgotten the question he was so nervous.

"I said, how is..."

"Oh fine," Peter said quickly. He looked up at the smiling face of the policeman. Shit, he thought. I'm busted.

"Good. I always liked him. He had a way about him. Always seemed to be in control, you know? Like nothing ever bothered him."

"Mmhm," added Peter. He didn't know where this was going.

"Yep, real even-keeled. Even if we were down by a few points at the end, he always seemed to maintain himself. Must have been his upbringing. Real cool customer that kid." Officer Fletcher was staring out the huge glass window as he waxed on about Peter's brother. Now he re-directed his gaze to Peter. "D'you play any sports, son?"

"Yeah, football and I think track."

Officer Fletcher just nodded. He looked around again at all the boys. They were silent and fidgeting nervously with whatever they could get their hands on. It seemed an eternity before he spoke again.

"Have a nice night gentlemen. Don't do anything stupid."

"Thanks," muttered Danny. Upon hearing this, the policeman turned on his heel and walked out the door to walk around the outside of the building.

Everybody let out a sigh of relief and Peter turned his attention again to Donny's fries. "How's come Tom gets a fry without asking and I get shit," he whispered to Donny.

Donny picked up the longest fry on his tray and placed it in front of Peter. "Now shut the fuck up."

Peter didn't respond and ate the fry.

"We should go, after this," said Weiland.

"Aren't you guys going to eat?" asked Danny.

"I'm not that hungry."

"Me neither," added Marty.

The boys hurriedly finished their meals. There was small talk of the basketball team and upcoming opponents. The girls stopped by and made small talk on their way out, but nothing came of that. There was a sense of unfulfillment as they made their way out to Peter's car a few minutes later.

As they shoe-horned into the car they resumed their piling-in positions from before. Peter noticed Tony and a couple of his cronies walking into the alley that ran behind the restaurant. He watched them disappear and wondered what they were up to.

"Come on, dude! Let's go," shouted Mitch.

Peter started the car and rather than exit out the restaurant's front drive, he decided to investigate Tony's disappearance into the alley. He slowly backed out of the spot and pulled into the alley. He could see some shadows moving up ahead. The few lights in the alley came from the rundown garages that were behind some of the rundown houses. Peter hadn't yet turned on his headlights. Seeing the figures just thirty feet ahead he wondered if this would spook them. He turned them on to illuminate the scene.

As far as the boys could tell there were four young men standing in a tight group and something was slumped at their feet. As soon as their shadows became definite forms one of the boys bolted toward the car. He looked very angry. Peter didn't roll down the window immediately. He was looking at the slumped figure. It looked somehow familiar. Peter only vaguely noticed the angry young man storming toward the car. He was searching the unknown victim for something. Then it hit him, it was the kid who sat behind him in biology class. He couldn't remember his name, it was no one he'd ever talk to. But the kid was smart. Quiet, but smart. Peter had copied his homework several times and had received his best marks when he did. What the hell could he have done to piss off Tony, he thought; he was just a scared sophomore who kept to himself. The young man arrived at the car and punched the window and Peter hit the button to roll it down.

"What the fuck do you want?"came the young man's harsh question.

Peter, who had been looking at the group in front of him, now quickly put his attention on the irritated young man at his window. "Uh, just leaving, man," was his uneasy reply. He looked out of the corner of his eye to see Tony deliver a vicious right hand to the victim's temple. Peter winced slightly.

The young man's eyes darted around the car. "Tom, that you?" he asked.

"Yeah,"came the muffled answer. Tom was squeezed onto the other side of the car.

"What are you guys doing?" asked the young man.

"Goin' home. What're you doing?" asked Tom.

Peter recognized this guy from Kallow. He had seen him in the halls. He was a senior and generally hung around with Tony. He had never talked to him but had nodded in his direction once or twice at keg parties. He looked rough and like someone to avoid.

"Some fag was walking through this alley when we were having a cigarette..." The young man turned his face to the illuminated scene. The slumping figure was easier to make out now. It was definitely a young person—skinny and smallish compared to his assailants. He had blood on his face and was now trying to prop himself up on one arm. He looked shocked and tired as he squinted into the headlights. His eyes were red and haggard-looking. A backpack lay next to him. The other figures surrounding him all looked familiar. They were either juniors or seniors at Kallow and they were all notorious for being people to avoid in a fight. Tony had fists clenched and stared into the headlights.

"Yo, who is it, Will?" he shouted.

"It's Tom and some other dudes."

"Whose car?" asked Tony.

"That Peter kid," replied Will. Peter hadn't even been aware that Will knew who he was.

"Tell him to cut the lights and we'll kick this fucker out of the way," said Tony, delivering a boot to the slumped figure's ribs.

"Turn off your lights, man," said Will.

As Peter turned off his headlights he caught one last glimpse of the anguished face, wincing in pain, blood streaming from the nostrils and the teeth a bright red. He wondered what it would be like to catch one of Tony's punches in the head. It frightened him slightly. The fear was short-lived, however. He was happy that Will knew who he was. A sense of triumph flowed inside of him as he slowly inched past the scene. Peter Darling was known, even by the upperclassmen, even by the tough guys. He hadn't been hassled by these guys; they liked him. He smiled to himself as he heard the thuds and saw the indistinct motions of Tony and his gang raining more blows upon the kid who sat behind him in Biology.

After impressing himself with a 2.3 GPA over the course of his sophomore year, Peter figured that high school wasn't that tough. He had friends, a spot on the football team, and decent grades. Of course his parents felt he could have tried a little harder in the classroom, but Peter was able to stave off their threats of groundings and punishments by pulling a "B" on a science exam every now and then. Peter also developed several relationships that he would hang onto until he was an old man. Most of these were with females.

Peter's knack for entering into platonic relationships with women was becoming commonplace. Most other males his age wanted to do nothing but kiss and grope and go as far, sexually, as their partner would let them; Peter seemed content to merely talk on the phone with girls, take them to the mall, and listen to them complain about their peers and boyfriends. This was as much as he could get and Peter figured that a little interaction with the opposite sex was better than none at all. Not to say that he didn't think about his girlfriends sexually—this was a regular thought process. As summer approached, Peter decided that he'd like to find a girl—preferably one who was quite attractive and sexually active. He was going to be a junior and he would need a few notches for the proverbial headboard.

"Hey, it's me," came the quick greeting.

"Hey, Peter, what's up?" asked Max. He had been sitting in the living-room, trying to decide on which jobs to apply for today. His mother had been harping at him for the past week. Now that school was out he needed something to do—or so she mandated.

"Nothin'. What're you doing today?" Peter seemed disaffected on the phone, but that was just his manner. He liked the impersonality of the phone. Face-to-face conversations were always more difficult for him. Having to articulate thoughts on the spur of the moment, as new avenues in the conversation opened up, was frightening to Peter. One would never have guessed this from his demeanor on the telephone, however. He knew what he wanted to say ahead of time. Consequently he kept his conversations concise, yet meaningful. The only time his phone conversations weren't "short and sweet" was when he was either talking to a girl or relating stories of what had happened over the busy weekend of partying. Then there was a giddiness to his voice. Not so now, at 10:45 in the morning.

"My mom's been all over my ass to get a job. Shit's hard. I'm supposed to go to OfficeMax, Target, Best Buy, Venture, and K-mart."

"You have interviews at all of those places?" asked Peter, mildly surprised.

"No, I just have to go fill out and drop off applications."

"Oh."

"What do you have planned?"

"Nothing. Absolutely nothing."

"Are you working this summer?" asked Max. He had noticed that Peter never seemed to be complaining about his parents wanting him to get a job like most of the other guys did.

"Yeah. My mom got me a job umping Little League," Peter responded.

"Aren't you playing baseball this year?" asked Max.

"Sure. I'll ump when we don't have games." Peter didn't elaborate on the stipulations of the job or how his mother procured it for him. He rarely gave these kinds of details. He figured that if they were boring to him, they were probably boring to everyone else.

"How much do you make?" Max wished his mom worked for the parents' organization that handed out cushy jobs like that.

"Ten dollars a game."

"How many games a week or day or whatever?"

"I can get about four or five a week if I want to," Peter replied, only vaguely interested in working.

"That's not bad money," admired Max.

"Yeah, I'll be happy with two or three games a week, though. That ought to be enough to keep some green in my pocket. Besides, it's hotter than fuck out there and the kids are retards."

"The kids? What about the parents?" asked Max. He had been to a couple of games and noticed the fanatical loyalty with which parents stood by their sons.

"Yeah, they get pretty stupid, too. They're not that bad at this level, though. Usually you just warn them once and they pipe down for an inning. If they act up again, threaten to throw them out." Peter's tone was even and nonchalant. He didn't see anything unusual about a sixteen-year old in the powerful position of umpire at a Little League baseball game.

"Think that'll happen?" asked Max.

"Maybe, most of them know me through my mom, though. I don't think they'll give me too much trouble."

"Oh. So when's the first game?"

"Tonight. I gotta be there at like 3 or something."

"Then what're you doing?"

"Spendin' that ten fuckin' dollars on somethin'!" came the excited reply. Peter couldn't wait to have money in his pocket. Spending money was quickly becoming a habit for him. It was never that he had a lot to dole out, but what little money he could scrounge up wound up in someone else's hands at an alarming rate. During school, Peter was allotted a certain amount of lunch money each week. That amount never made it to the lunch counter. It was given on a Friday and generally was spent by Sunday morning. Peter would then beg nickels, dimes, quarters, and even pennies for the following week in order to get money. The first half of lunch was used for "borrowing" money from virtually anyone who would let him and the second half was spent eating the food he had bought with money that wasn't his. He never once had to buy his own lunch. He also never missed a lunch.

"Where are you goin' with ten dollars?" asked Max.

"I dunno. Shelly wants me to stop by today." Shelly was one of Peter's numerous platonic friends. She was quite striking. A perfect body and not much of a brain—she leaned more toward the shallow end of the personality pool. Peter liked hanging out with her if only to admire her beauty. He also seemed to be able to carry on a conversation with her that lasted longer than thirty seconds, a feat most of her male classmates had yet to accomplish.

"Why?"

"I dunno. She said she'd be laying out today and if I wasn't doing anything to stop by." Peter didn't think this was anything too terribly strange. He perpetrated "drop-ins" all the time on his girlfriends. He knew Shelly wasn't interested anyway. She dated Weiland, one of Peter's good friends. Peter knew better than to mess with that relationship.

"She's sun-bathing and wants you to stop by for no reason? Is this a fucking porno or something? Are you bangin' her?" Max was somewhat surprised. He never was invited to anyone's house without a clear-cut reason, of which he thought sun-bathing did not qualify.

Peter laughed. "I wish. No, I think she just gets lonely. Weiland is working for his dad all day and won't be done until later and her parents both work."

"This is a fucking porno!" Max began to imitate the stereotypical soundtrack to a '70s porno film. "Oh, Peter, will...you...stop...by...and do me? Yeah, baby, ooh, don't stop," he crooned in a stilted voice.

Peter laughed harder. The notion of him as an adult film star was ridiculous, although he knew it would be a hell of a lot of fun. So he laughed at the preposterous notion, but also at the flattery that was implied by the statement—that he had the potential to be a porn star.

"Ooh yeah, stud, fill...me...up. Pour all of your...hot...love inside," continued Max.

Through his laughter, Peter tried to get Max to stop. "Shut up, dude. Her brother's going to be home."

"Oh my god! A three-way!" Max started in with the music again.

Peter kept chuckling as he talked. "Anyway, when do you have to do all of your job shit?"

"Any time. I think if I just do a few today I can save some for tomorrow. Hopefully that will keep Mom off my back."

"She still bitching about you not having any money?" Peter had never perceived Max's situation as much different from his. Max never appeared outwardly different from anyone else, financially. As a matter of fact, Peter didn't seem to notice an economic difference in any of his friends. Even the ones who lived in smaller houses, had older cars, and whose parents had divorced, seemed to have the same appearance as he did. He knew that Max had been given a car, which was a nicer situation than his own, so he didn't really consider Max's predicament too difficult.

"Yeah, it's been non-stop since, like, Prom. I might have a chance at Hy-Vee, but I won't know until next week." Max hated talking about his lack of employment.

"Why don't you come with me? I'll go with you to drop off the applications and then you can stop over to Shelly's with me." Peter finally got to this, the reason for his call. Despite his seeming ease around the fairer sex, he always liked to have someone else there. The third party was always relaxing. They filled awkward silences and offered new insight into music videos and syndicated sitcoms. Peter really wanted Max to go with him.

Max thought for a moment. His mom might be upset. He could sweet-talk his way around that, though. Then he considered the chance to see Shelly in a bathing suit on a hot June day. Lastly, he considered his friend, Peter, who really needed a straight-man—Max knew him well enough to figure that out.

"Okay. You want me to drive?" asked Max.

"I don't care," replied Peter. This meant that he wanted Max to drive.

"I'll drive—see you in twenty minutes."

"Sounds good."

"Do we need to stop and pick up film for the video camera?" asked Max.

"Video camera?" Peter had no idea what he meant.

"Don't you videotape yourself in the act of hot sex?"

"Fuck off," laughed Peter and hung up.

Max arrived at Peter's driveway to see him standing outside, staring at the landscaping near his front door. "What's up?" asked Max through the open window.

Peter stared at the tiny patch of dirt and foliage his mother had been working on that weekend. "Nothin'. This shit's so fuckin' stupid." Peter turned away from the small bushes, red mulch, and bright flowers and got into the car.

One classic rock song after another poured over the airwaves and Peter sang along with each one. He knew not only the words, but each breath of the singers of almost any classic rock song on the radio. Frequently he could name the artist and title, but he rarely did so unless asked. Max always admired this quality. Peter did not flaunt his knowledge of music history.

As they pulled up in front of the large suburban home of Shelly, Peter had no idea what to think. He was a little nervous. He always became nervous around girls, especially scantily-clad ones. What if she did want to do something with me? Peter wondered. What if she wanted to cheat on Weiland with me? How would it look if I showed up with a third wheel? Peter quickly dismissed these thoughts as ludicrous and led the way around the back of the house.

"Front door busted?" asked Max.

Peter stopped and wheeled on him, "No. She said she'd be around back," he said abruptly, as if Max had asked an all-too obvious question.

Max nodded. "Okay."

Peter moved around the corner of the house cautiously. He could see Shelly lying on her stomach on a chaise lounge. Her person was turned so the boys could see the top of her head first, then her glistening back, and so on down to her tiny feet. Shelly was barely 5'2" but had the curves of an adult woman. Peter and Max glanced at each other with raised eyebrows over the attractive young girl. She had neither heard nor seen them coming and therefore did not move to re-clasp the strap to her bikini top.

Once the boys were within two feet of her, Peter spoke. "Hey."

Shelly's head jerked. She squinted at Peter and Max as the sun was behind them. She quickly moved to re-connect her top. "Hey, Peter. Oh, hi, Max."

The chaise lounge was neon pink and white-striped. Underneath it were a spray bottle, suntan lotion, a small towel, and some nail polish. The garden hose was lying next to the chair in the glistening grass. It was apparent that Shelly had been using it to cool herself off. The boys absorbed the scenery. They looked around nervously as Shelly began to rise to all fours. Both of them happened to glance back at her and see her soaking wet bikini bottom, weighted with water, sagging off of Shelly's perfect waist. From above, they could see down the lower piece of Shelly's bathing suit. Both of their eyes bulged. Shelly was oblivious.

"Hold on, I'm going to go put on a tee-shirt," she said and pranced into the house. She effortlessly grabbed a beach towel on the way in and dried herself off.

Peter and Max were stunned. "Did I just get a beaver shot?" asked Peter, still staring at the chaise lounge.

"It was either that or the hairiest shadow I've ever seen," replied Max. He whispered quickly,

"Do you think she caught us?"

"Does it fucking matter?" came the harsh, excitedly whispered reply. "Oh my god." Peter did feel like he just got something for nothing. He always found Shelly attractive but he knew she was way out of his league. This was a gift from heaven. It was not often that Peter was able to see down a real live girl's pants. He was grateful whenever the opportunity presented itself.

"What should we do?" asked Max.

"I don't know. You wanna call someone?" came Peter's sarcastic reply.

Max was still stunned. Peter had not taken his eyes off of the exact spot where his new favorite memory had been revealed. "Should we go?" asked Max.

"Are you fucking nuts? What if her fucking top falls off next?" Peter had forgotten his nerves and anxiety from moments before. He thought Shelly hadn't noticed, but he did feel a little strange, almost as if the two boys should reciprocate and show her theirs.

"So, what should we do?"

Peter thought for a moment. His initial impulse was to run inside, tear off the remainder of Shelly's clothes and have sex with her. This, of course, was ludicrous, he knew; the thought, however, was exciting to him. He envisioned himself and Shelly on the countertop in the kitchen. Although there was a sectional in the nearby living room, his fantasy seemed to dictate that the cold formica was the best place for his sexual interlude. This initial thought was quickly pushed to the back of his brain by the idea that he and Max could tell Shelly what they had seen. She might then decide to sunbathe completely naked, since the boys had already seen the most mysterious part of her body. Again, Peter became excited. This thought was also put into the fantasy file for later when still a third thought poured into Peter's brain. The boys could say nothing and keep it their little secret. This seemed the most logical, though certainly not the most fun, of the three options.

"Why don't we just not say anything and keep this to ourselves," whispered Peter.

Max looked at him. "Why are you whispering?"

"Shhhh, she'll be right back," admonished Peter. "Just don't say anything. All we need is for her to know that we saw her box and then she'll tell Weiland and then we're really fucked!" Peter's whisper became increasingly louder.

"Oh, yeah. Good point. What if she knows we saw it?" asked Max, now whispering as well. The boys had not moved from their spots, as if their feet were rooted to the ground.

Peter pondered this for a moment. This was a fear of his. If Shelly had done this on purpose, and she was known to be a bit of a flirt, then it was conceivable that she did know the boys had seen down her panties. He wondered if this was some sort of diabolical plan to get Peter in trouble. Or perhaps it was Shelly's way of coming on to Peter. She hadn't known Max would be along. Maybe she set this all up ahead of time and meant for only Peter to see her. He became upset that Max had come along. He looked at him out of the corner of his eye.

"If she knows she would say something," said Peter.

"She would?" asked Max. He was a little amazed by this wisdom. "If I was standing in front of a girl and my dick popped out and I didn't want it to, but I knew the girl saw it, do you think I'd say anything?" whispered Max, his pitch heightening as he went.

Peter shrugged. "Who's the girl?"

Max rolled his eyes and spoke with his hands. "It doesn't matter who the fucking girl is!" he hissed. "What matters is that I didn't want her to see it and I sure as hell ain't gonna admit to letting her see it. I'm gonna pretend like IT NEVER HAPPENED. Then she has to think twice about whether it really did or not."

Peter processed this. It sounded logical, most everything Max said did, but he wanted Shelly to know that he saw it. He wanted her to know that he was impressed. That she could do that anytime she wanted. "So you think she doesn't know?" he finally asked, in a regular voice.

"Who fucking cares if..."

"Who fucking cares about what?" asked Shelly as she glided out from behind the screen door, an XXL t-shirt covering everything but her legs.

The boys were startled and looked at each other first, then at Shelly. She moved back to her chaise lounge and adjusted it to the upright position. She sat down and crossed her bronze legs.

"Who fucking cares if...my...aunt...has...a dick." said Max uneasily.

Both Peter and Shelly looked at Max as if he was from another planet.

"What?" asked Peter, horrified.

"I...uh..." Max stammered.

Shelly adjusted herself on the chair. "Have you guys been standing there the whole time?"

Peter was still looking at Max in disbelief. He didn't know what he had meant to do with that last comment, but it seemed that Shelly had moved the conversation in a different direction. He looked down at his tennis shoes planted in the almost putting green-length grass. "Uh, yeah, I guess so."

"Well sit down, silly," she said, playfully.

Neither Peter nor Max moved at first. They were both wondering whether Shelly knew about what they had seen. Peter moved first and headed toward the brownish-red picnic table with benches attached. He swung a leg through the opening and sat facing Shelly. Max followed suit and sat opposite Peter, both legs under the table.

"So, what are you guys up to?" asked Shelly.

"Uh, nothing?" replied Peter. His friend only looked at the table. Peter tried to avert his eyes from Shelly's gaze, thinking, at once, how gorgeous she was, and how guilty he might look.

"Is that a question or an answer?"

"Huh? Oh, yeah, heh, heh, sure it is." Peter said nervously. There was a long pause. Shelly looked at the two boys oddly, trying to figure out if something was wrong with them. Neither Peter nor Max looked at her directly.

"Did I hear you are umpiring?" Shelly asked Peter. She seemed genuinely interested.

"Word travels fast," said Max in a low voice.

"What?" asked Shelly. "Who's fat?"

"What? No one." Max spoke louder. "I said word travels fast." He nodded because he had nothing more to say. He went back to picking at the splintered wood on the picnic table.

"Oh," said Shelly, almost disappointed. "Will you be at Northwest?" Shelly resumed her questioning of Peter.

"Uh, yeah. I've got a game tonight actually." Peter still felt uncomfortable and aroused and curious all at once. He wasn't sure of what to say to Shelly.

"Speaking of baseball, have you seen my pussy?"

"WHAT?" blurted Peter.

"I said, have you seen Mike Steussy. It was just a question, silly. You don't have to yell about it."

"Oh, right," said Peter. He swore that he had heard her ask something else. "Uh, no. I hadn't heard. What happened?" He was relieved that she didn't ask what he had thought she asked.

"I don't know, I just heard something happened to him." Shelly shrugged.

"Did you hear anything?" Peter turned and asked Max.

"Me, no, I've been in a coma for the last two years," he replied absentmindedly.

Peter laughed. Shelly did not. She had a puzzled look on her face. The trio tried to make small-talk but the conversation seemed to be comprised of two or three short statements, an odd comment by Max, and then nothing more. After ten minutes of this, Peter became bored.

"What time is it?" he asked no one in particular.

"I dunno," said Max.

"It's about 11:45," said Shelly. She didn't look at a watch, since she hadn't one.

Peter wondered how she had known the time.

"Well, we'd better get going," said Max. "We've got a few errands to run. And I don't want to get ol' Blue here too tired for his game this afternoon." He started to get up from the bench.

Peter looked at him for a moment, wondering whether he should veto this obvious plea for an exit from his good friend. On the one hand, they were in the company of a pretty young lady and should relish every second of it. On the other hand, things had been awkward since the boys had seen down Shelly's bikini. Leaving might alleviate the uneasy feeling Peter had.

"Yeah, we should get going. Max has some job applications to drop off. We can't all work in the big leagues like yours truly."

"What time is your game?" asked Shelly.

"It's at 3:30, doubleheader," answered Peter.

"Maybe I'll stop by. My brother plays at Northwest at 6 p.m. Hope I see you."

Peter should not have been surprised. Many of his friends of the opposite sex had come to his baseball games. Now that he had seen Shelly virtually naked today, though, his feelings for her were a little different. He felt that he might have to impress her if she came to watch him umpire his Little League game today.

The boys made their exit and finished the job of taking Max's job applications around, all the while discussing Shelly's anatomy. Soon it was time for Peter to head off for his job at the Little League diamond at Northwest Park. As he drove to the park (which was within walking distance from his house) he thought about how he could impress Shelly. He knew that she was madly in love with Weiland, but he couldn't resist the idea of impressing a female. Garnering the praise of one of the fairer sex was always something he appreciated. It made him feel good and it made him think that he could be the all-American stud in which he categorized guys like Weiland.

Peter made his way to the diamond. He had changed clothes into his black AC/DC concert t-shirt and his cut-off baseball pants. He knew he would be sweating and these were akin to his workout clothes. He also knew that the Little Leaguers would be impressed that he was old enough to have gone to an AC/DC concert. He flipped his baseball cap around to face backward as he noticed the hustle and bustle around the diamonds. Each of the four diamonds was in use. The concession stand where his mother worked had a dozen kids straining on their bare toes to see over the counter. These were the future Little Leaguers who barely understood their older brothers' game, but who did understand that baseball meant candy from the concession stand. Peter's mother waved at him as he sauntered across the tall, green grass. He knew he was headed to Diamond Three, but he didn't know who was playing there.

As Peter moved inside the chain-link fence to lean up against the backstop and check line-up cards he noticed that one of the teams had the brother of a friend of his on the team. Jimmy was the younger brother of Cindy. He was a snot-nosed little punk who seemed to have none of Cindy's pleasant smile or easy-going nature. Peter had known Cindy and her family since she was in grade school. He had always gotten along with her and counted her as one of his friends.

Peter checked the line-up cards, occasionally checking the stands to see if Cindy had arrived. His desire was idiotic, he knew, but he held out hope that she might stop by, at least to say hi.

The first few innings went by without incident. The game was 5-3, in favor of Jimmy's team. Peter had been chit-chatting with Jimmy throughout the game. Jimmy was the team's catcher, so, every bottom half of the inning, Peter was right over Jimmy's shoulder calling balls and strikes. Jimmy, although five years younger than Peter, seemed to have a street savvy about him which allowed the conversation to become gradually more mature, until it eventually shifted to the subject of girls. It was the bottom of the fifth inning.

"So, you banged anybody yet?" asked Jimmy as he tossed a warm-up pitch back to the pitcher.

Peter was a little taken aback but had known that Jimmy's mind and mouth had always been a little beyond the average prepubescent child's. He had three older siblings who liked to party and didn't seem to mind if Jimmy hung around. Peter stood still, not sure if he should divulge this information or not. Shelly popped into his head.

"Uh, I think that's none of your business, son," said Peter.

Jimmy waited for another warm-up pitch. Once he caught it he gunned it down to second base, then turned around, looked up, and said, "that means you ain't gettin' any." He smiled a goofy grin through his red catcher's mask.

Peter furrowed his brow, flabbergasted by this young man's accusation. He wasn't sure exactly how to respond. "Uh, what?"

"You heard me," said Jimmy. He resumed his catcher's crouch. His tone was not antagonistic, but rather matter-of-fact.

"I've gotten plenty," said Peter. "Besides, I don't think kids at your age need to be discussing that kind of shit." He pointed a finger at Jimmy, trying to send a mild scolding his way.

"I'll bet I've seen more tit than you have," offered Jimmy confidently. He waited for the pitcher to go through his pre-pitch routine.

Peter laughed an uneasy chuckle at first. He felt that Jimmy was serious. He knew about the boy's reputation as a troublemaker and his popularity among the pre-teens at the elementary, but he didn't think he would start any trouble with him. Peter was surprised by Jimmy's condescending attitude.

"I'll bet not," replied Peter.

"I'll bet so," said Jimmy as another pitch popped into his glove. It was the last of the warm-up pitches so Jimmy gunned the ball to the third basemen. He got back into his crouch as the first batter came into the batter's box. The sun was still hot and the air was populated by a smattering of encouraging words from parents and coaches.

"I'll bet not," retorted Peter incredulously.

"Have you had my sister?" asked Jimmy.

"No! Of course not." Peter was startled by Jimmy's question.

"What's wrong with my sister?"

"Nothing, nothing at all," said Peter warily. He wanted nothing more than the game to get started again so he could get back to calling balls and strikes.

"Then why haven't you fucked her yet?" asked Jimmy. The batter, who had just entered into his stance now turned to face Jimmy, his eyes wide as saucers.

"I, er, I, uh..." Peter didn't know what to say. He instinctually crouched right behind Jimmy's helmet as he saw the pitcher getting ready to go into his wind-up. Peter put one hand behind his back, the other rested on the back-strap of Jimmy's chest protector. Peter was not comfortable discussing Cindy with her brother. She was cute, a little plump, but that only augmented her already large chest. She had a sweet disposition and was friends with all of the right people. She was someone he wouldn't mind dating, but her brother did not need to know this. The tiny pitcher reared back and hurled the ball into Jimmy's mitt. It popped when it hit the leather.

"Strike one!" called Peter. He glanced to his left. Oh no, he thought. Shelly had just arrived. She sat in the front row of the bleachers. This was just what he needed: Jimmy talking about fornicating with Cindy, and Shelly watching every move this umpire made from the stands. Peter didn't know if it could get much worse.

"I heard high school is loaded with girls. Why not my sister?" asked Jimmy.
"What?"

"I see you all the time with different girls, but never my sister. Is there something wrong with her?"

The second pitch came across, a curve ball that the batter swung at and missed horribly. The crowd "oooh"'ed. "Strike two!" came Peter's call as he pointed to his right and flicked his wrist. He wondered what had gotten into Jimmy. They had been moving along okay up to this point. Maybe Jimmy had been buttering him up for this line of questioning. Peter wondered if Cindy had been talking about him at home and Jimmy had overheard. Maybe he should ask her out. Then he remembered Shelly was watching and he snapped out of it. He was trying to impress her at the moment. The tension between catcher and umpire built.

The third pitch came across. "Ball one!" shouted Peter.

"You haven't answered the question yet, Pete," said Jimmy, throwing the ball back to the pitcher. The young man on the mound didn't like the call.

As Jimmy resumed his crouch, Peter leaned in, speaking through Jimmy's catcher's helmet into his right ear.

"I don't know. I just never...I don't know. Why do you care?"

"You think she's ugly don't you?" asked Jimmy. His tone was almost vindictive. "You think she's fat, and round like a..."

"Ball two!" barked Peter.

"I knew it!" came Jimmy's words, gritted through his teeth and the red catcher's mask. He threw the ball back to the pitcher so hard that his teammate looked at him strangely, wondering if that last pitch (which only missed the inside corner by a little) wasn't to his battery mate's liking—he was trying as hard as he could.

"Knew what?" asked Peter in a whisper. He leaned over Jimmy slightly as the catcher settled into his crouch. He was now more concerned with young Shelly. He tried to look as professional as possible. His muscles tensed. He imitated the umpires he had seen during Major League games.

"You think she's fat and ugly and that's why you won't fuck her," hissed Jimmy. The batter looked at Jimmy out of the corner of his eyes and winced.

"We'll see about that," said Jimmy. The pitcher wound up and threw the ball as hard as he could. It sailed wildly behind the batter. Fortunately he looked up in time to dance out of the way. The pitcher's face was contorted into one of rage. He had wanted that to be a fast ball, up and in, to blow by the batter. He wanted to show Jimmy how hard he could throw.

"Ball three!" shouted Peter confidently. He hoped Shelly could hear the tone of his voice. He wanted nothing more than to look good for her.

Jimmy ordered up the next pitch, another fastball, right down the middle of the plate. He settled into his crouch, intent on this full-count pitch. He made sure everything looked "normal." As the pitcher went into his wind-up, wild determination in his eyes, Jimmy said loud enough for both batter and umpire to hear—"Ass-fuck."

The batter looked down at the catcher, afraid that another wild pitch was coming. As the fastball came screaming out of the pitcher's hand it was clear it was the hardest fastball an eleven year-old had ever thrown.

Peter tensed to call a strike, noticing, out of the corner of his eye, that the batter had taken his eye off of the ball.

As the ball was halfway to home-plate, Jimmy lowered his catcher's mitt and ducked his right shoulder. In fact, he bowed almost completely over, leaving the umpire exposed. Normally, Little League umpires wear only a chest protector. The catcher acts as protection for the umpire's crotch and lower body. When there is no catcher, the exposed areas become vulnerable, especially with small, hard objects being hurled in their general vicinity. And so it was when Jimmy dipped to home-plate to let a fastball come hurtling at Peter's lower half.

Before Peter even knew what was happening he felt the surge of pain as the fastball caught him square in the groin. For as fast as it was coming, it didn't have much kick-back. The round sphere of leather and string hit Peter with a thud then dropped to the plate. Peter fell almost as quickly. He pinched his legs together and covered himself with his hands. Jimmy quickly popped up and threw the ball to first base. The batter stood, awestruck.

"You're out," Jimmy said emphatically, almost as much to the batter as to Peter.

"Aaahhhh, fuck!" Peter screamed. His face was bright red and he squeezed his eyes together as hard as he could. He lay on his side, yelling. "What the fuck? Owwwwwwwww, mother fucker! God damn it! Fuck! Fuck! Fuck! You fucking fuck! Fuuuuuuuuuuuuck!"

A couple of parents moved off the bleachers and onto the field to help the fallen umpire. Neither the catcher nor the batter moved. Jimmy smiled behind his mask. The batter couldn't believe it still. Peter lay in the dirt screaming invective loud enough for the neighboring diamond to halt play. The umpire there yelled over, "He all right?"

"Mother fucker! Fuuuuuuuuuuck! Owwwww shit! My fucking nuts! Mother shit-fuck! Goddammit!"

Two men tried to get Peter to sit up. He couldn't, or wouldn't. They tried to get him to calm down. He couldn't. He laid on his side in the dirt for at least five minutes, an eternity of swearing and gritting of teeth. The redness in his face and the severity of his yelling made the onlookers think that he would hyperventilate and pass out. Both teams had gathered round the fallen umpire, forming a perimeter about six feet away from him. They weren't sure of what this young man was capable. The parents stood in the bleachers and remarked at the longevity and ferocity of the young man's profanity. Some vowed that he would never work a Little League game again. Others, mostly men, kept saying what an unlucky bastard he was and how sorry they felt for him.

The two fathers who were trying to calm Peter had procured a small bag of ice and had placed it on Peter's groin area for him to numb the pain. They eventually carried him off the field over to the concession stand, where they knew his mother worked. Peter kept his eyes closed the entire time. He ran out of breath as he passed the bleachers where Shelly had been. He did not dare open his eyes and he only moaned in pain. Finally the fathers were able to get Peter to the concession stand and lay him upon the counter. Mrs. Darling moved the Blow-pops and napkin dispenser to make room. His mother attended her son with loving care and tried to comfort him. After the pain subsided briefly and Peter clutched a blue ice-pack tightly to his groin, he vowed to never work another of Jimmy's games.

Houston, We Have a Problem

So I'm trying to wrap my head around the exact reason why it means so much to me. Like Christmas...no, like driving faster than I'm supposed to...not quite right. I don't think it's like either of those (or the countless other trite analogies which have worn out their respective welcomes). It's more like a payday at a part-time job. Sometimes the check is a little more than one expects (overtime, accountant's oversight, some idiot punched in with the wrong employee ID) and sometimes it's a little less (oh yeah, I guess I did sleep in and miss last Tuesday; why did I ask to be sent home early?). In any case, it's mostly dependable. The check brings something I need. It's never the same amount twice, and it can arouse feelings of glee and gloom from week to week. And, although it appears to be relatively static, with small variation, I always hope it's something bigger, that one day it will show some astronomical sum upon which I can retire. Alas, on a Friday, it does not. Back to the grind for one more go around.

The dramatic side of me disagrees with this connection to work and money. (Far too ugly—too materialistic.) He says that the reason is because we connect so well—kindred spirits matched together by fate and the stars—in an odd paradox. This softer, more emotive portion of my psyche says that we are bonded by our solitude. Islands in the middle of a vast tumult, standing fast and alone, buffeted by the painful breakers only to be comforted by the warmth of the sun's rays; we sit stalwart, forever the rocks. In this geography we are connected to nothing greater, satellite to no massive entity. Together we are alone, seemingly adrift, yet still anchored at our base. Few have discovered us, even fewer seem to think our existence is noteworthy...

The realist in me says that no one does care. How could they? A grown man with such an obsession, a disease, a moral travesty if you ask the realist. Why does it warrant more than a footnote? Why can't I just see that to truly live is to cast off all such associations? Sever the limb to save the body (and mind). This trap has been cutting off the circulation for too long. Much greater futures lie in the distance, why not soar to that horizon?

The pessimist voice likes to dwell on the sad undertaking this has become. Even the word choice here: undertaking, like a funeral. The dreary doom and pain which pervades is all we shall ever know if I keep this up. I'd like to tell this part of me to lighten up, but I never do. Surely "deaf" and "death" are so close in (oddly) sound for a reason...nothing seems to comfort this part of my inner self. He thinks that I like pain, I've always liked pain, and therefore, I will always hold onto this chance that will never, can never come to fruition. It gives me something to complain about, and, secretly, if I didn't know that something was wrong, how could I exist? Surely there's something tragically afoul if I wasn't miserable.

The purist in me listens to these voices and opts for none of them. It's a boyhood fantasy, he says. It's born of fathers and sons, of summers and hope springing eternal. No one ever asks to endure hardship, it merely comes with this freshly mown territory. Roaring crowds and cool evenings, rickety organs and the sound of cleats on dirt, like a hundred pencils frantically scribbling love notes: "I love you, I love you, I love you." With this I cannot argue. The simplistic sweetness of all that has come before and all that will never change attracts me to this "game." (My whole self takes offense to those who fail to appreciate the nuance and beauty, but to each his own.) I have always been a bystander, a testament to the entrancing power within. Forever shall I be in its grasp, forever wondering why I can't put into words what this fascination means. From the pinnacle to the depths, despite my attempts to rationalize, I cannot and will not be released.

Thank you, boys of summer. Let's play ball.

Boys Don't Cry

I teach writing. As part of that undertaking I get to motivate my young charges to be descriptive, to use sensory details in order to make the reader feel the same way as the author does. I break it down as if it is easily accomplished. Picture it: the waiting page, a rising of the head, a pause for clarity, a flick of the wrist, and the subtlety of the moment is forever committed to paper, a lasting testament to feeling and emotion. Sadly, these young authors have difficulty making the reader truly feel. I can't blame them or be angry. I cajole and coddle and sometimes admonish, all in the name of achieving better description. I urge them toward making the experience more genuine for the reader. "Include more sensory details." My message seems clear enough to me: put the reader in the story, make them a part of it by making them feel it. Because of this seeming dedication to creating more descriptive writers, I think, I've become acutely aware of more sensory details around me. It's this...or age...or cynicism...or appreciation...I'm not exactly sure. More sights, sounds, smells, tastes, and touches stand out. Some of these raise questions—how could I put that into writing? How could I make it legitimate for the reader? What could I do to make the reader feel what I do? I think I've been cataloguing these for no one's real edification but my own. Perhaps now I'm ready to share a few...

I coach basketball. You may be deciding to turn a deaf ear or blind eye to the essay right now, passing it off as mere sport and not serious material. Remember, however, that this essay is about description, about feeling. I'll try not to be cliché or trite, but isn't that the maddening paradox of sports? Aren't the same dramas played out season after season (with only slight variations among personalities and on which teams certain fates befall)? After several years, isn't there a definite boredom in this repetition? By nature, isn't this making things too familiar—too cliché? There's the rub, though. It continues...and the sights and sounds and smells come rushing back anew, as if this is the first time for every player in the cast. To some extent, it is all new. A fresh start. A second chance. A new dawn. Once more unto the breach to feel what countless others have felt before.

There are particular sights and sounds and smells that are noteworthy. The summer is hot and (often) oppressive in Iowa. It slowly comes to me, secretive, furtive, the dampness in the air deadening the sounds of car doors outside the gym and stifling boys' voices as they call across the gym. The humidity moves stealthily, so much so that I don't notice it when I arrive in the gym. I'm clean and only a few drops of perspiration are trickling down the inside of my t-shirt, running crookedly, like single tear drops from the outside corner of the eye, almost gentle and tickling. It grows gradually as the players arrive for off-season workouts. The temperature rises when the sound of leather balls being pounded onto hardwood, their thuds uneven yet determined like some sort of mad factory punching out sheets of metal, fill the gym. The sweat now becomes a torrential pour as boys work harder, coaches yell louder. The coaxing is tied to the yelling. The encouragement is handcuffed to the critique. I forget how easy it is to take this for granted.

The feel of a ball in my hands: the passes leaving my fingertips, as hard as I can throw. Sometimes it pulls the skin back from my fingers. The tiny gap between skin and nail opening so slightly, a minute pin-prick paper cut that makes the whites of my nails grow larger by the end of practice. The pain is sharp when the ball leaves my hand and deadens for two seconds after. The area is irritated and tender, as fresh wounds are. I keep throwing hard passes, though.

The coach's whistle to stop a drill: short, shrill, commanding. It is like the traffic cop's tool, at once authority and instructor—"stop," "pay attention," "follow my directions (for your benefit)." Sometimes the sound is pleasant; if birds could understand joy (and comprehend that a quick verbalization to alert the world that they feel better than average is natural) they would sound like this. Sometimes it is vicious; the discontent behind the shriek seems to turn the air tense and red. I use the whistle judiciously and never tire of its piercing song.

The harsh stiffness of a practice jersey: I grab it when the player needs more than my words to move him, when I want to emphasize exact positioning and my precise intensity of emotion. I grab the side of the jersey and bunch it up in my hand, where the player's naked ribs heave with sweat underneath. A fistful of cotton-poly blend with a few days sweat soaked into it and stiffened is like burlap in my hand. It feels like nothing important, but it holds everything crucial.

The compressing wall of sound surrounds me on the bench. The cheers and jeers from home and visiting fans alike. There are conversations about the game, about players, about the weather, about classes. There are lamentations over missed calls. There are pleadings for sons to keep trying. The pitch is raised, like the hum of my car's engine while it sits in the garage. It is confined into space and enveloping that space, yet rhythmic and consistent. Going hoarse over this din, like Alexander addressing his troops, or William Wallace urging his men, feels right.

The smell of sweat in the team room: it wafts slowly into my brain. The boys clamor giddily for chairs after a victory, or slink slowly for them after defeat. The slight humidity returns. It's not repulsive or disgusting. At any other time social norms would call these boys smelly, dirty and "gross." I think the opposite. This is appropriate, pure and beautiful. The game is over and the sweat means hard work. It means a dedication to a goal; it means the never-ending trial that is sports. It is vindication that everything they've done up to this point is valid. Their flushed faces hold alternately hopeful and disappointed eyes. They lean forward, arms resting on knees to listen, sometimes looking at the floor, sometimes using the fronts of their jerseys to wipe the sweat from their brows. The smell is never repugnant and reminds me that nothing worth doing is easy. It is, in no small way, a reminder of the worth and value of what these boys do every day.

Finally, at the end of the season where we were ranked #1 for almost every week, the one where we lost once in the regular season, after the final game, I walk from the floor to the locker-room. The technicolor blur of faces and colors float by slowly, I'm on a carousel barely noticing the cotton candy held by t-shirt wearing children on the outside. I can hear only the sound of my heels collapsing on the pavement, like cement blocks being stacked. I can scarcely recall the twenty-one wins that preceded this game. My hand moves in slow motion toward the doorknob, its nicked and tattered copper coating wearing off; it feels warm in my hand. I am the last one to return to the locker-room. As the door opens it fills the room, the sound that only we can hear...

There are times when I think of what I want my students to describe and why. How much information is too much? Is there a point when enough is enough? Do writers need to exercise restraint? When? How? What if the reader should stay on the other side of the door, unknowing, unfeeling, in blissful ignorance? Would better description be a gateway to better understanding, that maybe others would want to go out and try new things, or could it be a warning of those painful experiences, those that need to be avoided? In lectures I try to simplify this by saying, "you don't want to include superfluous information that may bore the reader. If it doesn't add to the intended effect of the writing, then leave it out." What is the point of feeling, then, if we are allowed to edit certain parts of the experience? Now the description becomes a paraphrase. I'm not sure I know the answers here, but I'm considering this problem. I digress.

The sound is one that is indescribable, because it borders on unreal. In America, boys are pushed toward trucks and sports, playing war and ramping bicycles, being tough. They are encouraged to stand up tall, to never show emotion in the face of adversity: it reveals a certain, well, weakness. These boys that know enough to spend hour after hour in the gymnasium perfecting a skill, that are mature enough to work as hard for their teammates as they've worked for anything else, that understand they want to become men...they are, in the end, to be admired and praised for their sense of dedication to a cause. They return day after day in good times and bad and give supreme effort in search of success. Our success had taken us to 21-1; unfortunately, our success could not get us past the 9-14 team who was destined to go to state this year. These players reveal qualities that adults take for granted, qualities that help in the heroism and tragedy, qualities maintained by mere boys. And this is why the sound is so surreal. This is why, I think, you shouldn't feel what I've felt. This is why, I think, the sound of boys crying may be the saddest thing I've ever heard. This is why, I think, some things cannot be described with words. When there is no air in the room, when that pulsating knot in my throat clenches so tightly that I gasp for what is surely my last breath, when something behind my eyes pushes hot and hard and steadfast, when boys hide their heads in towels, the muffled sobs and slight shudders the clearest tell that, in the end, boys do cry, I'm certain.

In this moment, there are no words, there is only a singular feeling, a feeling that perhaps I shouldn't share.

JENNIFER HORN

A History in Words

1969: Entrance in Dubuque, Iowa, on All Saints' Day

1970: According to Horn family lore, first word is "dance"

1975: Five-year-old Jennifer discovers the typewriter and the U.S. mail; an early letter to Grandma and Grandpa Horn in Davenport, IA, reads as follows:

20 of august.

dear grandma and grandpa.
tank you for the xxxxx one-year xxx subscription
the national geographic world I thank you so much
I wish I could come xxxxxx to your house but I have
to start kindergarten.

I love love love lovelyou.
you lovexx love love love love jennifer.
love jennifer

1977: Early poetry (typed, of course) favors brilliant rhyming couplets in four-line stanzas (e.g., "Look at the snow. / Watch it blow. / Over the ground. / Around and around.")

Late 1970s and onward: Horn family dinner conversation frequently revolves around wordplay (e.g., an early 80s dinner conversation necessitates the precaution of shutting the kitchen window lest the neighboring DiPasqualis mis-overhear the Horn hilarity about "mastication")

1983 - 1987: High school years in Dubuque and Darien, IL, involve the repeated yelling of words while wearing uniforms (e.g., cheerleader and drum major), as well as sincere poetic emoting

Word Job #1: Pushing the envelope in creative Blue Light Special Announcement writing and delivery while employed in the Apparel Department at the Willowbrook (IL) Kmart during high school (e.g., even though the Blue Light truly did start on fire, regulations specifically prohibited uttering the word "fire" in Blue Light Special announcements; hence, the reference to "red-hot savings" and the very special close of the announcement, a whistled riff from the Doors' song "Light My Fire")

1987 – 1992: College career at the University of Iowa skips the originally planned ballet major (no words) and instead progresses from flute major (still no words) to physics/chemistry major (symbols instead of words), finally at the last minute ending in an actual degree in English education (all words, all the time)

Word Job #2: A semester spent as an arts writer for *The Daily Iowan* newspaper during college requires finding words under deadline to describe the incredible richness of artistic performances and garners a first (and only) fan letter from a reader

Word Job #3: A six-year stint as a secondary English language arts teacher in eastern Iowa schools

Summer 1994: Participation in the summer Iowa Writing Project, an intensive three-week writing workshop for teachers, while also dancing in the UI summer opera kicks down some interior doors, re-awakens a creative inner life, and introduces Derrick, Lisa, and Jen to one another, all of which helps to lay the foundation for the eventual Barcalounger Cowboys of St. Columcille's

Word Job #4: A shorter stint as science editor at Iowa City educational publishing company Buckle Down, with days spent in dogged pursuit of scientific truth and hot debate of lingual perfection (e.g., technically, one might, if one were exceptionally uptight, argue in defense of hyphenating the term "ice-cream cone")

Word Job #5: Employment at the testing company ACT, which acronym once stood for "American College Testing" but officially no longer stands for any words; favorite project to date has been developing and managing a suite of tests marketed internationally to measure skill in using business English

2000 and 2002: Entrance to the world of absolutely delightful daughters, the older being Bridget ("resolute strength") Caroline (depending on where you look up the meaning, "joy, song of happiness," "womanly," or "free man" — ?!?) and the younger being Muriel ("sparkling seas") Quinn ("wise and intelligent")

Today: "Tell us another story, Mike, pleeeeaase?" is how Muriel and Bridget often kick off dinnertime conversations; our stories today have family and friends in them, bicycles and mishaps, books and jokes, music and adventures to near and far places — and they weave our lives together.

Wake, be still

The turquoise bay curves,
tangential to the circle of the volcano,
and the train tracks mark still another arc between —
all is sun and blue sky and concrete,
shadows cast by the pastel apartment buildings
with their clean laundry waving from balconies
and the sharp green air of citrus groves
through cracked and dirty windows
that line the rows of molded plastic seats
bolted to the floor gently rocking, rocking,
steadily drawing the contours of earth and sea
and, this day,
I get to be there,
solitary in my winter coat and different words for all of this
than the man in the embellished black leather jacket
who boards and takes the seat next to me and my luggage.
He sits, and feels suddenly so close in the cramped space
that in just a few breaths the lines have softened and warmed,
and we both have become still and aware,
still, except for the swaying above the passing kilometers,
still, while the colors and shapes slide across the dusty windows,
still, until after all the full minutes
he rises for the next-to-last stop,
steps out to the platform,
looks back once —
and then there is just
the rocking, the swaying, the volcano,
the sunlight tumbling from blue into blue,
the lingering warmth I carry with my bags
up out of the last station.

Some months later, I wake in the dark for a reason I don't know,
yet I sense I should note carefully the time,
be aware, pay attention —
moonlight spills onto the blue of my walls, my sheets,
over the geography of my body,
I hear a soft swaying,
I sit up,
I turn so I can lower my feet and rest them on the gentle motion,
I let the waves roll through me to all the hidden places,
I am on the Circumvesuviana making my way north past the volcano,
I am being rocked beside a familiar stranger,
there is full warmth of recognition,
there is no train,
there is only the old wonder of the earth waking,
pressing us to sit up,
be still,
lay our hands on it,
pay attention.

Benediction in spite of

There are hazards in practicing
    the art of self-containment,
methodically emptying your pockets of
    the smallest fuzzy remnants
    of any sort of expectation,
keeping hope pushed back
    into the too-small drawer,
    pinched and quietly unruly,
as you walk through your town
    practicing solidity and calling it enough
    practicing living inside the lines of your skin
    practicing liking the lines of your skin
    practicing believing there is sufficient beauty and that
    magic is an untrustworthy itinerant, probably a fiction anyway,
    this is fine, you're fine, this is enough
    and your stride is strong and your back is straight and fine,
then, with another's hand laid on your arm, you're
    suddenly tripped to sprawling in the grass
    with the breath knocked out of you by that
    butterfly bolt of touch,
the warmth of contact racing to fill in all the lines in a wing-beat instant,
    face up in a sunlight downpour and without knowing how to breathe in it
and, still,
not wanting at all to get up and

walk away from that breathless place,
    but knowing it was nothing
    that must be carried home
    where you will add it to the overfull drawer,
    straighten the lines back out,
and resume your practice.

At the Grape Escape

The clientele is carried in
on gusts of February wind
that warm in the smooth, dim glow
of close-set red walls
and the occasional spark of light
through sleek, jewel-filled martini glasses.
An old man sits sideways on the divan,
slowly being buried
in the winter coats newcomers toss his way.
He is still, bent,
holds meetings in his eyes,
and thinks lustful thoughts
about the middle-aged social queen
in the out-of-season sleeveless sweater
as she holds court on her high-backed stool
and calls the hapless entertainment
off of his piano bench to receive his orders
at her side.
The young drunk in the corner
denies his drunkenness
by loudly pointing it out;
an exotic couple plays Chinese checkers on the bar,
each fantasizing about a stranger
while the other plans a move;
the piano player embellishes chords
to fill the space in song requests he pretends to know;
the artfully trimmed window
displays the town cop striding past
beneath his big-brimmed hat;
the French poster art
slowly curls in the frame.

River spring
(Love poem; Flood 2008, poem 1)

The river carries blue dawn and lingering city lights
on its slippery surface sheen,
and it is viscous below with lessening cold as it
transports the remnants of winter south,
where they will be tasted like dessert
in places where the kitchen tables have not been limited
to endless sacks of winter from the root cellar.

It slides past this place where we've arrived,
after long journeys that have left us open and strong,
where together we count eagles and look forward to things,
pedal home on a tailwind, read to each other tangled in bed,
where the sly dimples in your cheeks
and the slow meals seasoned with warm light in red wine
sometimes stop me like the new-green rush of gladness

at the sudden appearance of spring.

River rising
(Flood 2008, poem 2)

Driving my sunrise morning route
on the road laid flat
and smooth and bold
by human hands
at water's edge,
I see that the river
has been raised
like a chest
swelled full with pride —
or a hard breath held
for the moment.

From the road,
at earth level,
it feels suddenly
like I am next to the sea,
which glistens muscular,
overlarge and daunting.

I cross the everyday bridge
above the river water,
amid tallish things —
grain elevators, offices,
eagle trees and concrete monuments —
that seem to be growing shorter
even as I drive;

the air faintly sharpens
with unease.

Again
(Flood 2008, poem 3)

Rain.
Again.

Each time,
afterward,
it seems so manageable,
just looking at the trim vessel
of the rain gauge
anchored in the flower bed
next to the red orange yellow
ordered row of zinnia,
clear glass tube
that I brought into my kitchen
and washed
once the snow mountain over it
had finally finished its slow disappearance,
the order of the black lines,
metric and English,
both,
the perfect clean curve
of the meniscus in the glass,
the invisible science
of surface tension
making reading the level
conveniently quick.

But again.
Again.

I fling the caught drops
into the grass,
destroying the evidence
under the momentary reappearance
of the embattled sun,
hoping against hope
that, downhill to the river,

the thousands
and thousands
and thousands
of bags
bulging with shovelsful
of muscle and grit
and the most desperate sort of hope
will hold.

But again.
And again.

And, in the end,
what can be done
against an inexhaustible force
but shovel and lift
and lean into it and
shovel and lift
and shovel —
until the walls reach the sky
and strength reaches its end
and, with the stench of
rotten black river mud
clinging to our nostrils,
all we can do
is find our babies
our lovers our brothers and sisters
the way it was before,
and hold them close
as we wait.

Again.

Crest, withdrawal
(Flood 2008, poem 4)

The crushing impact
takes so
very
long
to finish
and fall
silent.

Days
and days
and even longer.

A collision observable
in excruciating,
indelible
detail.

And finally,
the point being made,
resistance rendered
utterly impotent,
the bully's knee is slowly
slowly
lifted
from the chest,
slowly,
just enough
to permit
small breaths
of foul scraps of air;
lifted slowly,
just enough
to allow the eyes
to turn a little
and begin to see
all
that has been
destroyed.

To meet a flood
is exhausting work.

And yet
the sky
is glorious blue
inlaid with
soft clean clouds
laced with
gold filament,
and the bird
finds the perch
to which it carries
the branch
that will
eventually
again
be within reach.

Lesson

She was trying to get herself to stop counting steps.

It was stupid enough just trying not to step on any cracks without that footstep counter in her head constantly ticking: one hundred thirty-seven, one hundred thirty-eight, one hundred thirty-nine...

She decided to try to remember note-for-note the song she was working on for her piano lesson, picture it on the page in the red Thompson book, remember the fingering. Come to think of it, some of those fingerings were stupid, too — if you had to play the same note three times in a row, why shouldn't you just use the same finger each time instead of using three different ones? Her teacher was nice enough, but she was so deliberate and orderly, from her neat gray hair to her tidy muted apartment, that it seemed like they'd always be working on notes and fingers and never get to the *music*. That was why she spent most of her piano time at home fumbling through the Mozart and Beethoven sonatas in an old book of her mom's. That stuff felt like real music.

She got stuck at the second bar of the third line of the song in the red book — thanks to those sonatas — and heaved her school bag up higher on her shoulder. She wondered if the grapes left over from the lunch her mom had packed were getting squished beneath her books.

It was a nice day for October, and it felt good to walk, although, on principle, she probably would admit this only grudgingly to anyone else — it was a long way from Jackson Elementary to her teacher's apartment, almost a mile and a half. She had also once again successfully made it past the scariest part of the trip: Central.

Central was the crumbly red stone alternative high school in a run-down neighborhood, and lots of those kids hung around outside after school. Their size and advanced age, as opposed to her nine-year-old-ness, were bad enough, but their attitude was worse. Attitude wafted from them as foul and toxic as the smoke from the cigarettes they all smoked. They never had book bags or tucked-in shirts. They just slouched and smoked and leaned on walls and other inanimate objects and watched stuff: cars going by; the school doors, in case of authority figures; more cars going by; each other, to see what would happen next; her, when she had to walk by. After the first couple times, when they made fun of her favorite — up until then — pair of corduroys, dark green and red and flowered, she revised her route. Now, by the time she got to the school, she had already crossed the street so that it served as a buffer zone between them. She had also gotten really good at looking straight ahead while she walked: head up, shoulders back, stride long. Impervious.

Now a few blocks farther along, she let the day soak in: the afternoon sun over her right shoulder, the blue blue sky tucked down behind the big houses on the limestone bluff above the street, the goldening October trees, the good and dry brown leaves on the sidewalk to *caarunnch* with a well-placed heel-ball-toe, the soft *cathunk* from inside the box as the traffic signal changed on carless corners.

She was almost to the garage door at the back of the funeral home when she noticed the boys on the other side of the street, walking in the same direction. Green pants, white collared shirts: St. Columcille's, just like the boy whose half-hour piano lesson was after hers, the boy who scoffed at stupid fingerings just like she did — she knew, because at the end of her half hour their piano teacher always reminded her to practice them, and he always rolled his eyes and made a face behind the teacher's back at this reminder.

She was a public school girl in a Catholic school town, and her multicolored and patterned clothes were as identifiable a uniform as the boys' plain two colors. There were three of them, maybe a year or two older than she. Their walking and talking was tumbly like puppies playing. A piece of cake after the Central kids. When she saw one of the boys notice her, she stopped looking at them and assumed her practiced, non-acknowledging posture and stride. Straight ahead.

A car went by at 25 miles per hour, and after that was when she heard the first one, the click and rolling away of a small rock hitting the pebbly concrete near her. She felt her eyelids press back into her eye sockets. She hitched up her book bag, secured it, and lengthened her stride. Straight ahead.

Another rock landed in the boulevard grass three feet ahead and on her right — overestimating her pace but a little short. Then another one on the sidewalk. She couldn't help it; she had to look at them. She didn't understand. She looked question marks at them — then remembered herself and resumed faster, straight ahead.

She was breathing quickly and shallowly. She tried to think how many more blocks it was to her teacher's apartment, but the only thought she could find in her head was *why*. She didn't know what she should do. *Why* got in the way of anything she could say to them, in the way of figuring out where she could go for help, in the way of finding some defense. Her left knuckles were white on her book bag straps.

Another, this one dropping on the toe of her brown school loafers. The shock of actual contact made her head snap around to look at them again, and as she did, the last rock caught her in the head, right above and just to the side of her left eye. The four of them were caught, snared for an instant, as though the arc of the last rock had crystallized in the air over the street and bound their eyes, three pairs to her one. Frozen. Blurring.

The movement of her hand to her head broke the bond. The boys spun away and ran between the old houses backed up against the foot of the bluff, toward the stairway built into the limestone. She ducked her head, and her feet started walking again; and when she took her hand away from her head, there was blood on it. Bright red and sticky. It shimmered in the trickiness of the tears welling above her bottom lids. Above her walking feet, she felt like she couldn't breathe, like she was choking on *why*.

She was afraid of anyone seeing it, so with her good hand, she reached up and undid the barrette holding back her long hair, stashed the barrette in her pants pocket, and pushed forward her hair, a little stringy after a busy day at school, so that it hung over the bloody place. She noticed she was still walking. Since her book bag was on the same side as her bloody hand, she had to use her elbow to keep it from falling off her shoulder while she kept her hair forward and kept the blood from running anywhere on her face. She crossed a street without looking. She saw the legs of the blue mailbox on the corner of her teacher's block. She was almost there.

In the orderly, hushed apartment, her teacher made her lie down on the good couch with her shoes on. Her teacher told her to lie still, then went to call her mom and bring back a damp, cool washcloth. She lay there trying not to get her shoes or any blood on the couch, staring at the dim ceiling, and feeling the weight of *why* throughout her entire body.

* * * * *

On Saturday, she went with her mom on errands to the mall so that they could have lunch at the Walgreen's Restaurant. In the code between them, she knew that it was her mother's way of trying to make up for what the St. Columcille's boys had done, as consoling as a silent bedtime backrub or a game of double solitaire after a tough day. It was nice, her mom all to herself, all those choices on the huge plastic menu, the plate of fries and the squirty plastic ketchup bottle, chatting about what was going on at school and the books she'd checked out from the library.

Afterwards, she wanted to look in the pet store, and her mom had to pick up a catalog order from JC Penney's, so they decided to meet out front. She would be able to see her mom outside in the car through the pet store window when it was time to go.

She didn't really like the way the pet store smelled — a little damp and full of gross food and weird litter box-ish smells — but she liked to meet the animals, especially the big birds you could talk to and the kittens. She liked to get up close to them and have private conversations, although something always nagged a little bit in the back of her mind that maybe it wasn't really nice to get so close to the animals in their cages in case they ended up liking you and it made them get their hopes up that you'd take them home and you really couldn't.

The hand-lettered sign in the front window said "KITTENS," and so she walked in, looking around in anticipation. They always seemed to move the kitten cage around, but it never really made sense why. Today the cage was tucked away next to the dark, damp fish section, and when she found it, she thought that they should change the sign outside to read "KITTEN WITH NO S." She felt sorry for it, alone in the cage, and bent forward to talk quietly with it.

It was nine weeks old, according to the sign, and starting to grow into its catness. It was fuzzy white with black spots, and she laughed to herself because it reminded her of a cow; if she could take it home, she'd name it Bessie or Heydiddlediddle. It had been sleeping curled up in a back corner, but at the sound of her voice, it twitched an ear, as though her voice were a bug to flick away, and then opened its eyes. It lifted up its head and watched her.

She tried to entice it up to the front of the cage so she could pet it through the bars. Remembering having read somewhere that the best way to catch a cat's eye is with horizontal movement, she started fluttering her fingers back and forth along the cage bars. At first only the cat's head moved, but gradually more and more of its body woke up and started preparing to pounce. When its little back end started wiggling, she knew she almost had it.

They played a while, and then she stopped to pet it. She could fit most of her hand — up to right before the bottom of her thumb — between the bars. The kitten sniffed her hand, licked off the last of the french fry grease, and rubbed its little jaw along her fingers.

Her absolute favorite part of a cat was the nose — its understatedness and compactness; the pale pink; the rough texture of the short, close-lying hairs, almost like their tongues; the dip at the top up to the forehead. She rubbed the kitten's ears the way she knew cats liked, if you do it right, and worked her way down toward the nose. They never let you just go straight for the nose. You had to work up their trust that you'd be gentle before they'd let you.

She rubbed the kitten's head the best she could through the bars, and since there was too much mall noise around to hear, she felt for its purr. She rubbed and scratched, and it leaned its warm, slight weight into her hand. She would feel bad to just leave it, but she was getting a little bored, so she looked around the store as she rubbed. Looking over her shoulder to the windows into the bird room, she saw the St. Columcille's boy who had the piano lesson after hers looking at the big parrot with his mom.

Without really looking back at the kitten, she cocked her middle finger behind her thumb and thwacked it right on the pale pink little nub.

She froze, her eyes now on the kitten, her hand still outstretched. The kitten jerked its head away and scooched a couple of steps backward. It crouched warily, looking at her through blinking eyes.

She remembered her mom and wiggled her hand back out from between the bars. Walking quickly toward the store entrance, her forehead itched. She reached up, picked off the scab, and flicked it from under her fingernail to the ground behind her as she left the store. Exposed to the air, the spot stung a little.

The big blue car was waiting, and she opened the door, got in, and slammed it shut in one swift movement.

"You spent a while in there — there must have been kittens today."

"Uh uh — they didn't have any left."

As her mom pulled away from the curb, she turned up the radio even though she knew her mom didn't like it — but then again, neither did she, really. Rolling down her window, she let the wind mess up her hair and rush over the raw skin and blow *why* all over her.

The Ice Cream Man

I love *the ice cream man!*
she proclaims from her green plastic wagon throne,
her young voice ringing clean
like a ripple from a pebble dropped splashless
into the calm of the neighborhood twilight.
Her beloved's white van has glided on
to troll the next street,
its speaker like a horizontal cow bell
over and over
clablaring one ragged Joplin phrase
that breaks weakly over the roofs,
scratchy and wobbly like a sun-warped 45
and slightly smudged
in the colored bomb pop sugar
that drips from her dimpled hands.

I'm gonna cause a car crash!
he screams gleefully,
crouched low over the handlebars, elbows poking up like cricket legs,
whizzing down the hill into the left-hand turn in the gap between cars,
imagining all the tremendous G forces pulling his cheeks taut,
his eyebrows toward his summer crew cut,
and the corners of his mouth back into a grin.
Waaaaiit uuup!
his pursuer's voice jiggles over the bumpy yard,
an undignified shortcut with no Gs
and no excitement of potential crashes
but leaving a great big bike wake that cuts a foamy swath
over the near-dew neighborhood
and points, slightly sticky,
toward the sweet promise of the distant white van.

Saturday Night — No Change

"Hi,"
he calls, singsong,
testing.
His short thin body
drapes and twists
over and around and through
the silent stadium's concentric railing,
absently,
the way old little kids do
when they're half playing,
half watching.
In the city twilight,
when the squinty day glare
and the alley dark night
are bridged by softness and
punctuated in neon,
his buddies trip and sprint,
a tiny kaleidoscope of T-shirts and no rules
flickering against the soaring, echoey bulk
that had cupped the sunny afternoon baseball crowds,
while the boy's dark limbs
poke bare out of their cuffs and
entangle in the wrought iron bars
to make the fence spring alive
for just a moment of its monotony,
a spider spindly and webbing.
"Mister,
you got thirty cents
so we can get a soda?"
With a sunburned hand,
Mister pats the pocket
inside his light summer dress pants.
But the boy knows this script well,
so even before the mister speaks,
he gets ready for the next scene,
de-spidering the rail,
poised to move on and web elsewhere.
Mister: "Sorry — no change."

For variety, the boy half-jokes:
"How about a five?"
and they both laugh a little.
He slips away from the fence, and
the boys' jumping, running, bumping kaleidoscope
grows one piece bigger and
disappears,
shifting, kaleiding
around the
ball
park's
curve.

Truth

We are covered in lies.
Ingenious things,
these lies,
like burs.
We pick them off
ourselves,
each other,
toss them out
the windows
of moving cars
on city streets.
Their stray hooks
remain embedded
in our clothes,
our skin,
and prickle quietly
when we undress
for each other.

A habit dying

His voice
is like an empty coffee can.
The love words he flicks out underhand
rattle hard and brief
like a flatworn penny or two
jangling to a quick stop
on the shiny tin bottom.

Containment

There is a small sliver of herself
that she keeps on the other side of her skin.
It paces back and forth
when it can no longer stand to be still,
holds glances a little too boldly,
makes brushing contact unnecessarily
while pretending not to notice,
imagines things —
she sometimes thinks to check the mirror
to see if it shows through the chinks.

She stands stretched in the window,
feels what her taut body looks like, and
takes her time pulling the shade
between the rising dark outside
and the bedside lamp inside —
she likes how *slow* makes her feel dangerous.

Discovered the next morning

Near midnight:

She put on her coat, adjusted her hat,
and draped her purse over a thin, tremulous arm
to shuffle forth in slippered feet.
The deep night was luminous
with powdery snow that welcomed her
and held her soft
and slowly still
until such time as she could be recovered.

So it is with us, my dear:

Coat, hat, all preparations made,
to step with mistaken certitude
into the beckoning lethal dream
that tenderly awaits.

Bus Stop

She's a dark spot toward the back,
from what she can tell
in the plate glass reflection
when the bus slides past the candy store
from its place in the night lineup on Main.
She sways on blue vinyl
and the bus is
a creaky tube of fluorescent light
nosing through cracked streets.
The seat back and textured metal wall
corner her shoulder,
and only her eyes need to move.
She watches the city pass.
The picture keeps
slipping out of the frame,
underexposed,
memorized,
the focus softening and crisping
with her breaths.
Overhead, the buzzer cord
flaps gently at the curves,
the window frame gives
a little rattle at the hills.
Her jacket collar
funnels warmth up to her face,
where her eyes register
her stop.
She gently sways.
She has never before watched
her stop drift past.
She thinks that the stops are
like leaves
carried south on the skin of a river.

Seasonal

Spring rises from the graveyard,

puts softness back on the trees and
drinks in our cups and
laughter in our exposed throats,
and it lures us closer to each other.

But I'm finding dozens of tiny insects
skilled in the arts of camouflage and tenaciousness
at home on the undersides of the cut flowers
I've filled my rooms with,

and there's winter creeping from within my chest,
flickering against the underside of my skin,
hot like the first blind touch of ice,
then racing like flame on a thin line of fuel,

a frozen breath spreading outward from the center,
leaving in its wake expanses of flesh drowned in ice,
fit and smooth and very still,
carrying an extravagant gorgeousness

of sparkle and gleam
that would crack and fall
with one well-placed tap
or accidental shiver.

When I was a kid, we had surreptitious contests
to see whose bare foot could stay still the longest
on an ice cube under the dinner table.
The winners knew how to embrace the burning cold —

gleaming fit and smooth and very still.

LIVE MUSIC 9–1

Rhythm blazes out the alley door
and starts the edges of the night to melting.
They warp a little first,
turn shiny, wavy, slick with neon.

Midnight, a rumpled bartender steps out the door,
slouches into a cigarette,
scrapes his palm across dark stubble,
and watches the night gather and trickle
past his shoes down broken concrete to the street.

The view from the second bar stool

The air is callused
and stained nicotine yellow
and gives the paths
of words and looks and bottles
fuzzed edges and scuff marks
they wouldn't have in the crisp black
outside the steamed-up door.
Rumpled plaid flannel,
dark stubble rising on a square jaw,
a partially peeled beer bottle label;
he pushes up his whole self
to angle toward her
next to him on the booth bench.
She faces straight across the table
and lets him look.
Her eyes fall on the studied, failed shot
at the pool table,
the loosened tie and wrinkled suit coat
leaning and twitching over the pinball machine,
the jukebox changing,
while her body warms barely perceptibly
in the places his eyes travel.
She lets him look.
She reaches for her beer,
his hand lightly touches her hair,
palm and fingers, darkened by the day,
stretch across the surface,
follow the fine brown shoulder length,
cradle her beneath her hair,
tentatively, gently, exquisitely.
She leans into his palm
and closes her eyes.

Baby Girls

We happily announce the arrival of

Bridget Caroline Horn Brown

Born 2:42 P.M., May 2, 2000
7 pounds, 1 ounce
20 inches

* * * * *

May 17, 2000
...Hope you are doing well! I'll call soon to gain your tips & wisdom before our turn to welcome a daughter. What fun to think that our girls may one day sit together at Sunday school!

Warmest wishes & blessings!
Sam & Carlyn

* * * * *

July 23, 2000

Because we know that you care about us, we want you to know that our wished-for, much loved baby passed quickly through our lives. Our daughter Mae was born on Friday, June 16 and died on Tuesday, June 20, 2000.

Late in my pregnancy, Mae bled in utero, which caused severe oxygen deprivation. At birth, she had major organ damage and devastating brain damage. She died in our arms.

"What we have once enjoyed and deeply loved, we can never lose, for all that we love becomes part of us." Helen Keller

Dear Jennifer,

I am so very sad to send you this news. How I'd looked forward to becoming better friends with you as we shared the joys of motherhood....

Carlyn

* * * * *

It's a gorgeous Sunday morning. October is taking its time in fall-ing, and the utterly blue sky breathes the promise of warmth in through the open windows around town. Five-month-old Miss Bridget and I head into the narthex of our church as I, awkwardly as always, carry her in her car seat, trying not to bang her in her into my leg too much.

Today is confirmation day for the ninth graders, and among the confirmation service crowd are Carlyn and Sam. I set the 20-some pounds of baby and equipment on the floor at our feet, and they bend down to see her. She studies their faces and smiles. I squat and unbuckle her, trying not to lose my balance, take her out, and hug her. Sam has never met Bridget before. So I hand her to him, and they begin to chat. After a few minutes of talking with Carlyn, I kneel back down to Sam and Bridget. When Sam turns his face to me, it is wet with tears.

Sam carries Bridget into the sanctuary; Carlyn and I follow with the assorted baby equipment. Sometimes I forget just how striking Bridget is — the three-inch Mohawk waving atop the alert and happy porcelain doll face — but I'm always reminded when we're in public. Her passing by seems to make the world smile the same way the passing breeze makes the leaves flutter on the trees. The row of high school girls, draped in cream choir robes and maroon stoles, turns and smiles at the baby as we sit behind them. I know how proud I am to carry Bridget through the world, even though her beauty and charm are someone else's handiwork and nothing I can take credit for; I am wondering what feelings are crossing Sam's chest as he, for this moment, carries a perfect baby girl through the world.

Bridget likes to talk. From very early on, she'd look earnestly at you and maneuver her tongue and lips in the sincerest conversation. Sometimes there was sound, sometimes there wasn't. After a few weeks of exploring the mechanics of her mouth, she moved on to expand her vocal range. It didn't take long for her to discover her upper register and the joys of making noises for the sake of making noises. She learned that you can add sound effects to the bubble-making process, and soon a sort of Bronx cheer became the unmistakable signal of Bridget frustration. Then she moved on to experiment with volume control. Every once in a while, a great blast like a truck horn will startle us, including, possibly, Bridget herself.

She practices her noises and learns new ones every day, it seems. In the early morning, baby noises float through the dim bedroom light and down the hall as she has quiet conversations with herself. When she and I drive to preschool and I sing our morning songs, she sings along. When she's tired, she makes a steady, low noise like a lawn mower a block away.

The last Sunday we were at church, Bridget spent the majority of the service being carried around outside the church. The acoustics of the sanctuary are amazing — a three-second hang time for an organ note — and they sent her nonstop baby song into every pew and corner. Perched against a shoulder, she moved through the rest of the church building and the neighborhood until she'd finished her long song.

This Sunday, though, she somehow knows she needs to be quiet so she can stay where she is. She studies Sam, then Carlyn. As they talk softly to her, smile, make faces, cry, she steadily watches everything and turns on the sunshine of her smile from time to time. She turns her head as far as she can to look across the pews behind her, to look up at the lights hanging high from the ceiling, to watch the cream and maroon choir row stand up together. She rests her head on her multiple chins and pooches out her jowls to study the wrinkles that form and smooth out in Sam's shirt. She reaches out to touch the pin on Carlyn's shirt. She holds up her hands for examination while rubbing them together, then jams them both into her mouth.

And she doesn't say a word.

Sam and Carlyn share Bridget. Carlyn shows Sam how Bridget grasps her finger. "She's so strong!" she whispers to him. Bridget teaches Sam that she likes standing best, so his solid hands hold her around the rib cage, and she wobbles her hula dance of imperfect balance.

Right around sermon time, Bridget gets a little fussy. She starts to squirm and makes small grunts and whines. The ancient parent instinct kicks in, and Sam begins to gently bounce and rock Bridget. After a minute, her left thumb finds her mouth, she tucks her head, and she nestles into Sam's chest. The three of us silently laugh at her honest and accurate appraisal of the sermon situation. Sam blows his nose.

Most of the sermon is an awful story about an orphanage somewhere in the former Soviet Union. A building full of children no one wanted or could afford to keep. A building full of children deemed damaged, flawed. There was the baby with the cleft palate. The one who was so unpleasant. The blind one the workers didn't bother with because it would just be a waste of resources.

Sam leans across Bridget's sleepy head and whispers to Carlyn, "I'd take any of them."

"Hannah Grace, child of God..." "Jacob Tyler, child of God..." The ninth graders look awkward and proud and uncertain as they are confirmed. I watch and remember my own confirmation, when I wondered if I was the only kid in the class who worried I didn't believe or understand enough of the Affirmation of Baptism, not sure what I really thought about the whole thing. These are the kids of the first Sunday school class that Carlyn taught. They are grown up, and she is proud of them as they share an experience she once thought Bridget and Mae might share. She tells me which girl would make the best baby-sitter.

Bridget sleeps against Sam's chest. His silent sobs bounce her gently, rhythmically. She is warm and peaceful.

There is a special hymn for the confirmation class, and I spend most of the time unable to read the words. The congregation sings, "I was there to hear your borning cry, I'll be there when you are old. I rejoiced the day you were baptized, to see your life unfold." Behind the sweet melody, I hear the awful silence of Mae's borning cry.

I shove wadded up Kleenex into my purse, and Sam hands Bridget back to me. She is fuzzy and heavy with sleep, one cheek rosy and wrinkled from his shirt. After the service, he and Carlyn help me get Bridget and all the assorted baby gear in order. Carlyn introduces Bridget and me to her recommended baby-sitter, who is tall in her white robe and her red corsage, whose face says she is thinking of Carlyn's baby girl.

Later in the day, I am holding Bridget, breathing her. I realize she smells faintly of Sam, cologne and warmth. I think of my own dad's scent, a combination of Mennen Speedstick deodorant and the certainty that he can fix anything that needs fixing. I wonder what scents Bridget will associate with her dad. And I hope that Mae could know that she was nestled in a good place during her brief stay.

Little Brother Lessons

After lights-out time,
from my top-bunk throne,
I send down words for him to learn
like messages hooked and dangling
from a fishing pole.
I command him to repeat
the things I know that he must learn.
He would like me to stop,
but still his little boy voice
burbles up sleepily in the dark
past stuffed animals
and Golden books and Matchbox cars
to my high-up perch.
My little brother.
My pupil.
I am six
and very smart.

My little brother stoops some now
because he towers so,
nearer than most
to doorway lintels and light fixtures.
These days when I can't quite reach,
he catches the hooks and
smoothes out the messages,
then holds them up for me to read.

He is my younger bigger brother
and very smart.

Toward the Man in the Moon

Last night,
after a life of not seeing him,
I finally saw the man in the moon.
As I drove through wide spaces,
there was a red-faced struggle with the horizon —
then he broke free and rose to white
and hovered above the belly of the earth,
where I recognized him at last
and grinned up at the prize
over the top of my steering wheel.

Harvest was in urgent progress,
field after field being gathered up
by black hulks carrying white spots of light
and kicking up slow shadow clouds of dust.
The man in the moon
bent his head to us
and breathed in the incense
of late fall.
At the edge of an inward breath
I suddenly felt the scent
of children yet to carry,
sleep-warm skin and fine tufts of hair,
and I couldn't wait to show them
what I'd finally found.

If we are lucky

They take me by surprise
when I suddenly see them showing through.
And when I glimpse one,
there is a quick and quiet catch
in my breath.
These small surprises are
like the fabric backing
where the velvet has worn away,
the color faded to slightly off,
not what is supposed to show.
They are the tenderness —
something nice but out of fashion,
snippets of myth
laid bare in shifted light.

And I think,
if we are lucky in our work
that takes us to that moment
when we finally gather up the courage
to offer their downy fledgling feathers to the winds,
this is what we prepare our children for:
to think tenderly of
the places they
no longer want to be.

Shared Custody

My daughter rides her bike
around one corner and up a short jog to the next,
turning around at the top
to pedal, hard and leaning over the handlebars
as though inviting gravity to climb on
her six-and-three-quarters-years-old back for the ride down —
all this a skill she has taken firm and joyful ownership of
in just the past two weeks,
still in the winter cold,
through false starts and tipped-over stops,
innumerable shin bruises and ripped-out play pants knees,
and her hallmark fierce determination.

She comes and goes from my view
as I slowly make my way
through minor tasks at the kitchen sink,
standing in the dusk falling through my window.

I know that when she's called inside,
her cheeks will be bright blooms of pink,
her lips pale cornflower cold,
and the backs of her unmittened hands sandpaper rough.
I know that she will be quivery with excitement
and dramatic with her stories.
I know what her hair will smell like,
with the cold and fresh almost-but-not-quite spring air
mixed in with earnest sweat
and last night's shampoo and conditioner.

But tonight is not one of my nights,
and she will go home through another door.
As I stand with wet hands and face,
I feel again how some problems
are simply unsolvable.

Pirates

In the tree
in the row
lining the drive
of the cemetery,
small pirates
climb treacherous rigging
while sailing vast seas
in exhilarating pursuit
of adventure
and treasure,
gold and fancy bracelets,
and tasty food
seasoned with
found fabric petals and
stirred to perfection
with a stick
in the knothole
at six-year-old height.

Arr, me mateys!
Load up the bombs!
Attack the giant squid!

They know
to retreat
when it is time
for the regular business
of the cemetery
to be conducted;
they abandon ship,
leaping
from green heights,
ponytails slapping,
to row nimbly homeward,

wordlessly neatening
fallen bouquets
and windblown trinkets
they find in their path
as they yield the right of way
to quiet people
getting out of their cars.

Having met

I have this feeling that
our kid selves recognize each other,
outliers both,
not comfortably at home
in the skin of the world around them
and, so, they found ways to slip out —
into the woods on a hill
into the wind on a bike
into the words appearing on a page.

I have this sense of
watching you approach through your years —
boy, man, soul,
sculpting your dolphin self, your flying self,
streamlined and sleek,
to leap and glide through the dappled spaces
where the shadows of meteors
and Queen Anne's lace and rippling currents
flash and weave skylit patterns
in translucent walls
where you've planted your house
on green banks.

I have this sense of
your presence as I approach,
finding my way back to the water
after nearly drowning in the desert
without the woods
the wind
the words to buoy me,
but remembering now
how to delight in my strength,
in my spirit,
what I know with my skin
hennaed with lace of wildflowers and light.

And now,
having met and walked a while,
sharing company but not a path,
trading flying lessons for delight
and road maps for small treasures,
I know what I carry,
kitchen warm and green-hills free,
within me,
anywhere.

Cherries

WASHED SWEET CHERRIES
off the main road a bit,
so we detour,
traveling with a dust flourish at the tires
like a magician's silk scarf
meandering up through the spaces
of the tall thin pines
that have tripped
off-balance over the edge of the dirt track.
We don't know if we'll find cherries down this road,
but we like that someone made the sign say "WASHED."
We stretch our heads out the front windows
and catch sundrops through the branches
on our tongues like rain,
washed sweet.

Opening Scene ~Telluride, CO

A sheep *baa*s from somewhere inside
the covered, dirty white pickup truck bed
parked at the curb
that he passes while walking east
toward the craggy end wall of the box canyon.
He's ambling down the middle of Main Street
atop a stride that swings
from hip sockets as loose-fitting as his brown pants
with the frayed fringe at the bottoms,
the purple and gold and orange tunic,
the scraggly, thin beard of 19.
Propped up on his backpack
above his stringy brown hair
is a cardboard sign that reads:
WHERE'S ANN?
He's running out of street.

Sparrow

Her head bounces
like an exquisite bauble
against her breast
as she struggles to escape the garage.

It is a bright roundness of eyes
set softly in small feathers
between the tidy curve of her head
and firm jut of her beak —

and it hangs from the point where
her neck has broken,
a terrible mishandling
of someone else's treasure.

It's difficult to navigate
now that her view
is limited to looking hard
at her twig feet on the concrete,

but she manages;
she rounds the corner
and I follow,
trying to think what to do.

She hops a ragged path
through brown side-yard grass,
then flies low through the linked fence
that keeps in the neighbors' dogs.

I tense to warn her away —
then stop,
ashamed to have been thinking
of the shovel hung on the wall.

These are not my choices to make.

Into White

In the face of
winter's early sighs,
fall died within the small, screened container —

supple leaves turned dull,
clover shriveled into brown,
and the captured wooly caterpillar disappeared.

On a weather-worn rail it sat,
wrapped hard in stiff, gray cold,
overcome by inanimation,

until, in soft opposition,
spring rose up
and shook from a brittle, curled-up leaf

a moth in even trade.
As she hung still, exposed,
on a bare wood wall,

a deliberate wisp of breeze
pushed through the screen.
She stretched.

Involuntarily, luxuriously,
she unfolded her wings
as they were meant:

to catch the fluid air.
And, spread to their full span,
her wings glowed the infinite white

of stark moon and crystalline snow
pressed to a powdery smoothness
designed for uncontained spring flight.

Poetry Shmoetry:
In the Basement, Decorah, Iowa

In an old brick building on Decorah's historic Water Street, we navigate, brown beer bottles sweating cold in our hands, toward periodic explosions of raucous ovation that have been blasting up from the basement and into the beer garden. After passing the barbershop, which is still doing a brisk business in a back nook of the building, and descending the turning, wide wooden stairs, we reach the basement and what the posters advertise as Poetry Shmoetry, a reading/slam. ("Recite from your favorites; share your creations; revel in the rhyme; commit random acts of poetry; short musical performances will also be welcomed.")

The room at the bottom of the stairs is dark and cavernous. Thick, square wooden posts hold up the building's first floor, a fireplace is dark in the stone wall at the front, and a small bar curves out from a front corner of the room. People sit in clumps with their drinks at longish tables like at a church potluck. There is a soft, ambient cushion of voices, but most people are listening to someone at the front of the room who is hidden from us at the moment.

There aren't any tables completely unoccupied, so we stand at the edge of the room to figure out where to park ourselves. Two women, who have the bearing of event organizers, slide a small table over from a wall to the edge of the rest of the tables. We move sideways a couple of feet so that we can see around the wooden posts, and the emcee of the poetry reading/slam comes into view. The women mean for us to sit at the table they've just moved, and I'm surprised and moved by their hospitality.

But my attention is divided. The emcee is in the prime of young adulthood, tight and wearing a short black leather miniskirt and a sleeveless, deep red, fitted top. His bosom is only slightly lumpy, his stomach is taut and flat, and he has really nice, smooth muscular arms and legs. The women slide chairs up to the table and gesture for us to sit. The emcee is tall in his high pumps, and he leans back straight-legged into his heels and bends from the waist while keeping his head up to speak into the microphone, not unlike a woman bending over to tease with a little cleavage. We thank the two women and sit down with our beers.

* * * * *

Apparently, it's nearly time for a break. The emcee — his name is Jake — takes a turn. First, stooping down slightly from his pumps, he reads a poem he's written. He writes of desire — someone else's for him, I think, if I make the assumption that the "I" is the poet — and of his arms "hilly with strength," which startles me because I've noticed. Then, because it's a favorite of his, he reads a howling

Ginsberg poem, this one about food. Well, maybe it's not *about* food, but that's all I can think of as the barrage of food images comes flying at me over the PA. Gluttony, overindulgence, excesses that tax everyone but the young to exhaustion. It's as though the poem's words leave a slight film of warm lard over the mouth and brain. Emcee Jake is cheerful when he finishes and tells us to be ready for more after this breather.

* * * * *

One of the women who arranged our table comes over to chat during the break. Her name is Toni; she's with the public library, a cosponsor of the event, and is transplanted here from Vermont. I am impressed that a public library is helping to sponsor an event at which alcohol is welcome, even necessary for some participants. The liberal university town I come from is too politically correct to allow this kind of aid for poets at a public library event. Toni tells us that we just missed the eight-year-old girl reading her own poem, which was marvelous.

Toni seems both pleased and uncertain about the way this event has turned out, seems both involved and removed. I wonder if this dichotomous feeling I get from her is an extension of her unchangeable status as an outsider in this small town while being involved in one of its more high-profile institutions. She is told I am a poet, which is a title I still don't feel confident assuming, sort of like the way it took me a long time to stop being surprised to be referred to as a woman rather than a girl. But with my notebook of early drafts and miscellaneous notes to myself sticking out of my purse, I can't claim that I have nothing to read. She steers me up to the bar, where Jake is manning the sign-up list. He asks if I prefer to sign up for the reading or the slam, and he doesn't put any pressure on me when I tell him I don't think I'm prepared for the slam. I've never approached poetry as a competitive sport before.

I make sure I notice the name on the list right before mine: Dennis.

* * * * *

The break is over; we have more beer. "This is a poem about death," the next reader says as he situates himself in front of the microphone, shifting his feet and folding back the pages of his wire-bound notebook. He's wearing blue jeans and a rumply button-down shirt, and he looks like he half expects to be beaten up, not by someone in the room, necessarily, but in general. And he also has that look of defiance that says he'd tell you he was better than you, even if you *were* beating him up. I can't pay much attention to his poem. I keep thinking about how I feel guilty about thinking it is so cliché that he is reading a poem he wrote about death.

* * * * *

"I added the third x a few years ago," Maxxximum Madcap — the cartoonist formerly known as Carl — will tell you. He has dark blond hair that flows in waves from his bald spot and very large, masculine glasses. In the dim light of the bar basement, I can see that his considerable chest hair curls above the top of his turquoise, spaghetti strap dress, which is covered loosely by a black, blousy jacket with pinstripes of gold lamé. His tall, black, strappy pumps fit perfectly at the end of muscular, hairy legs and make him at least six three — it's hard to tell exactly when I'm sitting down. He tells me, "No one thinks twice about you as a woman wearing those pants," gesturing to my springy-green-plaid capri pants, "and they shouldn't. I'm a guy who likes to wear dresses. So what?" I have to agree.

He's a friendly guy, very enthusiastic about the impressive turnout at this first in what he hopes is a long line of "Poetry Shmoetry" readings/slams. He is an editor of the fledgling local arts-and-opinion quarterly, *Valley Voice*, which is the other cosponsor of this event in honor of National Poetry Month.

Maxxx is also buoyed by the wild applause and hollering in response to his performance moments ago of an original limerick, self-accompanied on alto sax. It was a combination of prepared performance and improvisation. Host Jake assured the crowd that we could expect something great from this next performer, although, upon his arrival at the mike, Maxxx told us he wasn't so sure how great it'd be. After the first part of his performance, which revolved around wetting his reed and to which the audience responded with enthusiastic applause, his limerick began. Reading from a notebook placed on a music stand, he spoke the first line slowly and robustly, with drama.

"There once was a lass from Nantucket..."

He paused, put the mouthpiece — with wetted reed — to his lips, and sent his sax off on a freeform, mood-enhancing journey, bending and waving his body with the notes. He broke off the sax improvisation at a high point:

"...Who kept all her jewels in a bucket..."

And he climbed back on the sax for another wild ride.

Maxxx has no illusions about his poetic abilities, but he does trust his sense of humor.

When he was done, he grinned and bowed; the audience loved it and let him know. As he and his sax walked offstage, emcee Jake gave him a quick kiss.

* * * * *

Earlier in the day, the massage therapist — a quiet woman wearing Birkenstocks and no makeup — discussed the fact that the town is a little too small and buttoned up for her; she stays only because her high school freshman daughter loves it there. Massage therapy is relatively new to the town, and business is pretty good because there isn't much competition. She can't predict how it will be once the novelty wears off, when people stop giving gift certificates for massages. With reserved, Norwegian Lutheran guilt in the bones of almost the entire town, she says that lots of clients have a hard time even admitting, "That feels *good*."

I think that tonight we must have entered a different town from the one she lives in.

* * * * *

The on-the-spot poetry writing team of college students is taking longer to finish their poem than they had expected. The emcee calls them up, but they holler that they're not ready. He moves on to the next person on the list, a nervous-looking man who checks with Jake to verify that the limit is three poems, then starts with a poem he's written that ponders the meaning of a squirrel in a tree.

More death: A college girl gets up to read. She tells us that this is a poem about death. She considered death last semester.

I'm trying to pay attention, but I'm also trying to figure out what to read when it's my turn. My turn must not be too far away. My notebook has only rough drafts. In pencil. The basement is dark. In between sips of beer and rounds of applause, I am trying to figure out exactly what I've written on these pages. I'm trying to remember what revisions I made after these penciled drafts, revisions that were revised again, revisions that ostensibly made them better poems. I'm trying to figure out which poems to read. I'm trying to think of pithy, clever introductions to the poems I choose. I'm trying to figure out who I want to be in front of this room of strangers.

* * * * *

The next one is a skinny guy, young, with really short hair and a small bit of a dark goatee. The posters say you can read your own poetry or someone else's. This guy nervously tells us that he's decided to sing two things. Songs are poems, too.

He's a little tall for the mike, so he stoops. The first song is an Irish ballad. I think that we're in a good place for this — a bar, a basement, with friendly strangers, lots of feelings, and beer. His voice wobbles around the pitch a little; it's like a kid walking a curb with his arms outstretched, teetering sharply to crazy angles to keep his balance. As he gets farther into the song, though, his voice finds more secure balance. It's a nice voice, unadorned.

The second song is an Elvis song. It takes me a minute to understand that it's Costello, not Presley. By this time, the guy seems to have succeeded in largely ignoring the rest of us in the room. He sings strong, with a late 20th-century Top 40 slide in his voice, and I imagine him singing about uncooperative love into a pop-bottle microphone in his bedroom late at night.

* * * * *

Emcee Jake introduces Dennis. Which means that, suddenly, I am next. I think I should be gracious and considerate and pay attention to Dennis. I have no idea what he read.

The audience is applauding Dennis. Emcee Jake is telling everyone that Jennifer is next.

I've decided to read two poems; two poems will allow me to be more-dimensional than if I read just one, right? I've dog-eared the pages of these two poems, even though it turns out they are on consecutive pages. I've penned in a couple of revisions and words I couldn't read easily in the dim. As I walk around the edge of the room up toward the stage, I'm trying to remember what I came up with for my pithy, clever introductions and also to look confident. Emcee Jake gives me an encouraging smile.

At the microphone, I tell everyone that I'm on vacation, so I figured I might as well read because no one here knows me. They *laugh*. I read my first poem, the one funny poem I have. At the end of the second stanza, when you're supposed to figure out what really bizarre thing has just happened in the poem, I pause and think, *Rats, it doesn't go over without being able to read it on the page* — and then they *laugh*. I read the last stanza, the one that's kind of over the top, and they laugh, a lot, and *clap*. I have a brief, pathetic, out-of-the-movies moment when I have to make sure that I don't exclaim aloud, "You *like* me — you really *like* me!"

Then it's time for the serious poem I've chosen, one of the poems I'm most proud of. I make myself not rush through the reading. I try to read what it means. I wonder what meaning the people in the room find in it and whether it's what *I* think the poem means. I come to the end, the revised end as best as I can remember it, there's a small pause, and then applause. And yelling. And I'm relieved and happy. As I walk away from the microphone, emcee Jake gives me one of those end-of-the-game high fives along with his smile.

* * * * *

Only two on-the-spot college poetry writers remain in the room; they decide to just go with what they have, and they read to us some striking images. A young woman reads about the surprise of a plant growing from a seed she planted when her roommate left, and then reads her poetic feminist treatise. A man gets up and plays a hammered dulcimer, the poor man's harp.

They are all relieved and happy and enveloped in a mist of applause by the time they sit back down.

Someone asks me if I've published any of my poetry.

The three brave slam competitors read one by one; two read their own poetry, one reads someone else's. The judges are blustery but gentle.

When the slam champion is announced, there is great cheering. People chat, finish drinks, begin to drift away. We wend our way back up the stairs, where the barbershop chair *still* has a customer in it.

We start down the dark street, trailing bits of poetry behind us.

* * * * *

What a beautiful thing, to be a star for just a little while for speaking poetry in a public place.

Simplifying

Her sigh
knocked the moon loose from the horizon
and it floated up to hover above the trees,
translucent, fragile.
Another quick puff of breath
blew the stars from dim earthbound rest
to hang suspended, winking,
like house dust blown from furniture,
and begin the slow descent
toward morning.
She paused still a moment,
inhaled the cool,
then slung the night around her shoulders
to darken her from sight.
She began to dig
in steady rhythm:
dig in, toss dirt,
dig in, toss dirt,
dig in, toss dirt.
When the hole was deep enough,
she set aside her shovel
and reached in past her cloak
into herself
deep
and what she pulled out
she laid gently in the hole.
She reached in several times
and used both hands
to cradle the things that shone faintly
in the light that is the best the night sky can do.
When she'd finished,
she tugged the night again tightly around her,
knelt at the hole,
and scooped the dirt with her hands
to cover softly what had filled her.

In the morning,
when her fists had lost their grip on the night cloak
and, uncovered, she watched the sun
quiver in its shape as it squeezed fluorescent
up through the horizon,
she felt her insides shift,
settle into the empty places,
and the light hurt her someplace past her eyes.

Morning Triptych

He drops the glimpse caught in the corner of his eye:
she's late and half jogging down the side street,
her business pumps-filled bag bouncing off her hip.
He fills his eyes up with the road and lays his boot sole on the floor;
his bus growls up the hill past her on a diesel cloud.

There's a big silver rig parked on the shoulder of the on ramp
between prairie towns, in the middle of a two-week run.
He opens the driver's side, emerges pantsless in the doorway,
and lets it swing in the morning sun, grinning at wide eyes accelerating past.

On my way in, I drive impatient in the left lane,
steering with my knee as I write notes to myself,
and I don't swerve for roadkill. Thumpthump.

Falling Time

The sky was moving too fast
in the wrong direction;
time spattered the windows,
then gathered in rivulets
that ran down to the tulip husks
and nourished their decay,
brownly bent over the foundation dirt.

She removed her socks and shoes,
lined them up next to the door,
and stepped out into the deluge,
tipping her face open-mouthed
to the wrong-way sky
so the weeks and minutes and decades
could tumble down her throat to her soles.

She stood still to let the downpour claim her
and watched the falling moments with closed eyes,
swallowing smells and sounds and colors,
feeling earlier and later and now all at once.
She heard a tulip bloom,
breathed a warm quilt beneath winter's weight,
and felt regret and doubt and fear

lift away from her
with the silent roar
of a feathered flock
rising from budding limbs
to soar through new spaces on the sphere.
She stood, upturned, lightened, unmapped, and,

gently, it began to rain.

LISA ROBERTS

When I was between eight and eleven, gearing up to the height of my preteen drama queen years, I made myself a scrapbook out of my sister Sarah's discarded drafting homework (nice, thick paper.) I wrote a scathing condemnation of one brother: "I hate Alan, and a million times more!!!" There was a heart-rending account of a young girl and her misunderstood woe: "They don't understand. It was a bone-on-bone pain." In a separate journal appeared this poetic gem: "Blue is blue./ Green is green./ In nature, these two colors/ are often seen."

Since I apparently left my work lying out and about (probably thinking to share my talent with the masses and receive their praise), my siblings read it and enjoyed it in a way that has haunted me for years.

Thus began my journey as a writer and my not-at-all pathological search for positive feedback and validation.

Read and enjoy.

No Spawning Involved

We used to play a game called Salmon. I have no idea who made up the name or why, but I know other families played it and called it something else. It was a version of hide-and-seek, and it had to be played in total darkness. For us, actually, it was only ever partial darkness since we usually played while Mom and Dad did the dishes. (They never got a dishwasher. Mom said it was because you could count on everyone to disappear when it was time to do the dishes so it was practically the only chance she and Dad had to be alone.)

One person would go hide while everyone else shut their eyes and somebody counted. Then we'd all slink off separately to search. When the twins, Gary and Gordon, were little, they got to look with someone else. When they got older, they followed someone else around until they got yelled at. If you found the hider, you joined him. The last person to find everyone else hid first the next time.

I was just a little scared of the dark so this game was the perfect amount of excitement and suspense. If I was hiding, my heart would pound, and I'd try so hard to breathe quietly that I had trouble breathing at all. At least when you hid, you knew when someone was close to finding you. Looking was scarier because you didn't know when something might jump out of a dark corner. The adrenaline made my knees wobble, and I'd have to screw up my face along with my courage in order to stick my hand underneath beds and into closets. It was hard not to scream when I touched flesh.

The basic assumption of the game was that a person would choose to hide in the deepest, darkest depths of the house. One time, though, when it was Gary's turn to hide, Mom stuffed him in the cabinet under the sink, and then she and Dad went back to doing dishes. We looked all over the place and ended up in the kitchen asking for hints from the parents, who only chuckled and implied that Gary must be much smarter than the rest of us. We ran off to check other places, but all roads led back to the kitchen. After some time, Gary popped open the cupboard with a red face from much suppressed giggling and lack of oxygen. He was king of the salmon that night.

Feeding Seven Children

You might think feeding seven children would be difficult. Putting aside the economy of it, just the actual physical gathering of that many hands and feet and mouths could be a daunting task. For the most part, however, the accompanying appetites guaranteed bodily presence whenever the food was put out.

Delicacy and gracious manners, while perhaps not utterly lacking in our culinary education, were not overemphasized at the kitchen table. I remember fondly the aroma of many childhood favorites, having sensed them briefly while inhaling the first serving on my way to the second. Getting seconds was a competition of sorts, forming a habit that leaves me reminding myself that chewing is good for your digestion and can be quite a pleasant part of the whole eating experience.

During the school year, Mom made cold lunches (taking school lunch was a highly unusual occurrence) while Dad got breakfast ready. It is a credit to her that I did not know for years and years that my mother was not a morning person and did not enjoy this one-woman assembly line duty. Be that as it may, it was an unchanging part of my mornings to come into the kitchen and see Mom standing near the Amana Radarange with five or so lunchboxes and brown bags lined up in front of her, filling them with dried beef sandwiches, apples, and homemade chocolate chip cookies, while Dad got out the cereal and the toaster and juice and other stuff, happily listening to WHO news radio.

In the summers, the siblings were responsible for fixing lunches, Dad being at work and Mom being engaged in various mom-type activities—a never-ending mountain of laundry, grocery shopping, or cleaning (usually in a house miraculously bereft of children for the moment. Mom didn't actually ever ask for help, but you never knew when she might. Actually, I personally thought I could be most helpful by getting out of her way, and perhaps my siblings shared this selfless thought.)

The kids took turns making such tasty entrees as Campbell's Chicken Soup with Stars, the ever-popular dried beef sandwiches, and bloodballs and gravy, which was our name for Salisbury steak. Anita probably christened it so; she was the oldest and took some pleasure in squirmy ideas like that. Anyone's delicate sensibilities that might have been offended were overcome by our plebeian taste buds.

Dinty Moore beef stew, Spam, and other canned items usually formed the basis of most summer luncheons, though occasionally one of our more advanced siblings who had been through some form of home economics class would try to get creative. Creamed chipped beef made with milk and dried beef was a particularly revolting attempt, proving that some ingredients just cannot successfully be substituted for others, even when you're feeding a bunch of pigs.

Velveeta was the cheese of choice in our house, no doubt because of its comparative cheapness, but perhaps also because of its smooth and creamy texture. It goes amazing well with any fatty meat product, and fatty meat products were a great favorite of ours.

About every other Friday night we made pizza with the Chef Boyardee cheese pizza kits. It came with a package of mix for the dough, a can of sauce, and a little can of parmesan cheese. Unbelievably, I found out some families actually made it and ate it exactly that way.

Hamburger was the usual topping. We did drain off the fat. The technique was first to mash all the meat up into the corner of the electric skillet and tip the thing up on the opposite leg. There was a glass jar to spoon the grease into. Mom kept it capped and sat it up on a high shelf on top of folded paper towels on top of a plastic lid. Variously colored layers of fat congealed on top of one another into a fairly disgusting but sort of interesting semi-solid mass. The jar, because we tried not to waste things, had to be full before it got thrown out. Fortunately, given the amount of food we went through, this usually happened before it went rancid.

The basic pizza also needed onions and Velveeta. (Try saying it with an Italian accent.) I didn't know for a long time that other people put mozzarella on their pizza. I loved the Velveeta. It bubbled up and browned on the top while underneath it oozed cheesy goodness all over the place. Our pizzas, in fact, tasted a lot like cheeseburgers, which was, in my opinion, a good thing.

Cheeseburgers, of course, had their own honored place in the menu lineup every Wednesday night, without fail. We fried them up in the skillet in cold weather, grilled them outside, otherwise. Actually, the majority of the family just had hamburgers. At some point, I decided that it was not a rule that only Mom and Dad could enjoy America's favorite cheese product on their sandwich.

Potato chips, as you might guess, were a favorite side dish in our household, and my brother Alan perfected the art of ultra-thin cheese slicing to go with them. The ultimate Velveeta snack, though, was a slice of bologna with cheese in the middle. Popped in the microwave for forty-five seconds, the meat curled up into a little bowl filled with melted Velveeta and a little extra bologna fat floating on top.

No one in my family has had a heart attack. I suspect it's only a matter of time.

Skating

We used to go skating on the pond every winter. There were five pairs of figure skates to share, two male and three female, I think, stored in boxes on the shelves under the basement stairs, an out of the way, slightly dark and spooky spot, suitable for stashing stuff you could only use a couple months of the year.

We'd all hope for a good hard freeze before the first snow of the season. That gave you the best black smooth ice, the kind you could see down into a foot or so. Naturally enough, some years we weren't that lucky, and snow falling on top of the freezing water left a rough, pitted surface. Even if the freeze came first, snow put you to the extra work of shoveling clear a rink.

Going round and round in a little circle was never all that satisfying. It couldn't match skating down the length of the pond, building so much speed that you slid on the edge of danger, constantly looking out ahead to jump the odd branch from a partially submerged tree. Sometimes the pressure cracks left a ridge, too, and would catch a blade.

Pressure cracks were both scary, booming out like a gunshot, and reassuring, since they never happened unless the ice was strong enough to hold you. Dad wouldn't rely just on them, though, so before anyone could go skating for the first time, he'd head down to the pond to measure how thick the ice was. He'd pick a spot not too far away from the overflow where the ice was likely to be the thinnest and we were supposed to keep away from anyway. I don't know what you call the tool he used, one of those cranks with the funny bends in the middle. I realized much later most people use it to make holes for ice fishing. I know you had to turn the handle around forever, and it took a firm thunk down to get the blade to cut into the ice.

Once given paternal approval, it was time to suit up. We all had our own pair of overalls and dug into a communal drawer of socks and mittens, scarves and hats. Fortunately, Mom kept these in a reasonable state of cleanliness, no small feat given the incredible snottiness of our noses.

The socks were probably the most important element and almost never failed to disappoint. These were your basic knee-high sport socks of the era, the kind with three bands of color around the top of the calf, and had been used and reused to a uniform thickness slightly above transparency. You might not notice it so much slogging down to the pond in boots, but there was ample opportunity to reflect on their shortcomings later.

We didn't have a bench or anything down by the pond for changing into your skates. The best bet was usually to find a hummock of dead grass in the unmowed parts on the slope of a hill, swipe the snow off and sit down, hoping to create a semi-dry area. It was nearly impossible to keep your socks completely dry while stuffing your feet into the cold leather of the skates. Depending on the age and condition of the sock and the size of your feet relative to whoever had the biggest feet and stretched them out, they either bunched up uncomfortably in the toes or were pulled to maximum thinness, allowing the cold to be transmitted to your skin immediately. And, not being a glove family, our fingers were thoroughly red and numb from the lacing, which you would invariably end up tightening in five or ten minutes anyway. When you replaced your mittens, you first curled your hands into fists and stuck them into your armpits, staving off hypothermia for another few minutes.

After walking through snow to the edge of the pond, I always wobbled and skated on the insides of my ankles the first time out. If kids had the brains to appreciate being young, they would give thanks repeatedly for flexible ligaments and tendons. Practice eventually allowed me to stand straight up. After a minimal number of concussions, it also taught me not to lock out my knees, and that way I could feel the ice and stay straight up.

Sometimes I wondered, usually when the wind chill was below zero, if I really wanted to be out there. I sort of learned to skate backwards, but it's not as if I was throwing axels and Salchows and spinning around like Dorothy Hamill. My repertoire outside my Olympic skating fantasy was so severely limited that it wasn't hard to get bored. Still, at certain moments, it was worth any amount of headaches and trouble and flirting with frostbite. Once in a great while came a sunny afternoon when the wind wasn't blowing, and the ice was mostly clear. On those perfect days, it felt like flying to speed from one end of the pond to the other, heart pumping and the cold bite of the air in my lungs. I'd crouch down and hug my knees until I coasted gradually to a stop, then get up, turn around, and do it all over again.

Stuck in the Gravy

I went to kindergarten in the afternoons. The bus stopped out on the gravel road in front of the driveway. I missed it once when I was busy rolling a marble around the bathtub.

The bus driver then was a farmer who, I suppose, was a perfectly nice person when he wasn't driving a bus. He used to give us big candy canes at Christmas that I felt guilty taking because I didn't really like peppermint and my family didn't celebrate, anyway. Blob Elliot, whose real name you can probably guess, received his nickname from my big sister Anita. (Sometimes we refer to her as the creative one.) Blob scared me, mostly because he was quite large. In the afternoons, too, he had to yell sometimes, because then the bus was full of big kids, and once he got up and walked to the back to straighten somebody out.

But when the bus pulled up after lunch in that blissful year that was kindergarten, it was nearly empty. I think one kid got on before me. He was short, though, and quiet so you never saw much of him at any time. I slipped on quickly and sat quietly on the green vinyl, mostly looking out the window but occasionally sneaking a peek at Blob in the mirror over his head.

Kim Nelson got on about a mile and a half or so later once we were on the highway, then Kevin Stewart over the top of the next hill, and Ricky Schoole at the trailer court at the bottom. Just past the second feed store, after the next set of two quick turns, the bus stopped to pick up my best friend Carol.

Carol's dad owned a hog shipping business, and theirs was the last house before the city limits so she was the last kid we picked up every day and the first kid we let off. Lucky Carol. We missed the bus once together after school, and our teacher took each of us by one hand and ran us out over the grass to where our bus had stopped in the street. Naturally, we were much embarrassed by the event and never let it happen again.

Our kindergarten teacher was Miss De Heus (rhymes with nice), a vision of utter perfection to me, and better known to my family, courtesy of the creative one, as Miss De Hoos. Calling her that bothered me to no end and, in the typical boneheaded kindergarten way, I told Miss De Heus that my big sister Anita made fun of her name. She said something soothing and after I announced it at dinner, there was a lot less Miss De Hoos-ing going on around me.

The kindergarteners got their own door that went right outside to the front of the building. There was a coat-hanging area with hooks just inside, above which the life-size cardboard bricks were stored. I loved those bricks, later biting Tammy Smith, a round-faced little blonde with burn marks on her arm, over some issue arising from their use. Or maybe I bit her because she wanted to play with the pointy-chinned little boy of my dreams at the time, Eric Quayle.

I kissed his cheek once when we took our turns at the art easel, draped in big white shirts from our fathers. Judy and Anita helped me write love notes covered with hearts and instructed me to stash them in his cubby.

I do not recall exactly how this affair ended, but I can tell you that I both bit and kissed again within the year. I bit some bruiser out on the playground for kicking my ball, and I kissed some pale little redhead on the bus just before he got off at his stop. I wonder now what the heck my report card said.

Study

We didn't call it going to church; we called it going to study. The building was called the Kingdom Hall. That's just what we said, and it always sounded normal to my ears until I got old enough to understand what other people thought.

I mostly liked going to study. Before they remodeled when I was about twelve, the Hall was a rectangular blond stone building that I liked to imagine was the Ark. I pretended each of the blocks was a cubit and wondered if the real Ark had any windows. They don't mention any, Dad said, so likely not or not many, anyway. There was a little concrete porch out front of the building that couldn't have been an afterthought to the design but looked like it. I guess the skinny black metal railings prevented it from blending in. The door was good, though. It wasn't particularly impressive, but it was solid, closed with a satisfying thunk, and had one of those cool little brass mail slots with the flap.

When you opened the door you were looking straight down a short entryway and right up the center aisle to the stage. We were never late, and you wouldn't want to be with that kind of arrangement because half the congregation would turn around and stare. There was a rod for hanging coats, but normally we just took ours with us. We almost always sat in the second or third row back from the front on the right side. The Kingdom Hall didn't have pews, God forbid, because that would be too much like Christendom. We had old theater seats, reupholstered and repainted. Depending on your neighbor, you more or less shared an arm rest between you, which caused some furious but quiet conflicts. Dad used a hand signal in these and other cases, holding the middle two fingers in with his thumb and waggling the index and pinkie fingers up and down. Sounds kind of goofy, but he meant business, and you ignored it to your peril. The one and only spanking I remember getting was at study and came from a fascination with how my saddle shoes sounded on the checkered tile floor while I hung on to the back of chair and slid back and forth. One spanking was plenty.

Some Witness families, though, I suppose like some Catholic and Protestant and Jewish families, held pretty strictly to "spare the rod and spoil the child." One lady used a coat hanger to whup her children. I wonder if that was to alleviate the sting to her hand or increase the sting to their bottoms. Those kids got taken to the basement more than once or twice.

The basement in the old Kingdom Hall was icky, and that's where the bathrooms were. Of course, going to the bathroom is a time-honored time killer, if you have a sincere face and don't go to that well too often. The stairway to the basement was not too narrow and not too steep, and once when I fell asleep at study I woke up with a big, noticeable jerk because I thought I was falling down those stairs. When you stepped off the wooden landing at the bottom, you were in a room that had been paneled off from the rest of the basement. The floor was concrete. That front room and the bathrooms were as clean as they could be, but they always smelled musty, and the sink had that rusty discoloration from the water no matter how many times the sisters scrubbed it with bleach.

Singing was always my favorite part of going to study. Mary Brodine played the piano or Nelly Ver Duff, but my dad pinch hit occasionally for certain songs. We sang three times on Sundays and Thursdays: once at the beginning, once in the middle, and once at the end. The songbook had more than one hundred songs and was bound in a thick dark pink paper that got as soft as a blankie with repeated use. The piano was an upright in dark wood that I wanted to play in the worst way, but when we were little we stayed away from it. One time after the meeting, Nellie played and sang "Walking in a Winter Wonderland" for me (changing Parson Brown to Brother Brown). I was very surprised to find out you could play anything other than meeting songs on that piano.

My second favorite thing about going to study was drawing and writing in notebooks. I don't remember exactly how or when that started. I suppose the most likely explanation was that it was a device to keep antsy children quiet. It continued long past the point where we should have been able to sit still and listen. Even back when I was in grade school, there were some good little girls and boys taking notes and writing down the scriptural references during meeting. Occasionally I would do this, too, usually under some duress from bossy big sister Judy. She took shorthand and, though no one else in the family but Mom could read it, I have no doubt that it stuck faithfully to the speaker's topic.

We did not each get a notebook, I know, but on the other hand I don't remember having to share very often. We couldn't play games like tic-tac-toe for any amount of time since then it was too obvious that we couldn't be paying any attention. Gary and Gordon drew war pictures. Sarah took notes mostly (another good girl). Anita, the only acknowledged artist among us, drew all kinds of stuff. I can't recall Al doing much of anything, which some might call foreshadowing but, then again, might just mean that since he usually sat on the other side of Dad, I just didn't know what was going on over there.

I liked to draw pictures of ladies in dresses with big, poofy long skirts with their hands hidden well behind their backs. Sometimes they wore dangly earrings, and sometimes they showed off their high-heeled shoes, standing, of course, in first position. I also loved to do math problems. When I learned about decimals, I would do huge division problems that went all the way down the page. I traced my hand many, many times, trying afterward to fill in all the wrinkles accurately and drawing myself beautiful rings with big, oddly shaped stones.

Just one time that I remember, Mom took the notebook and drew an endless line of little circles that curved back and forth all over the page. I was fascinated and added that to my own repertoire.

It's been a long time, but the right kind of notebook brings it all back.

Sacred Waters

Mom and Dad put a pool in the backyard around the time I was nine or ten. Prior to that, swimming was the once in a blue moon trip to the Maytag Pool, a gleaming jewel in the crown of Maytag philanthropy, a vast aquamarine playground with an aluminum fence right there in the water separating the little kids' end from the big kids' end, which came complete with a high-rise, death-defying diving board.

Once when I was explaining to my mother that I was actually a shy person, she referred to the Maytag trips as proving the opposite, as I apparently had no qualms in appropriating little girls to play with. I vaguely remember playing catch with one curly-headed stranger who couldn't help but be a great improvement on my built-in playmates: the little brothers.

The most memorable thing about Maytag Pool was that when you exited the locker rooms, having, in my case, mashed your clothing into a little wire basket with the belongings of two or three sisters, you had to walk through a slippery tiled tunnel of cold showers, and the sun on the water and concrete nearly blinded you when you came out.

My second clearest memory is a little boy with a fake arm. You'd think having grown up with a little brother whose legs didn't work, I'd have been immune to the staring response but, no, I stood and gawked at that kid splashing and playing with the water dripping off his shiny peach plastic arm. I never saw a less real-looking arm until one year at a teachers' meeting when I was, thankfully, old enough not to stare.

Swimming was also, at least once or twice, the pond. I'm not quite clear on the timing, though. I seem to remember learning to swim in the pool, and one has to wonder about parents who blithely allow their non-swimming offspring to jump into a pond. Secure in the continuation of their DNA, they may not have been overly worried about turtles taking me like they did goslings every spring while the geese were still young enough to reproduce. More likely, I suppose, I used a set of Dad's homemade floats. No wimpy water wings, these consisted of a pair of sealed gallon milk jugs connected with a couple feet of nylon cord. They rode you up out of the water about a foot high, a considerable advantage when crossing the inevitable patch of moss, particularly the slimy stringy variety that, even if you tried to avoid it, always seemed to find you.

Swimming in the pond looked like it ought to be fun, especially on a hot July day with the sun sparking diamonds off a bright blue surface. Several things conspired to make this a cruel myth. First of all, that blue is only an illusion. Pond water is murky, smelly, and harbors stuff that lurks down in the cool layer where your feet might dangle when your legs needed a rest from all that kicking.

Second, we didn't have much in the way of sand. There was a little bit at the jumping off place, a good spot to watch tadpoles, but five decent steps sent you into the slick sticky ooze full of organic decaying goop that felt almost exactly how you'd think greasy grimy gopher guts might feel, only cooler.

There was a bit of a beach on the west side, our destination. It actually stuck up out of the water that summer, owing to the terrific drought we'd been having. That made it safe to wade around the overflow, too. A good six inches of the pipe was showing, greatly reducing the likelihood of falling in accidentally. Curiosity being what it is, you couldn't say the chances were quite down to zero. The mud around there is the only place I remember picking up leeches, however, which pretty much clinched it for me as a stop to avoid.

At any rate, after the pool went in, pond swimming became a distant memory. The pool was a thing of beauty, nestled into the slope in back of the house, in front of the kitchen window. You could see every inch of the bottom, painted white, and the lovely sky blue walls. It had a standard diving board and two gleaming silver ladders, one in the deep end and one in the shallow.

They did have to take out the weeping willow, a crying shame, but Mom says it was dying anyway. We had a swing set underneath it, the site where Gordon, having gotten terribly excited by something Mom brought home from the store, once leaped up, dropped his pants, and started peeing.

We all peed outside more once the pool went in. Some of it was, inescapably, in the pool itself, but most of it went on behind the two pine trees on the north side, planted close enough together to provide a little privacy. For a long time, I thought we killed the grass back there, but now I think it was just the thick blanket of pine needles. Peeing out there was preferable to the alternatives, which were squatting over the drain in the basement, assuming it was unoccupied, or drying off completely to walk through the house.

The pool was surrounded by about a foot of some smooth stone and then about two and a half feet of rougher concrete. On the south side, when the water splashed up, it made a puddle that warmed up to sauna proportions in the sunlight, the only problem being that you might snag your suit if you rolled around at all.

Around the west end and sloping off to the south was a retaining wall, off of which it was possible, if only slightly dangerous, to dive into the deep end at an angle. I do not remember ever doing this, possibly through a deep sense of self-preservation, having chipped my tooth diving into the shallow end somewhere towards the beginning of my swimming career.

Alas, the Golden Age of the Swimming Pool came to an end. Actually, it died a lingering and ugly death. Mom and Dad, having taken up running, found they enjoyed a little skinny dip afterwards to wash off the sweat. Evidently, they did not want to be observed in broad daylight by the enquiring eyes of their nosy offspring.

So, Dad built a pool house. That might conjure up ideas of an extended pool season, an ability to use the pool in less than ideal weather. Actually, swimming in the rain (not lightning and thunder rain) is fantastically cool, but the pool house took care of that, along with the intersecting prisms of sunlight cast on the bottom that a kid might look at longingly while walking the perimeter in a stupid pink dress before going to study on a perfectly good for swimming late afternoon in the summer.

Dad had the best of intentions, it must be said, and even rigged up solar panels to heat the water, a system that never worked quite the way he wanted it to. The pool house was a dim, dusty, slightly moldy place, whose one attraction—jumping off the board, grabbing the nearest beam and swinging from it—quickly paled. The pool, one of the first in-ground models of the area, developed plumbing problems that, in fairness, had nothing to do with the building, but it was all downhill from there. I don't think the water was ever as clean afterwards, and any puddles splashed up on the side stayed dark and cold on the cement.

Credo

She married right out of high school and started having babies five years later. She quit secretarying then and concentrated her considerable energies on home life. With seven children, I guess it's no wonder that keeping things clean took on a special importance.

Mom did laundry on Monday, Wednesday, and Friday. I loved it. The floor of the basement was covered in sorted piles of dirty clothes. Since they were dirty, Mom didn't mind if I walked on top of them trying to get all the way around the room and back without touching the floor. She fed the piles into the washer one at a time to the comforting thumping of the agitator. The tub was usually open to the air so I could see churning suds and carefully hold doll clothes into the warm soapy water.

The wringer on the washer was interesting and dangerous. We heard cautionary tales about mangled fingers, and I believed them. I remember once that a particularly tiny doll dress got stuck going round and round on the roller. Mom had to stop it then and unhook some doohickey and crank on something else to open the assembly and fish out the offending garment. Then she reversed the process and got back to the rhythm of feeding clothes in with one hand, guiding them out with the other, and letting them fall into the first of two rinse tubs. Once a load was all soaking in clear water, she rotated the wringer arm and fed them through to the second tub to get every bit of soap out of the clothes. After another wringing, they went into a big wicker basket to carry out to the clothesline if the weather was good.

Before she hung anything up, Mom walked up and down holding the wires of the clothesline with a rag. I can't remember when it dawned on me that she was dusting them off. I thought she did it because it was fun. The bucket of clothespins came out, and up first went the diapers and sheets. In and out of that basement door she went all day long. I wonder how she did it when there were still babies in the house. I can only picture wash day from the freedom of childhood, trying to run between the sheets in the sunshine without being touched as they billowed out in the wind.

If the weather was bad, the laundry hung on the clothesline Dad had rigged up inside. There wasn't as much space, and Mom periodically mopped up the little flat puddles that collected under the dripping clothes. On rainy days she didn't like it, but she used the dryer much more.

As the clothes dried, she brought them upstairs. Things that could be were folded on the kitchen table and put away. When I was older, I helped first with diapers (we used diapers long after there were no babies left, but that's another story) and then I helped match socks and fold underwear, Mom's least favorite task. She used to mark the toes of the boys' socks and the tags of the girls' underwear with a code. Mine was three dots.

Shirts and dresses and pants were hung up in a little extra space in Anita and Judy's room where they waited for ironing. She usually did that during the next day, I think, but sometimes after the supper dishes were done, she'd pull the ironing board out of its special cupboard and set it up in her usual spot alongside the kitchen table behind Judy's and Dad's chairs. She used distilled water in the steam iron and was always careful afterwards to pour what was left into a clean mayonnaise jar that sat to the left of the sink by the radio.

She dusted and vacuumed twice a week, with Wednesday being the big day and Saturday the light one. Though I do not in any way approach Mom's standard of cleanliness, I still assess furniture before buying for the ease of its dustability.

Mom recently said Aunt Miriam is a bit compulsive about cleaning. I laughed because she said it as if she wasn't. At Mom and Dad's fiftieth anniversary party, she noticed the punch had dripped on the floor and stooped to wipe it up. While she was crouched down, she commented that the walls probably hadn't been cleaned in years and gave them a quick scrub, too.

At Country Kitchen in our hometown, where Mom and Dad are regulars, the waitresses love her. She stacks the dishes (the family appetite accounting for the clean state of the plates) and dries up the rings from the water glasses. I came out of the bathroom there once to find her cleaning the dust off the top of the paper towel dispenser.

She picks up trash everywhere; every little bit helps, she'll tell you. She takes a Hy-Vee bag along when she runs. We've stopped the car on the highway, if there's no one coming, to grab a can from the side of the road. Five cents, she'll announce, but I think she'd do it anyway.

If it's an obsession, then I guess she's got it pretty well under control. When we were little, she cleaned because it needed to be done. The transition from Mom doing it to our doing it for ourselves took place at different times and at vastly varying degrees. She didn't nag us to pick up our toys; she was just a good example. I can recall some exclaiming over grass-stained jeans, but Mom, who started running when I was about eight, could appreciate the need for athletic endeavor on the playground.

She's still running--just won her age group at the Alliant 8K in Cedar Rapids on the 4th of July. Taking it up when she was fortyish was a landmark in her life and in ours. Mom had a letter sweater from Newton Senior High, Class of 1952. She lettered in speech and debate. There were no sports then for girls in Newton. She was a good runner right from the get-go, too, and although this became another expected part of her being my mom, it was the first time I remember taking pride in her accomplishments.

Because she and Dad worked out when he came home from work, this marked the increase in responsibility that we began taking for cooking dinner and cleaning. Actually, she pretty much abdicated responsibility for cooking, having never particularly enjoyed it, though I've heard she makes a mean lemon meringue pie. I still never really had to take total responsibility for cleaning my room or doing my laundry until I went to college. She dusted, she vacuumed, she straightened up. But that wasn't all there was to her, thank goodness.

Keep yourself and the world around you reasonably clean, and find what makes you happy. That's what I believe, and I learned it from my mother.

First Grade

Mrs. Olsen taught my first grade. She had short dark hair with just a hint of bouffant to the top. This being 1972, I guess that wasn't as out of style as it may seem, but, even as a six-year-old, I was aware that Mrs. Olsen was not exactly cute. She wore glasses with thick dark rims and had rabbity teeth. Her elbows and her hips stuck out funny somehow, and she wore sturdy, sensible shoes. I liked her just fine, but she was no Miss De Heus, of course.

First grade was not an extremely interesting year, but there are a few highlights. One was seeing Mrs. Olsen's underwear. She was wearing a skirt, and there was something sticking up between the waistband and her shirt. I cannot describe the something with any precision whatsoever, but it was universally acclaimed to be her underwear and was the source of much guilty enjoyment and finger pointing.

Another memorable moment was someone leaving "a big log" in our little bathroom. It wasn't me, to the best of my recollection. In fact, I was not quite clear on what the person meant by "a log." By the time I understood, Mrs. Olsen had flushed the excitement away and was in the midst of a lecture about what to do when you were finished going to the bathroom. In my house, we just called that "poop."

In first grade, I got to go to second grade math with Mike Wigans, whom I didn't particularly like, and John Paulson, whom I most certainly did. We sat in a little row of our own in the back and chattered among ourselves. Whether or not this experiment was deemed successful, I do not know. The next year we were in a combined second and third grade, and I know we didn't leave the room for math. Of course, that year I experienced a mental block in learning subtraction, causing me a limited amount of pain and suffering which does not come into this story at all.

My first grade school picture is atrocious. It looks as if someone was interrupted in the process of scalping me. Even I thought I looked like my brother Gordon in it. This is odd given that one of my enduring memories of first grade is sucking on a hunk of my hair. I enjoyed the taste. Mrs. Olsen did not enjoy the aesthetics of this, however, and when it got to the stage of getting a sore on the side of my mouth, I decided to give it up forever.

Finally, there's the fish. Mrs. Olsen had a big aquarium with a large fish, a medium-sized fish, and some little fish. In a shocking dose of reality, we came to school one day to the somewhat disturbing sight of a large fish with the tail of a medium-sized fish sticking out its mouth. The big fish stayed alone for the rest of the year.

A Friendly Contest

My family is a gaseous one. That's not to say we're entirely composed of gas, but at times it has certainly seemed that way. We weren't even one of those poor families that had nothing to eat but beans and thus had an excuse. Most of us just appear to have inherited digestive tracts that will handle most any comestible in large amounts and will produce methane readily and steadily as a by-product.

As my siblings and I were inherently a dignified group, we did not stoop to crude language to describe our vaporous contributions to the general atmosphere. We called them "friends." And, if you were contributing frequently in a particular time period, you were said to be "friendly." I have no idea from where arose this quaint terminology, but it suited us quite admirably.

Another happy little phrase we used in these situations was brought to us from the lips of a sweet and innocent child. I was baby-sitting Tyler Shaffer one day when—oops—out slipped a little friend! Before I could say anything, my charge, being at the tender age of two, piped out, "Tyler did it!" I imagine he had been blamed regularly in his own home, and, from that moment on, he was a routine contributor at ours.

We all learned that to produce "friends" at school was a humiliating experience, and, while we did not discuss technique, I am sure that my siblings all became masters of the slow, silent release. I reflect now that this was probably an art practiced by many, although, as a child, I was certain that I was among the very few and tried very hard not to have my talent discovered. At home, naturally, things were a bit more relaxed. Ordinarily, this meant only that involuntary emanations were accepted graciously and with some humor. On one memorable evening, however, our standards were lowered to an appalling degree.

Three members of my family, who shall remain nameless to protect whatever shreds of dignity they might retain, entered upon a "friendly" contest. They assumed the posture most conducive to gas production: elbows on the floor, chest low, rear high. And then they began to produce in their three vastly different manners. One was able to produce only large eruptions that made up for their scarcity by their incredible amplitude. The second was able to produce a medium amount of medium-sized emissions. The first two contestants, however, were seriously hampered in their efforts by the difficulty associated with engaging in the aforementioned activity while being convulsed with laughter. For the third member of this shameful trio was producing no audible noise whatsoever from the rear but kept grunting out numbers in a steady stream. At the end of the agreed upon time limit, the count was twelve, twenty-seven, and one hundred seventeen. So far as I know, this record still stands and has not ever been challenged. But, you know, there's always next Thanksgiving.

Dad

One morning during high school, I think sometime during track season my senior year, I got up early to study for a test. It was probably about six o'clock. I sat down at the desk in the TV room and turned the lamp on. I want to say it cast a warm glow or lay a golden puddle of light across my notes, but I suppose that's just because this is a good memory. At the time, I certainly wasn't thinking about the lighting. I was worried about getting through the material before it was time to get ready for school.

I didn't normally do homework in the morning, but we'd had a meet the night before, and I was too tired to study when I got home. Getting up the next day seemed like a much better idea. I've always been a morning person, anyway, and I got that straight from Dad.

That morning, when he came out of the bathroom, he stuck his head through the kitchen doorway and asked who was up and what was I doing. Studying, I replied, rather shortly, and bent back to it. I don't even remember what subject this was, but, though I did well in all my classes, I distinctly remember the slightly sick feeling of concern I had about this particular test.

Dad disappeared back into the kitchen, and, without really noticing, I heard the familiar noises of him moving around, cupboards opening as he got out dishes to set the table. He clicked on the radio, set to WHO with its recognizable musical intro to the news, and filled the teakettle with water.

It was Dad's unenviable job to wake the brothers, two of whom were pretty much never happy to greet the morn. Then he walked into the TV room on his way back to the kitchen. He paused behind me at the desk and put one hand on my shoulder. He murmured something encouraging, ruffled my hair, and walked off. I almost cried.

Dad, true to his generation maybe, was never much of a touchy-feely guy. When I was a little girl, he used to let me dance on his feet. I stood on his insteps, holding his hands, as we walked around the kitchen. He used to lift me up with one arm, letting me dangle, which I recall as feeling deliciously dangerous without any real fear of falling. But that was when I was little.

I've never been in doubt of my father's love. He showed it in lots of ways and lots of times. He had a special way of whistling "Pee-Wee," his nickname for me. (He also called me "Troublemaker." I'm 95% certain he meant that endearingly.) He and Mom were at nearly every one of my track meets and swim meets, a comforting presence with a particularly loud cheer.

Much later, grown-up and married, I hugged my dad one day, sort of awkwardly, and embarrassed him when I told him I loved him. It's not a routine that we repeat, maybe with some relief on both sides, but it was important for me to let him know.

One Golden Set

My high school swim team worked out at the local YMCA. It was on the southeast side of town, and living north of town off Highway 14, I got up at 5:12 to be at practice by 6:00. Travel time included a couple of miles in the wrong direction to pick up Robin Shaffer, a trip that once provided my first ever sight of cows mating. The only other time I nearly drove off the road was because of the most fabulous aurora borealis I have ever seen. Even when we got into town with the streetlights you could still see it glowing almost right up to the zenith.

Naturally, getting to practice wasn't usually that exciting, mornings or after school. I do remember one goofy afternoon in taper time when we drove in and around the circle drive the wrong way whooping and hollering. Mrs. Kirchhoff, Rae's mom, happened to be walking out at the same time. She flagged us down and spoke sternly to me. I think she might have been kidding, but I was properly chastened.

The best memory I have of swimming, though, came just before taper. Taper, let me pause to tell you, is the athletic equivalent of the Promised Land. You've worked hard all season (slackers excepted), and you've kicked it into an even higher gear for the last couple of weeks, then you start resting. Coach said sometimes an athlete will feel tired or let down at first, but for me, it always felt wonderful and powerful and semi-delirious. As I said, however, the best thing happened just before that, the last week before taper my senior year.

I was undoubtedly the fifth-best swimmer on the team. First came my fellow seniors, Janet and Kristin, and then a couple of sophomores, Rae and Heather. Maybe Rae should have been second, based on raw ability, though she struggled with nerves at big events, or you could conceivably build a case for Heather, but, regardless, solidly in fifth position came me.

I was swimming that afternoon in lane three behind Kristin. We started from the shallow end and, unlike the boys who walked halfway out, we always started at the wall to get the full distance. It was a metric pool, one of the few in the state, which I always thought gave us an advantage, both at home meets, because the other teams were pysched out by the extra distance, and at away meets, because 25 yards really does seem a lot shorter than 25 meters.

Our coach, Julie, had the digital clock set up on the bleachers at the end of the pool. It was about the middle of practice when, sitting down to reset the counters, she announced that this next set was going to be hard. Julie always told it like it was, and we trusted her. Ten hundreds on the 1:15. If you've never been a high school girl swimmer in the middle of Iowa in the middle of the eighties, that probably doesn't send chills down your spine. Swimming a 100 is a lot like running a 400, if that helps. Earlier in the season, we'd gotten about 15 more seconds of rest, but Julie had been bringing the time down steadily. Do your best, she said.

I gave Kris the usual five seconds of cushion before pushing off. We finished about that far apart at first, too, and I was coming in as the clock hit 1:10. As the set wore on, though, I started catching up to Kris's feet in the last length. She didn't kick with much bubble, and she had a funny little crossover hitch. Maybe it was the shark effect, hunting prey, but I continued to feel strong and out on top of the water. I sped up into the flip turns and streamlined hard coming out. God, I felt great! It wasn't fair of me to make her continue to lead, but I did, even when I started finishing up at the wall at the same time, coming in around 1:11 or 1:12.

To be accurate to history, Julie might have added on some seconds in there somewhere, but it hardly matters. When we were done, I was completely exhausted, but I had the most tremendous feeling of exhilaration, intensified, I'm sure, by the unaccustomed thrashing of a better swimmer. Kris did make me lead the next set, whatever it was.

I guess a real go-getter would have been dissatisfied with subsequent performances. I dropped time after taper, of course, but I never swam my leg of the 400 free relay in a time consistent with the promise of that set. I'm not unhappy, though. It felt good when it happened, and it feels damn good to remember it now.

I don't swim anymore—too much hassle—but, once in a great while, instead of walking, I run. And sometimes I go hard enough and long enough to give me a little taste of the big endorphin rush I got from that one golden set in October.

Gramma

She's lost the thread
that connected her causes to her effects,
wanders the hallways,
doesn't know who I am.
Vaguely she feels an impulse to escape, but
they've locked all the doors to keep her in.

Ironically Enough

Having undergone a righteous cleansing
of his once-sordid soul,
he casts benevolent condescension
on the unenlightened and unreformed.

Unrepentant,
I soldier on.

Vigilant Vegetarian

At the next table over,
an obnoxious woman
is proclaiming to her children
that she would
never
eat a dead body.

I think I'll order my steak rare.

Teacher of the Year

Most of the time, I'm a practical, realistic person. Most of the time, I'm a decent teacher. Every now and again, though, I am moved to make that extra effort to be great.

Such was the case on the Wednesday before Thanksgiving break. The students were restless, yet it was only a pre-Thanksgiving sort of restlessness, nothing compared to the candy-snarfing excitement of Halloween or the gift-getting anticipation of Christmas. It was nothing, in short, that I couldn't handle. No special arrangements needed to be made; I would be teaching regular lessons that day. As it worked out, I would be teaching the very last lesson of the Flexibility and Strength unit on the very last day before that kit had to be turned back in.

Had I but given this a little more thought, I would have taught it the day before. As with most units, there is one lesson that is the bane of my existence. I was, however, in the midst of one of those great teacher kicks and thought this was the year I would conquer Stiff Joints, on only my fourth try. I carefully read through the directions, days before I would actually be teaching. I assembled the needed materials and planned my attack.

Stiff Joints had a station for knees, a station for hands and wrists, and a station for elbows. Each station had three simple, everyday activities to be done first normally and then while wearing a splint. That's nine (for the mathematically challenged among you), nine things to do. That's a lot for a fourth-grader. These activities were listed on a handout, but, great teacher that I was, I knew that I would have to demonstrate all nine, and I did. I knew that I would have to show clearly how to put the splints on the joints, and I did. For the crowning jewel in my teaching consciousness, I recognized that here was a lesson that would need step-by-step directions painstakingly explained and displayed on the bulletin board for frequent referral. All these things I did, and not grudgingly; I delighted in my greatness. I was doing all there was to be done.

Then, in one unguarded moment, it was all undone. I let them choose their own partners. Foolish, foolish, foolish me. Most students chose someone they could work with and paired up quickly. But, as usual, there were two oddballs (I know what you're thinking: the Teacher of the Year wouldn't call names. Well, isn't this better than using their real names?). They were forced to work together. I had misgivings, but I let them go. Could anyone fail to do a good job, given the excellent directions and modeling I had provided? The answer, of course, was yes.

To be fair, nearly everyone was doing just fine, but every time I looked at the oddballs—let's call them Bonehead 1 and Bonehead 2—they were doing the wrong thing. First, they didn't go to the right place. Then, when they finally got there, they weren't putting the splint on the knee right. When I came over to help them, lying at their feet was another splint—broken in half! "Who did this?" I snarled, which is exactly the wrong thing to say if you really want to know.

"Not me," said Bonehead 1.

"Are you sure?" I asked pointedly, since if anyone in the class would do it and deny it, it would be her.

"I swear," said Bonehead 1. Bonehead 2 was looking everywhere but at me. I glared at them and at the other four kids at that station.

"Someone had better tell me who broke that splint, or I am going to be very angry." (You may have noticed by now that the feeling of greatness had abandoned me.) No one claimed responsibility, and no one tattled, so actually it probably was broken beforehand, but I was still irked. I left that station and walked over to the hand-wrist area. What to my wondering eyes should appear but another broken item! Actually, it only turned out to have fallen apart, but, as it was a pencil sharpener, in doing so it left pencil shavings all over the table. I brought the class to an abrupt halt and launched into my second little tirade of the day.

"Class," I said, in that dangerously calm voice that means you're not really calm at all, "what should you do if something breaks or falls apart?"

"Try to fix it?" suggested one of the braver non-boneheads.

"That would be an excellent idea. And," I went on, gazing around, partially mollified by her answer, "if you can't fix it?"

"We could ask you for help?"

"Yes! Yes, you could ask me for help! And when should you ask me for help? Should you wait until I discover the problem on my own, or should you raise your hand and let me know right when it happens?" I was working myself up again, as my eye fell upon certain irresponsible members of the class whom I suspected of having perpetrated this particular crime.

"We should let you know right away," answered someone.

"Right. Then do it. Get back to work." I fixed the pencil sharpener and resumed my stroll around the room, heading towards the elbow station. There were Boneheads 1 and 2 fumbling around in a fog. "What are you doing?" I asked, needlessly since it was apparent they had no idea. I began tirade number three, because right in front of them were those directions I had painstakingly explained and written on the board. Not waiting for them to actually form coherent sentences, I inquired as to what they thought the purpose of my giving directions was. Did they think I just enjoyed standing up in front of the class talking? Didn't they have any idea that they were supposed to listen? "If," I finished, "I look over here in two minutes, and you aren't doing the right thing, you will not be participating in the rest of the activity." I left.

I suppose I should mention again that the rest of the class was really doing as well as I could have expected. The next ten minutes or so passed with me giving what I would describe as the normal amount of help to the people trying their best to do the activities correctly. I tried not to look at the Boneheads.

Finally, Stiff Joints was more or less completed by more or less everyone, and we had decided that having stiff joints does, indeed, interfere with normal movement. It seemed to me to have been a relatively long and painful way to discover that, but at least we were done. I showed a little film about the brain, and the morning was over. The day, unfortunately, was not done.

In the afternoon, we switch classes and do the same thing again. Fortified by lunch, I had regained at least a smattering of that great teacher feeling and resolved to fight the good fight. The time I was even more detailed and careful in my explanations. I showed twice how to put on each splint. I gave the tell-me-right-now-if-it-breaks speech before anything was broken. I told them how some people in my class had trouble following the directions even though they were written right there in front of them. I was confident, but not falsely so, I thought. Betrayed by that confidence, I once again let them choose their own partners. And, once again, nearly everyone chose smartly.

I began to walk around the room, starting this time at the elbow station. Some unnamed teacher's instinct, though, pulled my head around to the knee station, and, sure enough, there were Boneheads 3 and 4, making the same stupid mistakes that 1 and 2 did.

I found myself repeating the exact phrases I had used in the morning. What are you doing? What is the point of my writing the direction on the board if you aren't going to follow them? If I look over here in two minutes and you aren't doing the right thing, you will not be participating in the rest of the activities. I was confused by the second helping of idiocy so soon. I tried not to look at the Boneheads until the lesson was over, and, at last, it was. All that was left before recess was that nice little film about the brain.

When I say film, I mean the kind you had to use an actual film projector for back in the old days. (I resist the impulse here to explain how much I've grown since the old days.) I threaded the movie into the machine, gave my little introductory spiel, and turned it on. That was when I realized the gods were against me, perhaps in an effort to teach me a lesson. The damn film started jumping. I hung on to the last little shred of cool I had and rethreaded the machine. Still jumping. A boy behind me asked if the machine had a focus. "It's not the focus," I said through gritted teeth as I began to hit buttons and jiggle parts at random. Still jumping. The boy behind me spoke a little louder, "Does that thing have a focus?"

The rest of the story is not pretty. (Even less pretty than the middle.) I completely lost all vestiges of professionalism. I whirled around and yelled at the kid, "IT'S NOT THE FOCUS! Didn't you hear me the first time I said that? Do you ever listen when I am talking? That is so frustrating!" I'm sorry to say that I may even have continued on a little longer in that vein.

The kid got very quiet. In fact, everyone got very quiet. When that finally sunk into my enraged brain, I shut up. I looked around the room. Everyone was looking at me. The projector finished rewinding, and the end of the film flapped as the spool turned. I flipped it off and looked around the room again. I knew I hadn't been a great teacher today, but I also knew one sure way to make the kids think I was. After a few more seconds of silence, I looked up at the clock and said, "Let's go to recess early."

Residue

Summer has evaporated
and left behind
a residue of missed opportunities.

Kitchen drawers unorganized,
closets full of clothes I don't (or shouldn't) wear,
bedroom walls an unchanged shade of dispassionate gray.

In place of accomplishment, there were
mornings on the porch with the newspaper and the cats,
afternoon naps that let me stay up hours into the starlight,
books and walks at sunrise and sunset.

A life full of relaxation.

But still,
here at the end,
I think

summer has evaporated
and left behind
a residue that's bittersweet.

Still

We planned to play kickball after swim practice on the last Friday afternoon of summer vacation. I brought the brand new yellow playground ball from my classroom, with my last name written in big, black capital letters. It sprinkled as the girls and I jogged, and the light rain blended with our sweat instead of washing it away. Grass clippings from the football field stuck to the track and to the bottoms of our shoes.

I was running with the team partly because I had no other time to work out. School had already started for teachers, and practice in both the morning and the afternoon ate up my free time. I was keeping up today with the extra slow Friday pace, but my ankle, knee, and hip hurt from the other four days of wishing I was sixteen again. I knew that when classes started for the students on Monday, I wouldn't be doing this anymore. I've given up showering in high school locker rooms and rushing to do my face and hair before driving off, too fast, to school. I felt old.

We finished up and walked two laps, then went to find a place to play. Alicia nixed the baseball field for mud; our second choice was taken by cross-country runners doing sprints. We walked down the hill and used water bottles to set up bases in the thick grass. The rain faded in and out.

I wasn't going to play because the teams were even at six, but Beth named me all-time pitcher. I was happy with that. Kickball was one of my two favorite games in elementary school, dodgeball being the other. I never liked being a captain, but I almost always could depend on being chosen first. It had been a long time, though, since I was a player. Being the pitcher would be safe.

The ball was wet from the grass, and I had to pitch hard to make it roll straight and smooth. Most of the girls, unlike little kids, wouldn't run up too far to kick the ball and, consequently, didn't get the distance that they could have.

Tara kicked the ball up high and short. It was coming towards me, off a bit to the left. My feet didn't slip on the wet grass as I turned with my eye on the ball. I could see the girls in the infield coming toward me, but I knew they wouldn't get there in time. Decision made, I jumped. It was, for that moment, just like it used to be. I didn't care that my shirt might get dirty. I didn't think about coming down. I really hoped I wouldn't drop it. For that moment, I flew.

I caught the ball. My forearms took the force of the landing, and I scraped my left elbow and wrist, but I held on. The girls reacted in various ways. Tara was concerned for my bloody elbow. Beth fell down laughing on the grass. Katie and Heather pointed out the blades of grass and dirt stuck to my neck. I told them all, of course, that they were not to do what I just did. We didn't want anyone to get hurt. The game went on.

I was a player. Still.

The Right Thing to Do

Jeff didn't show up to the preseason meeting for coed junior high swimming or to the first day of practice when my defenses were up. He came on the third day: loud, irritating, and mentally handicapped. I was not thrilled. He argued with every direction I gave him that day, claiming to be a great swimmer, very fast, protesting that he had swum twelve laps, those other people were just slow. Within ten minutes, I wanted to kill him, but I was legally obligated not to let him drown. His strokes weren't completely awful, except for his breaststroke, and I did desperately need boys for the team. But when he told me I was supposed to call his mother, I was firmly resolved to tell her a kid like that couldn't be on my team. One coach with forty-one seventh and eighth graders could not have a special needs kid who couldn't count and wouldn't take directions.

Unfortunately, his mom turned out to be really nice on the phone and apologized for not having prepared me for her son. She said to kick him out of practice if he didn't obey, this threat having worked well for the football coaches. She took the wind right out of my sails by acknowledging (in a nice, motherly way) that Jeff was, at times, obnoxious. Before I could chime in with hearty agreement, she went on to say how much he wanted to swim and how he was looking forward to the season. I felt my resolve slipping. As I sat in the guard office holding the phone and wondering how this child could have come from a woman whose very voice dripped intelligence and elegance, I realized there was no way I'd be getting out of the Jeff Vandorpe experience.

In the next two weeks, I found that Jeff was not really that awful. He was annoying, yes, but no worse than your average junior high boy. Despite my best efforts, his breaststroke kick continued to be illegal, but as the day of our first home meet approached, his freestyle was actually coming along quite nicely. I was frantic about everything else—timers, flags, scoring—but I was fairly confident that Jeff was going to do just fine if I put him in the open 100 free. Fairly confident that, even though his start pretty much resembled an ape stepping off a cliff, and his flip turn was really an open turn done under water, his stroke, at least, was decent. I had taught him that, I thought, at least.

Turns out, as so often was my experience in coaching, that the least was too much to expect. Jeff had a case of the nerves. Last off the blocks, he emerged from the water and threw his head around to get a large breath. Then he took off at a pace much, much, much slower than he swam in practice. That was frustrating, but what I noticed next was actually painful to watch. Jeff's left arm never emerged from the water. For one hundred excruciating yards, Jeff stroked correctly with one arm and appeared to be pushing himself backwards in the water with the other. The audience and I, both thinking unkind things, I'm sure, about the competence of Jeff's coach, had plenty of time to observe this technique.

Coaching is really a difficult thing. You give out a lot of your heart. I, at least, ran my feet ragged on the bulkhead trying to watch everyone so I could help them improve. You repeat and reteach and repeat. You think you have the kid prepared. And then, for all your hard work and effort, this is how you are repaid: He forgets everything you have ever told him and makes you watch three-and-a-half minutes of one-armed swimming.

I didn't yell at Jeff, of course. I couldn't; he was happy. And why not? He'd just swum in his first swim meet ever. I'm sure neither of us will ever forget it.

Not Exactly Tripping the Light Fantastic

When I took the junior high teaching position, one of the things I was looking forward to was going to a dance. I never got to go any dances when I was in junior high myself. My oldest sister Anita ruined my chances of that. She got to date and go to dances and did something still unknown to me that took my parents right to the breaking point. I remember a huge fight that involved yelling, tears, and the laying on of hands. Dances were out.

I suppose being forbidden imbued them with a wholly unrealistic aura of mystery and magic. It was impossible to take this parental edict stoically. Along with not celebrating holidays, which people already thought was weird, I was also the oddball who couldn't date or go to the dance. Dances were all about boys, of course. There was a little slice of me, though, that was relieved not to have to go and be rejected for prettier, more popular girls.

What I heard about the dances was both appealing and slightly frightening. They took place in the cleared cafeteria and consisted of clumps of girls and clumps of boys with some small amount of dancing and, reportedly, some intermixing of a different nature occurring in dark and secluded corners. But mostly the conversation centered on who asked whom to dance and if so-and-so liked whoever. Again, dances equaled boys, and boys equaled excitement.

I did not have that in the forefront of my mind, of course, when, as a teacher, opportunity finally coincided with my schedule and I signed up to chaperone. In fact, I said yes partly because I felt guilty for having said no every previous time. Friday after class, all I really wanted to do was go home, eat chips, watch TV, and forget the names of my students. But there was that part of me that expected this to be fun.

One of my algebra students, a student of some brains but very little academic ambition, had told me he was in charge of decorating the foyer. I had no idea what to expect. There was a teacher in charge overall, so I guess my vague notions of bleeding skulls and skateboards, which would have represented his personality very well, never actually had a chance to materialize. The theme was "Viva Las Vegas." He and his helpers had taped playing cards around the door, hung giant dollar bills from the ceiling, and liberally strewn the space with crepe paper. It was surprisingly cute and appropriate.

I had time to observe this before I had to report to my post. I had asked to be a "roamer" or, in other words, a person who gets to walk around wherever they like. I was, instead, assigned to the locker room and the gym. The locker room had to be open for about the first half hour so kids could stash their coats in their gym lockers. This was not a plum assignment, as evidenced by my sharing it with a student teacher who desperately needed to take the contact lenses out of her bulging red eyes. Distracting as that was, I managed to observe a large sample of interesting behavior. The girls tended to come in waves and demonstrated varying degrees of giddiness. One found it necessary to shout across the room to me that she HAD found the algebra video interesting and that she HAD stayed awake and focused for the WHOLE thing. Of course, we know what that means.

(I wanted to smack her for that, too. It's not particularly easy to find videos that go with algebra. I was making the effort to vary instruction for her benefit, the thankless twit.)

Lots of girls walked up to about six inches away from the mirror, leaned in, examined their faces closely, leaned back, and either fluffed their hair or adjusted their shirts. Lots of shirts needed to be adjusted, too, since the dress code did not appear to be in effect. Many girls were wearing skimpy tops made of thin material. Many girls looked like ladies of ill repute in their skimpy tops made of thin material. A pretty fourteen-year-old leaned over and inadvertently showed me nearly the entire back of her thong. At least, I think the effect was inadvertent. I probably should have grabbed her and let her know how cheap and easy she looked. I can only imagine the effect that little outfit had on the boys.

Finally, I got to lock the room and assume my post in the gym. They always call these social events a dance, but it's really a party. The gym is where they set up games, in this case all having something to do with our Las Vegas theme. It did bother me just a tiny bit that we are teaching our kids how to play black jack and roulette, but, hey, Iowa City is a progressive place. And Las Vegas is supposed to be such a wholesome spot to take the kids now.

The games enjoyed a steady stream of the geeks and the less mature. Not too interested yet in the opposite sex, they were enticed by chocolate coins, the opportunity to win a free pop, and various cheap little prizes, plus bubblegum.

There being plenty of supervision available, I decided to make a foray into the dance area. It was dark, exceptionally loud, and full of people standing around. Unlike the reports from my junior high days, the boys and girls seemed relatively well-mixed. Small circles broke into dance when a "good" song came on. In less than five minutes I told one boy to remove his hands from his girlfriend's pockets and another, in not so many words, to remove his crotch from the vicinity of her rear end. I made a quick exit then without looking back.

The locker room opened up again for the last half hour. At first, just a few disillusioned girls wandered in. One kicked the trash can over before she saw me. Boys suck, I guess. (I could have told her that and gone into voluminous detail. She really wasn't interested in my perspective.)

As the dance ended, the waves washed back in, mostly happy and making plans for the weekend. The same girls rechecked their hair and tops in the mirror. I'd seen one girl at the beginning of the night putting on eyeshadow which apparently her parents had approved, and I meant to see if she washed her face, but if she did, I missed it.

I probably expected to feel some sort of magic at my first junior high dance. I wasn't looking for love, of course, but I guess I thought I should still feel that mysterious aura. Maybe the junior high kids felt it. It didn't look like the innocent who-likes-who scene I imagined it should be. These kids have a much clearer understanding of what sex is, in part because more of them are experiencing it or watching it on screen. It's wrong to let your daughter, particularly your junior-high aged daughter, go out looking as if she is ready for sex. It's unfair to focus solely on the girl, but I wonder who'll be raped and who'll be pregnant and who'll be making hard decisions about abortion before too many more years go by.

Probably a lot of kids at the dance were just having fun. Maybe I'm just another member of an older generation looking at the younger generation with disapproval for not being the same. But I don't see much good coming out of this, and I don't see much hope for change. Back at the dance, I shooed out the last few stragglers and left, unsettled and disappointed.

On Praising Poetry
(Happily back teaching elementary school)

We wrote some poetry today in science class. One might say that we were blatantly killing time (which would be ironic, seeing as the unit is called Measuring Time), but I prefer to see it as infusing language throughout the curriculum. I was sorely in need of some infusion today as the only activity we had to do was marking our sun clocks. Tracing the shadow left by our tinker-toy gnomon only took about five minutes every hour. It would have been no problem if I only had to worry about my own class, but I teach another section, too, so I had a good thirty-five minutes to fill.

As time passes, so do the seasons, I reasoned, so I shared some poems about them, including a depressing and slightly disturbing verse by Ted Hughes. (Is he the one who couldn't love Sylvia Plath? I wondered silently.) Clearly he was not a fan of autumn, given *The Seven Sorrows*, complete with pheasants hanging on hooks, heads in bags. Mollie's class, I'm pretty sure, hasn't had quite the same exposure to poetry as mine has, so I shared plenty. My directions afterwards were to write a poem about a season. "It can rhyme or not. It can have lines all the same length or not. It can be in a shape or not. Just write a poem."

"Can it rhyme?" someone asked, reaffirming that there is, in fact, such a thing as a stupid question.

At the end of the period, an intrepid soul volunteered to share.

> My favorite season is summer,
> It really is no bummer
> In the summer, you get dumber...

Here Emily broke off, looking embarrassed, and said, "I couldn't find anything else to rhyme." The rest of the class, of course, loved it, but I sensed a teachable moment.

"Perhaps," I said gently, "if you have to search so hard for something to rhyme, and you're unhappy with what you chose, you should consider rewriting the poem without the rhyme." She nodded, as if in understanding.

Kayleen chimed in, also nodding. "Yeah," she said, comprehension dawning in her face, "you could maybe just write, "In summer, everything is funner."" Mercifully, it was then time for them to go.

Later in the afternoon, I repeated the lesson with my class. They agreed with me that Ted Hughes was a downer, but I reminded them that those are feelings worth exploring, too. So, same directions, with, thankfully, no one asking this time if the poem could rhyme. Off they went, writing, writing, writing. Boom, up they started to jump, excitedly forgetting to raise their hands, coming up to share with me.

"Delightful," I said to Colin's quick three lines, "but it needs something more."

"Nice," I said to Cody's four-line stanza where the last line repeated the first, "now go make it better."

Eventually, I told them all to get up and go find someone to share with. A line also started to form on either side of me, and I read and reacted at double-quick speed. There was one teacher veto: Quincy had someone dying in a hospital from the shock of a hurricane, accompanied by the last few beeps of the heart machine. If he'd been the least little bit serious about it, I would have let it go, but he was just looking for an easy laugh. I gave out some I-like-its, even more I-like-it-buts, one I-don't-really-think-all-these-things-fit-in-one-poem, and one wholehearted I-love-it!

The I-love-it was loud, and it surprised the kids. I think it may have surprised me even more. A couple of kids were looking a little jealous, so I seized on another teachable moment.

I told them I knew there were some teachers out there who would listen to nineteen poems and say that they loved them all. "But," I said, "you got me."

They laughed, but I had a serious message. For one thing, I won't say I like something unless it's true (though I could sometimes be a little more tactful). For another, I cautioned them, my loving or hating your poem only means that you've made or not made a connection with me. (Keeping firmly in mind, however, that pleasing your teacher is an important and useful school skill.) Poetry, I reminded them, like all writing, should first of all be satisfying to yourself. So, even though you may stretch so hard for a rhyme that you fall on your face a bit or you kill off unsuspecting old people in the midst of nature's fury, the important thing is to go out and write.

No thunderous applause greeted this wisdom, predictably, but I felt like maybe I'd planted a seed, and the class moved on.

Three Points or More

On the twenty-seventh of February this year, I kicked a field goal. It wasn't a real field goal, of course, but I found that to be a distinction that did not matter at all.

The Grant Wood Jazzy Jumpers performed at school that Friday afternoon, robbing my students of their coveted P.E. time. To assuage their pain, I took them outside after the assembly into the unseasonably mild February sunshine. Temperatures in the forties that week had melted all but a few pockets of snow and left the top layer of ground spongy. Little boggy puddles were scattered around, and small patches of mud were left where previous feet had gouged.

Knowing our time outside was limited, the usual football crew set up for field goal kicking parallel to the swings, affording the non-football players an excellent view and cheering opportunity. As usual, two kids ran down in back of the second temporary building to stand in for the goalposts. Another kid was in charge of holding the ball, and the others lined up to kick it.

Having outgrown the days when I'd rush headlong out to play, I picked my way sedately through the mushy grass and took position at the end of the kicking line. I had tried this game before, rather unsuccessfully, and I knew enough to protect my place in line. Kids don't tend to see adults as participants in their games, I've found, which doesn't bother me much as I actually expect them to see me as existing on a somewhat different (and higher) plane. It does annoy me when they cut in front of me at the drinking fountain, and I have my strategies for dealing with that. Lining up to kick the ball has a specific rhythm to keep, however. The kicker goes out and becomes a goalpost, and the goalpost runs back to get in line. That's the kid you have to watch out for, and I announced a couple of different times that I was in line behind Spencer or Ben or whoever.

Colin always does the Nate Kaeding thing: back up so many paces and step over. I was not so precise, but I do favor the angled approach. I took my hands out of my coat pockets for balance and ran. Left, right, left, boom. The kick had that immediately satisfying thunk that flooded throughout my whole body. There was an instantaneous sensation of success when I knew that what I had done was just exactly what I wanted to do.

My arms flew up, my students cheered, and that football sailed up over the imaginary crossbar, straight and good and true.

The Perfect Swimsuit

My friend Stephanie called me up the other day and told me her swimsuit shopping days were over. She had found two more swimsuits she liked. Added to the perfect suit we found together last year that meant she would never have to look for another one again. Hey, I tried to tell her, swimsuits are ephemeral. They come, the Lycra wears out, and they go. You don't understand, she said, I'm not ever doing this again.

Stephanie is mildly obsessive about having the perfect swimsuit. Her previous perfect suit was an elegantly-cut black one-piece with some netting along the thighs and armpits to give it a little racier interest. It was a great suit, and it looked great on her. I mentioned it was black, didn't I? Well, it started that way. When she unveiled it for not the first time at a combination pool party and baby shower some four or five years ago, the suit was brown. Now, there's nothing wrong with a brown suit, but this was various shades of brown created by the powerful fading effects of sunshine and chlorine, and it did not look artistically done. Put this together with the pilling on the rear and when she mentioned that she needed to get a new suit, I tactfully agreed.

Stephanie searched for a swimsuit. I bought two at Target that year. Stephanie kept searching. The next year I ordered one that I loved from Victoria's Secret—the most money I'd ever spent on a swimsuit. Stephanie looked high and low. I threw out some old bikinis and bought a cheap new one at Wal-Mart to take to Cozumel.

Last year, she and I went up to Cedar Rapids when the swimsuits arrived in February. She was determined on this trip to find the perfect suit or die trying. I was along to haul her sorry carcass home if she failed. Stephanie had decided that she wanted a bikini with a boy leg bottom. She thought the style should look good on her. She tried on many, many swimsuits. The boy leg bikinis were mostly looking as if they were built for ten-year-old girl bodies (which often still look like they have boy legs on them.) At this point, or actually much sooner, I would have abandoned the boy leg idea, but when Stephanie decides something should be, she'd rather beat her head repeatedly against a dressing room mirror than give up.

After several hours, Stephanie got tired of taking her clothes on and off, and I got hungry. We began to trudge back through Lindale Mall towards our exit, contemplating a quick stop at the food court. Suddenly, Stephanie's head swung to the left. Maybe we should try Von Maur, she announced, and veered off that way.

We probably took ten steps into the store, and there on a mannequin (Stephanie's favorite place to find her outfits anyway)—spotlighted, no less—was

The Perfect Swimsuit. It was, if you can believe this, a preview model for the next year. The suit was sold the minute she laid eyes on it and what followed was only about twenty minutes of making sure she got the right size. For just the right finishing touch, I agreed that she should buy the matching mesh T-shirt. (I excel at spending other people's money, although, in her case, I barely need to use any persuasion at all.)

Stephanie was, and is, very happy with The Perfect Swimsuit, now in its second season, and continues to claim it will meet her needs for many years to come. In fact, forever. This summer, however, even though she was not even looking, she did find two Perfectly Acceptable and Attractive Swimsuits to round out her collection. And she is taking very good care of them so they really ought to last. Forever.

I tried to tell her about one of my favorite suits. The one that I always rinsed twice in cool water after wearing, and washed in Woolite periodically, and blotted carefully with its own special towel and lay flat to dry. It lasted four years. Then one summer, when I opened up the drawer, the rear of the suit was transparent and the elastic in the straps had cracked. I tried to tell Stephanie about that, but then I thought, swimsuits are like summer. I'd better just let her enjoy it while it lasts.

(Lisa Roberts currently owns six swimsuits.)

Not For Another Five Years

I'm not really one to get fussy about my age, but thirty-five sounds a lot older to me than thirty-four. Maybe it's by virtue of being another complete fistful of years. Maybe it's because people treat it like the last big signpost on the march to forty.

About ten years back or so, at another significant year, my doctor started asking me at the end of every annual exam if I wanted to have blood work done. No, I didn't. At that time, the insurance only paid something like forty bucks every third year towards a physical so I was sure I didn't want the extra expense.

Still, I felt a little twinge every time she asked, probably the hypochondria flaring up. So one year around thirty somewhere, I announced that I would have the blood tested when I turned thirty-five, comfortably in the future. The decision was made, which didn't stop Dr. Rankin from asking every year, but which prepared me in advance for meeting the question.

My thirty-fifth birthday was in June. My appointment was in July.

The Monday of that week I went to visit Jim's uncle who was in the hospital following a stem cell transplant. I made a characteristically tactful beginning noting that Richard's color looked better than when I saw him last, and they informed me that was a burn from his particular cocktail of chemicals. He dozed off under the influence, and I settled down for a chat with his wife.

She explained the harvesting process to me, how they take the blood from one arm, run it through a machine, check the results against a color chart, keep the stem cells, and pump the rest of the stuff back into the donor. After contributing various mild expressions of disgust and drawing my arms up into the praying mantis safety position, it occurred to me that Nancy might conceivably take offense at my reaction to the medical marvel that was, after all, attempting to save her husband's life. I told her that when Richard decided on the transplant, I thought about coming down to be tested as a donor. I knew I probably wouldn't be a match for him, but I meant it as a gesture of support. Unfortunately, I wasn't able to follow through with the idea of big needles being poked into my veins. Merely talking about it with her gave me the shivers. It was then that I realized my big appointment was just two days away.

Now, I do have a little unpleasant history here. The last time someone drew blood from me in significant amounts was just fourteen short years ago, and I remember certain details of it really well. Unfortunately, I remember waking up and finding out the people present had decided to save my head from hitting the floor instead of saving the godforsaken vial of blood. They had me lay down for the next bloodletting.

I was pretty determined, however, that since I wasn't sick this time, not repeating the scene was mostly a matter of mental action. I did fast, but I made sure to hydrate well, and I wore loose-fitting clothing. I'm sorry to say it was to no avail.

The nurse, sweet, soft-spoken, tiny little thing that she was, came into the room carrying her little caddy of doom. I looked away quickly, but not before I saw an array of fluid-filled vials.

She directed me to pull my chair up next to the examining table and put my arm up there. That helped give the patient some support, she explained. I, in turn, explained to her about the fainting episode, which was why, I said, I would only be looking at the opposite wall. That's okay, hon, she replied and directed me to go to my happy place.

While I was examining the window treatments, she poked me with the needle and started a little conversation to take my mind off the blood coursing through my violated vein and out of my body. She asked if I was ready for school and what grade I taught. She told me what a great year her children had in fourth grade. I was simultaneously thinking of asking her which school they attended and telling her about Monday's conversation about stem cell transplants when I noticed that I couldn't hear anything anymore. Strangely, my little nurse was holding both my head and my elbow. Through the buzzing, I heard her tell me that I had passed out and that she was holding me up. I felt my mouth say, "How embarrassing," though it came out all fuzzy and weird.

Just writing about it brings back a rather unpleasant shadow of the sensation. I broke out all over in a cold sweat and turned, according to eyewitnesses, as white as a sheet. I wanted to observe this phenomenon myself, but even I knew better than to go vertical at the moment. In fact, I was perfectly willing to let the tiny nurse and the backup she called for manipulate me into place on the table. I would have lay happily on the floor, but I suppose they reserve that option for the very worst-case scenario.

Sometime afterwards, resting comfortably and restored with candy from the pharmacy next door, I recalled that I have, to a much lesser degree, even felt faint on two widely separated occasions when getting my finger pricked. And once I nearly passed out in third grade when I got a nasty cut on my wrist. Somehow I had very successfully blocked those episodes from my memory.

I have learned two important things from this experience. First, I have a distinct talent for forgetting, and second, no matter how much I may hope to the contrary, I am a total lightweight with my blood. If it comes down to amputating my own limb to save myself when a tree falls on me, I will have to bleed to death. I'm not even going to carry a knife.

Suzanne, the nurse, called the other day to let me know my test results.

Everything was normal, she said, except that my cholesterol was slightly elevated. I needed to watch my diet, eat more fruits and vegetables, and cut down on the fatty foods. It wasn't until I hung up the phone that I realized the little vampire's last words to me were, "We'll check it again next year."

(Lisa Roberts has successfully survived subsequent blood-lettings.)

Poetry for Physicists

Have you been pondering the nature of black holes?
Wondering if there ever will or ever could be clean energy?
Looking for the ultimate nuclear deterrent?

The Z Machine may answer.

A forceful magnetic field sets off a blazing burst of x-rays,
initiating the implosion of a dab of heavy hydrogen,
fusing hydrogen into helium like water into wine,
releasing enough energy
to light a single small bulb on your Christmas tree
for a very, very brief time.

Physicists are hopeful.

I Was Present at a Drowning the Other Day

I had been riding with Jim on patrol when the call came over the radio. A man had gone into the water off a boat and never come up. We were back in the neighborhood streets of Tiffin, Jim just having waved at a group of men in their lawn chairs circled up around a barbecue. The weather was perfect, and I had a knot in my stomach for the swimmer. That's how I tried to think of him at first, as a swimmer, but that's not how it turned out.

We tore out of Tiffin, picking up speed and running with lights and sirens. The back roads were twisty and almost deserted. It might have been fun, but I was holding onto the armrest caught between hoping a deer wouldn't jump out and wishing we could go faster so that I could save this man.

The more-traveled roads were even more alarming, as the traffic sometimes didn't move over fast enough for a squad car doing eighty-five in a thirty-five. I found myself amazed and disgusted at the other drivers' behavior. Some of them clearly weren't paying any attention at all.

We listened to the voices on the radio. The dispatcher was having trouble getting information from the woman on the boat who called the emergency in. She wasn't sure where she was, she thought maybe halfway between Mehaffey Bridge and Sugar Bottom but didn't know which was closer. We got behind North Liberty Fire towing boats and had to stop one that was fishtailing all over the road. There were flashing lights at the Mehaffey boat ramp, but something he'd heard made Jim decide Sugar Bottom was the better bet.

Pulling into the campground, we saw everybody walking in the direction of the beach, attracted by the first lights and sirens through. They wouldn't get off the road, sometimes, and Jim cussed. Down at the boat ramp, a crowd had gathered, and I stood out of the way while Jim checked in with his superiors. At first he got sent up to keep the road cleared for the ambulance and other emergency vehicles coming in. Besides the Johnson County cars, Solon responded and North Liberty, of course, and the park ranger and her assistant came down.

They started putting boats in the water to drag, and the lieutenant called Jim down, thinking they'd need him for that. I stood on the side of the road between Jim's car and the fire truck. The sun had gone down by now, though the sky was still pink. The volunteer firefighters set up floodlights, and I saw that one of them was a man who worked at the Physical Plant for the school district. I think he recognized me, too, but I didn't want to bother him. I hoped he didn't think I'd just come down to the water to gawk.

The ranger brought the boat in, a ski boat with four girls on it. You could tell which one was the girlfriend, and I felt my heart breaking for her. I wondered if I should get my jean jacket from the car. She was barefoot and wearing a strapless black cover-up over her swimsuit. She looked tiny and vulnerable among all the uniformed officers.

They'd been drinking on the boat. Jim got the unenviable job of trying to take statements from the other three women. The first one had on a white skirt and orange shirt, and she tried to tell Jim she wouldn't be able to write down a statement and sign it because she didn't have her glasses. I was still standing out of the way, probably about ten feet. I couldn't hear everything Jim said, but she was loud. Her friend, already on a cell phone, rummaged around in a big beach bag and came up with sunglasses.

They must have been prescription sunglasses, I guess. The loud one put them on and got in the car with Jim, but she wouldn't shut the door. I could see them through the windshield, talking, and could tell my husband was trying to be patient. When she was done, he sent her to get her friend. The orange shirt was all up in her friend's ear trying to tell her something, and Jim came out of the car, annoyed, and said he'd appreciate it if she didn't try to coach her friend. They exchanged more words as she came over. Again, I couldn't hear much of what Jim said, but she said she was sorry. She admitted she'd been drinking, and she said she was just trying to protect her friends.

As the sky got darker, a woman came up alongside me. She wanted to go to those kids, she said. She couldn't have been all that much older than they were, really. She didn't think they'd want some stranger coming up to them, but she wanted so much to go give them a hug. She couldn't stand that people were staring at them, sitting in their lawn chairs and staring at them, but I wondered where she thought these people had to go. We were standing just a yard or two away from someone's campsite. You can bet they had been planning on taking it easy by the fire and watching the water anyway.

I couldn't condemn anyone for looking. When the sirens went off, they didn't know what was going on, and they were curious. No one wanted anyone to be hurt; no one wanted anyone to drown. Some of the others looking on surely had to be feeling as I was: impotent in the face of disaster, wishing we could do something more than just stand there but wanting to know for sure what was going on.

The floodlights on top of the fire truck drew thousands of bugs, but I wasn't getting bitten. There was a lot of smoke in the air from campfires and maybe that helped some, too. The weather stayed perfect, and I felt a little guilty for noticing that it felt good to be safe and dry.

Transformed

Golden dust dances
in
chaotic Brownian motion,
receptive
to faint breezes,
illuminated
by a
spotlight of sun.

www.ingramcontent.com/pod-product-compliance
Lightning Source LLC
Chambersburg PA
CBHW030404020726
47493CB00003B/939